Had he changed his mind about the bargain they had made?

It was surely a little late to have second thoughts? Did she mind? Rosamund was shocked to discover she minded very much indeed. She felt hurt and betrayed and very, very lonely. Had she expected him to be a conventional husband? But she had known from the beginning he would not be that, so why was she disappointed? Was it because he had not referred to their agreement at all since the wedding, and she had hoped they might come to a deeper understanding of each other—especially as he was so courteous and careful of her? It hurt to think such niceties were simply his natural good manners and meant nothing.

He had bought her.

He could do with her as he wished, and if it amused him to keep her on tenterhooks then she would have to endure it…

Born in Singapore, **Mary Nichols** came to England when she was three, and has spent most of her life in different parts of East Anglia. She has been a radiographer, school secretary, information officer and industrial editor, as well as a writer. She has three grown-up children, and four grandchildren.

Recent novels by the same author:

RAGS-TO-RICHES BRIDE
THE EARL AND THE HOYDEN
CLAIMING THE ASHBROOKE HEIR
  (part of *The Secret Baby Bargain*)
HONOURABLE DOCTOR,
  IMPROPER ARRANGEMENT
THE CAPTAIN'S MYSTERIOUS LADY*
THE VISCOUNT'S UNCONVENTIONAL BRIDE*

*Part of *The Piccadilly Gentlemen's Club*
  mini-series

LORD PORTMAN'S TROUBLESOME WIFE

Mary Nichols

First published in Great Britain 2010
Large Print edition 2011
Harlequin Mills & Boon Limited,
Eton House, 18-24 Paradise Road, Richmond, Surrey TW9 1SR

© Mary Nichols 2010

ISBN: 978 0 263 21848 0

Harlequin Mills & Boon policy is to use papers that are natural, renewable and recyclable products and made from wood grown in sustainable forests. The logging and manufacturing process conform to the legal environmental regulations of the country of origin.

Printed and bound in Great Britain
by CPI Antony Rowe, Chippenham, Wiltshire

LORD
PORTMAN'S
TROUBLESOME
WIFE

Chapter One

Summer 1761

Rosamund looked about her at the mourners, standing with glass in hand, or slowly perambulating the drawing room of her Holles Street home, and wondered why they had all come. They could surely not expect a bequest for everyone knew Sir Joshua had frittered away a fortune. Perhaps they hoped to pick up a little gossip, something to pass on over the teacups when they next met their friends. Her father's death had been sudden and violent and surely there was more to learn about that?

He had been found in Tyburn Lane in the early hours of the morning, evidently on his way home after a night out. Everything pointed to him having been run down by a vehicle, which had not stopped. 'Rolling drunk,' everyone said. 'Not looking where he was going.'

Maximilian, her brother, had been closeted with the family lawyer in the library for the best part of an hour, leaving Rosamund to attend to their guests alone. There were some cousins she hardly knew, fancy people who looked down on her, whispering amongst themselves, calling her an ape leader and plain to boot and hoping they wouldn't be expected to give her house room. A few of her father's acquaintances had turned up to offer condolences and no doubt to find out their chances of being paid what was owed to them. No one truly mourned the passing of the irascible man, except his daughter. Rosamund had kept house for him ever since her mother died seven years before and, believing he needed her, had never married. At twenty-six, she considered herself well and truly on the shelf.

'What are you going to do now, Rosamund?' Aunt Jessica interrupted her reverie. Mrs Jessica Bullivant was her father's sister. She was dressed in a black silk mourning gown; its caged hips made her look broader than she was tall.

'I expect I shall stay here, at least for a time.'

'Here, child? You cannot live alone.'

'I will not be alone. I shall keep Cook and Janet.'

'They are servants. No, Rosamund, it is not to be thought of. I know someone who might offer you the post of companion. Of course it will not pay much, but you will have bed and board and little enough to do. After looking after Joshua, it will be child's play.'

'Companion!' Rosamund shuddered at the thought. She was outspoken and used to her independence and there was no one less independent than a paid companion at the beck and call of her employer twenty-four hours a day. 'No, thank you, Aunt. I am sure Papa will have made provision for me. There will be enough for me to live frugally without having to resort to paid employment.'

'I doubt that. Everyone knows my brother was a profligate. Did he ever give you anything more than pin money?'

'I did not need anything.'

Her aunt snorted at this loyalty. 'Being companion to a lady is better than unpaid employment, which is what you have been doing for the past seven years.'

'I did what any daughter worth her salt would do.'

'And now you are long past marriageable age.'

'I know that, Aunt. I have no expectations in that direction. I shall do good works.'

Her aunt laughed at that, causing everyone else in the room to stop talking and turn to look at them. She immediately became serious and put on a mournful expression. 'If I did not have my dear Miss Davies to look after me, I would take you in myself, but I would not, for the world, hurt her feelings. And truly my little house in Chandos Street is not large enough to accommodate us all.'

'I know that, Aunt, but I thank you all the same. I shall manage.' The last thing she wanted was to move in with her domineering relative.

Rosamund, seeing the lawyer emerge from the library and hurry out to his waiting carriage, slipped into the room where her brother sat with his head in his hands, his full brown wig pushed to the back of his head. Hearing her enter, he looked up. He was not mourning, he was dry-eyed and furious. 'That…that…stupid old man…'

'You mean Mr Tetley?'

'No, our father. He has left nothing, Rosie, nothing but a heap of debts. How could a man be so gullible? He let people persuade him into worthless investments, refused to listen to wise counsel and lost everything.' He gave a cracked laugh and picked up a canvas bag which chinked as it moved. He threw it down at her feet. 'Except this.'

'What is it?' She bent to untie the cord that

closed it to reveal a heap of gold coins. 'But there's a fortune here!'

'No, there isn't. They're counterfeit, every one. Tetley says they must be surrendered to the judiciary.'

'Oh, dear. But how does Mr Tetley know they are counterfeit?' She picked up a guinea to examine it. 'This looks perfectly good to me.'

'It is clipped.' He delved in his coat pocket and produced a genuine coin. 'See? Put them together and you can see the clipped coin is smaller and the milling is fresh with sharper edges.'

'I do not understand.'

'Neither did I, but Tetley explained it to me. The coiners snip or file off the edges of real coins and mill a new edge on to them. Then they are passed into circulation again and the spare gold melted down and used to make new coins, often by just covering base metal with a layer of gold, then stamping the head and tail on them and milling them. Like this one.' He delved into the bag and produced another coin. 'It is apparently a very profitable undertaking.' His grunt of a laugh was humourless. 'So long as you don't get caught, of course.'

'But how did Papa come by them?'

'Your guess is as good as mine. I would like to

think he sold something and was unknowingly paid in counterfeit coin, but he might have been aware of what they really were and intended to pass them off…'

'No, he would never do that,' she insisted. 'He was gullible and difficult to deal with and sometimes mean, but I will not believe he was dishonest.'

'We shall never know, shall we? The point is what we decide to do now.'

'Take them to a magistrate as Mr Tetley said.'

'And be asked a lot of questions about how we came by them? No one will believe in our innocence. Counterfeiting coin and distributing it is treason; we could hang for it. I'll take charge of them until I can decide the best thing to do with them.' He took the coin she still held, popped it back into the bag and tied the neck tightly. 'One thing is certain: we cannot use them to pay Father's debts.'

'No, of course not.'

'In the meantime, you have a fortnight to quit the house…'

'Quit the house?' she repeated, shocked to the core.

'Yes, Father mortgaged it and the mortgagors are foreclosing. We can make enough selling the furniture to pay the immediate debts and that is all.'

'You mean I am destitute?' She could not believe the father she had loved had left her penniless, but then he had not expected to die as he did and no doubt hoped to come about.

'As good as.'

She was silent a moment, trying to digest the information. 'I suppose that means I shall have to come and live with you?' The prospect was not pleasing. Max had a demanding wife and six children, none of whom were well behaved. She could see herself becoming an unpaid nursery nurse. Even the lot of companion was preferable to that. Suddenly her secure world was collapsing about her.

'You could find yourself a husband.'

'Max, who would marry me? I am twenty-six and have neither looks not fortune. You are not being realistic.'

'Someone must be willing to take you on. A widower, perhaps, someone needing a mother for his children? There are plenty of those about.'

'What about love?'

'Love, Rosie? Can you afford love?'

The question was a brutal one, but Max had never spared her feelings, and he was right. 'No, but finding a husband in a fortnight when I have nothing to offer is surely outside the bounds of possibility.'

'I could perhaps rake up a small dowry so you don't go empty-handed.'

'If you can find money for a dowry, then give it to me. I can use it to set up a little business.'

'Now who is not being realistic! What do you know of business? All you are capable of is keeping house.' He stood up and went to the mirror to straighten his wig and tweak his black silk cravat. 'The trouble is that time is not on your side. But leave it to me, I may yet come up with something.' He strode out of the room and back to the mourners, followed by a very dejected Rosamund.

She was too numbed by Max's revelations to attend to their guests as she should, but Max made up for her deficiency, exhorting them to take refreshments, and conversing amiably about the deceased, telling stories about his life, listening to them recount theirs. At last, realising there was nothing more to be learned, the guests departed, leaving Rosamund to sit down, surrounded by the debris of plates, cups and glasses, half-empty bottles of wine, stewed tea and crumbs. Max, clutching the canvas bag, was last to leave, together with his wife and noisy children who would not have normally been allowed to come, but they were thoroughly spoiled and their demands acceded to if they were loud enough. Rosamund hardly noticed them go. Janet came in to clear away and tidy the room, a task Rosamund would normally have helped her with, but she could not raise a finger.

She mourned the passing of her father, but she was also angry with him for being such a gullible fool, and even more angry with those so-called business associates who had sold him useless shares and ruined him. And who had given him that bag of counterfeit coins? Why had her father kept it instead of bringing the criminals to justice and obtaining some restitution? He must have realised they were counterfeit or he would have used them to pay his debts and buy them a little extra comfort. But supposing he had, supposing he had already spent some of them? Would she have angry tradesmen on the doorstep, demanding proper payment? Or worse, a constable or a Bow Street Runner with a warrant for her arrest? Would pleading ignorance save her? She needed to know, but she would have to be careful in case she uncovered something not to her father's credit. She prayed that was not so and he was entirely innocent.

Max was disinclined to do anything about it.

The only other person who might be able to help her was Mr Tetley, so she set out next day to ask him.

'My dear Miss Chalmers,' he said, when she was shown into his office and offered a seat. 'May I offer my condolences on your loss? I am sorry I did not have the opportunity to do so yesterday, but business had to prevail and you were engaged with your relations. And no doubt your brother explained matters to you.'

'He did, but I should like to hear it from you.'

Mr Tetley sighed, but patiently went over everything, exactly as Max had explained it. 'I am unconscionably sorry that you cannot be given more time to order your affairs, ma'am, but my best endeavours failed to allow you more than two weeks to quit. No doubt Sir Maximilian will look after you.'

Hearing her brother spoken of as Sir Maximilian brought her loss home to her more effectively than anything else and she had to force herself not to cry. There were things more important than tears. 'Thank you, Mr Tetley.' She paused to gather herself. 'I am mystified by that bag of gold coins my brother showed me. How did my father come by it?'

'I have no idea. I knew nothing of it. It was your

brother who found it locked in a cupboard in Sir Joshua's library. I am afraid he was angrily disappointed when I told him they were all counterfeit.'

'So you cannot throw any light on it?'

'No. I can only suppose your late father sold something, a picture or jewels or something of that sort, and that was the payment he received.'

'Then those responsible should be brought to book and forced to pay good money for whatever it was.'

'But we have no idea who they might be. And such men are dangerous. I would not like to confront them. No, my dear Miss Chalmers, I advise you to leave well alone. Take the bag to a magistrate, say you found it, wash your hands of it.'

'My brother has it and he will do what is necessary. But can you tell me anything about the shares Papa bought that were worthless?'

'There is nothing you can do about those either if they were sold and bought in good faith. Playing the 'Change is a gamble at the best of times.'

'Could the two things be connected? The buying of shares and the mutilated coins, I mean.'

'I doubt it.'

'But you must know the names of those who

sold my father the shares. You were, after all, his legal adviser.'

He grunted a laugh. 'When he decided to take my advice, but very often he ignored it, as he did in this case.' He opened a drawer in his desk and took out a folder tied with red ribbon. He untied it and laid the folder open. 'The name of the organisation is the Barnstaple Mining Company.'

Rosamund gave a brittle laugh. 'Mining gold, I suppose. What is the name of the signatory on that document?'

He consulted the paper. 'Michael O'Keefe.'

'That sounds Irish. Do you know anything about him?'

'Nothing at all, Miss Chalmers. It might not even be his real name.'

'And where is the office of this company?'

He looked at the papers again. 'The only address I have is the Nag's Head, Covent Garden. It is unlikely to be a bona fide address. I advised Sir Joshua against investing, but he would not listen.'

'I cannot believe my father would be so gullible. The whole thing is decidedly smoky.'

'So I told him.' He paused. 'Miss Chalmers, what are you intending to do?'

'I do not know yet.'

'Do nothing, I beg you. You surely have enough to occupy you, ordering your affairs before moving out of Holles Street.'

The meeting of the Piccadilly Gentlemen's Club at Lord Trentham's London mansion was drawing to a close. It was no ordinary drinking and gaming club, but one dedicated exclusively to the tracking down of criminals and bringing them to justice. Officially designated the 'Society for the Discovery and Apprehending of Criminals', its members were all high enough in the instep not to require paying for their services. Not for them the taking of bribes as other thieftakers were known to do; they did it for the love of adventure and to make the country a safer place for its inhabitants.

Set up ten years before by Lord Drymore, then simply Captain James Drymore, its other members were Viscount Jonathan Leinster; Harry, Lord Portman; Sir Ashley Saunders; Captain Alexander Carstairs and Sam Roker, James Drymore's servant and friend. Each had their own area of expertise, but this year they were especially concerned that the wedding of George III to Charlotte of Mecklenburg-Strelitz on 8 September, and their coronation two weeks later, should not be marred by more crime than usual. They were, among other matters, on the look out for pickpockets and criminal gangs who might be planning to take advantage of the crowds come to witness the processions and take part in the celebrations afterwards.

Harry's particular interest was in counterfeit money and he had been instrumental in bringing several gangs before the courts. But there were always more to take their place and what better opportunity for passing counterfeit coins could there be than among the crowds flocking to see the processions? He was indefatigable in pursuit of these types of criminals, though you would never think so to look at him. He wore a full-skirted coat of amber silk embroidered with gold thread. Lace flounces fell over his hands from the wide cuffs. His embroidered waistcoat had a long row of pearl buttons from the neck right down to his knees, though only half of them were meant to be fastened. His cravat was starched and frilled within an inch of its life and his breeches and stockings were white, tied at the knee with yellow ribbons. His pose was relaxed, the long fingers of his left hand, loaded with rings, lay idly on the table. The other fingered his quizzing glass on its ribbon about his neck. To anyone who did not know him, he was a macaroni of the first water.

'I'm off to the Old Bailey,' he said, when the

business of the day was concluded and everyone was preparing to leave. 'The Dustin Gang are on trial and I would know the outcome.'

He picked up his tall hat from the floor at his side and stood up. The high red heels of his shoes and the height of his white wig made him seem at least six inches taller, even though, at five feet eleven, he was by no means short. Most men of his acquaintance found it more comfortable to shave their heads for wearing a wig, but as he often needed to go out and about without one, he put up with the discomfort to appear the fop. The real Harry Portman was a person very few people knew.

'Are you to give evidence?' Jonathan asked.

'No, don't want to blow my cover, do I? Do you fancy coming with me?'

'No, Louise is expecting me home.'

'I will come,' Ashley said.

They left together and a greater contrast between two men would be hard to find. Ashley's clothes were muted in colour, though they were superbly tailored and he wore his own dark hair tied back in a queue. Unlike Harry, whose face was powdered and patched, Ashley's was tanned and rugged. But appearances were deceptive because they were equally athletic, equally observant and sharp-witted, able to react swiftly to any given situation. It was simply that it amused Harry to play the fop.

At first his dandified mannerisms had been a front to disguise his deep hurt and the terrible guilt he felt over the death of his wife six years before, but then he found it useful when pursuing criminals. Seeing him mincing along in his fine clothes, they thought he was a fool and it pleased him to let them think it. Naturally the members of the Piccadilly Gentlemen's Club knew better.

'How did you bring the Dustin Gang to book?' Ash asked, as they emerged on to the street and looked about them for chairs for hire. The road was busy, but they could see no chairs and so began to walk, or rather Ashley walked and Harry picked his way daintily between the dirt and puddles.

'By becoming one of them.'

Ashley laughed. 'You! Why, you would stand out a mile. I cannot believe they were taken in.'

'Oh, I can be one of the great unwashed when it suits me, Ash.'

'I believe you, though many would not.'

'That is as it should be. My long association with the theatre has stood me in good stead when it comes to putting on a disguise and acting a part. I do believe if I had pursued it, I could have become as famous as David Garrick.'

'Why did you not?'

'The responsibilities of an estate, dear boy. I came into my inheritance when my father died in '53, and it behooved me to marry and settle down to bring forth the next generation of Portmans.'

'I did not realise you were married and had a family.'

'I was married less than a year. My wife died giving birth to a daughter.'

'I am sorry, Harry, I did not mean to pry. I always assumed you were a confirmed bachelor as I am.'

'It is no secret. I simply do not talk about it. Beth was too young, barely seventeen. No one had told her what to expect and she did not understand what was happening to her when her pains began.' He paused, remembering her screams which went on and on and the strident way she had cursed him. 'God will punish you for this!' Her words were punctuated with screams of pain. Feeling helpless and unable to stand any more of it, he had gone out to walk about the garden until it was all over. He should have been with her to comfort her, but no, men had no business anywhere near childbirth and he would be told when he could come in. Why had he not insisted?

Instead they had called him in to look at her pale, dead body. It had been washed of blood, but a heap of linen thrown in the corner was saturated with it. He tried not to look, but his eyes were drawn to it in horror. He had not wanted to know his lustily yelling daughter and had packed her off to a wet nurse and after that to a foster mother. She wanted for nothing, but that did not make him feel any less guilty about it. 'No woman, let alone one so young, should be asked to give up her life to gratify a man's need for an heir,' he told Ash.

'You are being too harsh on yourself, Harry. You could not have known what would happen and next time it will surely be plain sailing.'

'There will not be a next time. How can I put anyone, particularly someone for whom I have the tenderest feelings, through that torture?'

'Women do have a choice, my friend, to marry or not to marry, and most, if you ask them, would certainly say they want to be married and have children. It is their lot in life and they know it.'

'You are a fine one to talk,' Harry said. 'A bachelor of, how old?'

'Thirty-two. I have given up expecting to meet the lady with whom I could contemplate sharing my life. I am too set in my ways. We should drive each other to distraction and as I have no great estate to worry about, there is no need.'

'But you have mistresses?'

'Naturally I have. But there are ways to prevent conception.'

'What use is that to a man who needs a legitimate heir?'

'But you must have an heir somewhere,' Ash said.

'So I have, a muckworm of a cousin who has no care for the land, nor the people who depend upon it, and would ruin his inheritance in a twelvemonth with his gambling.'

'Then you must prevent that and marry again.'

'I am not like to die in the immediate future.'

'I hope you may not, but you can never be sure, can you?'

'No.' The answer was curt, and spying a couple of chairs for hire, Harry beckoned the men over and they climbed in, effectively ending the conversation. In this fashion they were conveyed to the Old Bailey where they took their seats to listen to the trial.

The room was already crowded. Some of the audience had an interest in the case, but many came to the proceedings simply out of curiosity. Until the entrance of the court officials they talked, ate pies and fruit and noisily speculated on the fate of those to come up before the judge.

Those of the Dustin Gang who had been apprehended were brought into court and ranged in the dock. There was Alfred Dustin, his wife Meg, their twenty-four-year-old daughter, Matilda, and her husband, Bernard Watson. All were charged that 'they not being employed at the Mint in the Tower, nor being lawfully authorised by the Lord High Treasurer and not having God before their eyes, nor weighing the duty of their allegiance to our lord, the King, and his people, did between the first day of May and the tenth in the year of our Lord seventeen hundred and sixty-one, feloniously and traitorously forge and counterfeit forty coins of pewter in the likeness of silver shillings and sixpences'. They all pleaded not guilty.

The first witness was the landlady of their lodgings who had gone into their rooms to clean them when they were out and had found a mould filled with chalk, some clay pipes, much burned, and two sixpences, which had been stamped on one side but not the other. When Bernard Watson came home she had taxed him with her finds and he had admitted to her that he was counterfeiting and had shown her how the coins were made.

'He had a mould,' she said. 'It was filled with

chalk and had an impression of a sixpence in it.
He poured in pewter, which he had heated in a
tobacco pipe over the fire. He said good-quality
pewter was best and he obtained it by cutting up a
tankard. When the piece was taken from the mould
he nicked it with a clean tile to mill the edges,
then he scoured it with sand to make it look bright.
Lastly he put it into a pot of water boiled with a
powder he called argol to make it look silver.'

'What did you say to this?' the judge asked.

'I told him I would have none of it and they must
all find other lodgings.'

'You lie,' Bernard Watson protested. 'I never
made a false coin in my life.'

The woman turned to the judge. 'Your honour,
as God is my witness, I tell you true.'

'Then what happened?' the prosecutor urged
her.

'He said he would pay me well to pass the coins
off when I went shopping, but I refused and said
they must all leave.'

'And did they?'

'I left the house and went to fetch a constable.
When I brought the constable back, they had
packed up and gone and taken all the sixpences
with them.'

The constable was called next and told the court

that he found nothing except a broken-up pewter tankard and the bowl of a pipe with a residue of pewter in it. He saw no counterfeit coins.

'God, I do believe the rascals will get off,' Ash murmured.

'Patience,' Harry responded, flicking invisible fluff from his sleeve.

'Where did they go?' the prosecutor asked the witness.

'They went to a house in White Lion Street. I got the address from a man at the Nag's Head, who heard them speak of it. I went there with Constable Bunting and we broke down the door and found them all gathered to make coins.'

'I suppose you were the man at the Nag's Head,' Ash whispered to Harry.

'Shh,' Harry warned him, smiling.

Other witnesses were called to corroborate. Their defence that they were making buttons and buckles to sell in the market was thrown out. Alfred, Meg and Bernard were sentenced to hang; Matilda's plea that she was not aware her parents and husband were doing anything but making buttons was accepted and she was set free. She left the court vowing vengeance against whoever had ratted on them.

Harry and Ash did not wait to hear the next trial,

but made their way out to the street and comparative fresh air. 'I did not know it was so easy to make false coins,' Ash said. 'But surely the profits are minimal.'

'Not if you make enough of them. Take a counterfeit shilling or even a sixpence to a shop to buy something for a ha'penny or a penny and receive the change in good money and you soon make a tidy profit. Usually the coiners employ what they call passers-off to go into the country with a supply of bad coins with which they buy goods needing change.'

'Not worth the candle,' Ash said.

'Not for such as we are, but for the lower sort a welcome supplement to low wages and, for those with no work at all, better than starving.'

'The young woman was very angry. Do you think she will try to carry out her threat?'

'She has no idea who turned them in.' He paused. 'They are small fry. The really big profits come with clipping gold coins, but for that you need to be supplied with real coins to make a start and it is altogether on a more lofty plane. That is what I'm going after next.'

'What have you discovered?'

'Not a great deal as yet, but I was handed a clipped guinea at the wine merchant's the other day. It had been used to purchase wine. Unfortunately he could not remember who had passed it to him. He has promised to let me know as soon as he sees another one.'

'You can't do it more than once in the same shop, surely?'

'It depends how observant the shopkeeper is. And if the rogue thought he had got away with it he might be tempted to try again.'

They had been walking back towards St James's as they talked and turned into White's and the subject of coiners and, indeed, of crime in whatever form was dropped in favour of playing cards. Harry drank and gambled in moderation; he found that men in their cups often let fall titbits of information that helped him in his work for the Piccadilly Gentlemen. And there was nothing to go home for. He could attend soirées, routs and balls, he was always a welcome guest, simply because of his title, wealth and unmarried status, but he became tired of gushing mamas throwing their daughters in his way. He found himself reiterating that he had decided not to marry again, but that did not stop them trying to change his mind.

He could, of course, find one of the hundreds of ladies of the night to amuse him for an hour or two, but he had always found paying for that dubious pleasure distasteful. He went frequently to the theatre and enjoyed supper with the cast afterwards, but there was a limit to the number of times he could view one play, especially if it were not particularly well done. It was easier to spend his evenings at one or other of his clubs.

A four was made up by Benedict Stafford and Sir Max Chalmers. Benedict was a pimply youth of no more than twenty, heir to a Viscount who kept him on short commons, which everyone knew. Harry had never met Sir Max, but he was well dressed in sober black, relieved by silver embroidery and a white lace cravat, matched by the froth of lace emerging from his coat sleeves. With his sharp nose and chin and thin legs, he reminded Harry of a magpie.

'You have the devil's own luck,' Stafford complained several hours later when Harry scooped up his pile of winnings. 'Unless you take my voucher, I can play no more.'

'Naturally I shall accept your voucher,' Harry said, using the high-pitched voice of the fop, though he drew the line at a lisp. 'But if you have scattered too many of them about, I wonder when I might be paid.'

Benedict laughed. 'That I cannot tell you, but

you are in no hurry, are you? I believe you to be prodigious high in the instep.'

'So I may be, but neither am I a fool.' He was idly looking at the coins he had won as he spoke, but not so much by a flicker of an eyelid did he betray the fact that one of them was clipped. He wondered which of the players had put it there and if he was aware of what he had done. The trouble was that it was easy to pass clipped guineas without realising it; they had once been genuine and their only flaw was that, after clipping, they were smaller and weighed less than they should. He put it in his pocket. 'I like a man to pay his debts.'

'Then I withdraw,' Benedict said huffily. 'Any other man would demand satisfaction for that slur on his honour.'

'I am relieved you do not,' Harry said, smiling lazily. 'I abhor violence.'

'I will toss you the dice for my share of the pot,' Ash told the young man. 'If you win, it will give you the stake to go on playing.'

'And if I lose?'

'I will take your voucher.'

'Agreed.'

The card game was suspended while the dice were called for. Harry spent the time studying his playing companions. Benedict was a young fool, wanting to impress, to be counted a man about town, but he would not have the stomach for passing counterfeit guineas. Max Chalmers was different. He was thirty or thereabouts, not ill looking, though his expression was surly. His clothes were well made and his powdered wig one of the best; a vain man, he decided, then chuckled secretly at himself for his own pretensions.

'Allow me to offer condolences and congratulations, Chalmers,' Ash said while they waited. 'I believe you have recently come into your inheritance.'

'I thank you, though there is little enough to salvage and I am left with an unmarried sister to provide for.'

'Is that such a burden?'

'It would not be if our father had not invested foolishly and left no portion for her. My wife is not over-fond of her and is reluctant to offer her a home.' He sighed. 'If only I could find her a husband. You do not know of anyone requiring a wife, do you?'

Ash looked meaningfully at Harry, who frowned at him, but he took no notice. 'What can you say in her favour?'

'Not a great deal,' Max said gloomily. 'She is

twenty-six and not beautiful, but I suppose you could say she has a good figure...'

'Why does your wife not like her?' Harry demanded.

'She is too opinionated.'

'Mmm, a bad trait indeed,' Harry said. 'Is that why she has never married?'

'It could be. But she has been housekeeper to our father since our mother died. To give her her due she is very good at it. The house always ran like clockwork. That is half the trouble—if she comes to our house, she will want to impose her own ideas...'

Harry laughed. 'Then you have a problem, my friend.'

'Marry her off,' Ash said.

'So I would, if I could find someone to take her.'

'Is she healthy?' Ash persisted in his questioning.

'Never had a day's illness in her life.'

'It seems to me,' Ash said thoughtfully 'that your contention that she has little in her favour is false. She is a good housekeeper, can hold her own and is healthy enough to bear children. Is she particular as to a husband?'

Max laughed. 'She cannot afford to be.'

'You mean she would agree to a marriage of convenience?'

'If one were offered, I think I could persuade her.' He paused, realising he might have sounded unfeeling. 'Of course, I would not let her to go any Tom, Dick or Harry… Oh, I beg your pardon, Portman.'

'Granted.'

'I would wish to know she would be dealt fairly with, not kept short of pin money or treated like a skivvy,' Max went on. 'She is, after all, a lady. Our family can trace its lineage back to Tudor times.'

'Dowry?' Ash asked, ignoring the kick Harry gave him under the table.

'Alas! There you have me.'

Ash chuckled. 'Not much of a bargain, then. How do you propose to bring this marriage about? Advertise her for sale?'

'That's a thought,' Max admitted.

'How can you be so callous?' Harry burst out, forgetting his usual languid air. 'She is your sister and a lady; surely she deserves your protection.'

Max looked startled by this outburst from a man who had the reputation of indolence and a studied lack of finer feelings, except when they were his own. 'Naturally she does and until she marries she shall have it, but she would be happier married, of that I am certain.'

'We should like to meet the lady, should we not, Harry?'

'Speak for yourself,' Harry said brusquely, wondering how much longer the waiter was going to be fetching the dice. The whole conversation was becoming offensive.

'You?' Benedict queried, addressing Ashley. 'I thought you were content to remain a bachelor.'

'So I am. I was thinking of someone else.'

Max laughed. 'A man-matchmaker—whoever heard of such a thing?'

'I would not go so far as to say that,' Ash said.

'I should think not!' Harry put in. 'I beg you to forget it.'

But Ash had the bit between his teeth and was not about to let go. 'It cannot hurt to meet the lady. Socially, of course. She need not know.' He turned back to Max. 'Where and when could this be done?'

'She is in mourning and not going out in society, but she likes to walk in Green Park of an afternoon. If you care to be there, we could come across each other by chance and I could make her known to you.'

'When?'

'Tomorrow afternoon. Shall we say two o' clock?'

'Capital! We will meet you at the gate and take a stroll together.' Harry's kick was even more vicious than the previous one and drew a cry of 'ouch' from Ash, which he hastily covered with a cough.

'Where has the pesky waiter got to with those dice?' Harry grumbled, looking about him.

'I have changed my mind,' Max said. 'I will not wait, if you will excuse me.' He left the table and strode away. He was quickly followed by Benedict, who was glad to escape without writing out a voucher. Harry noted it, but decided not to pursue him.

As soon as they were out of earshot, he turned to Ashley. 'Just what are you playing at, Ash? If you think I will stoop to buying a wife, you are grossly mistaken. I will not go.'

'It seems to me that you will be doing each other a favour. She cannot want to live with that coxcomb of a brother. You could provide her with a comfortable home and she could provide the heir you need without disturbing your sensibilities.'

'I wish I had not told you anything about my wife,' Harry said. 'I beg you to refrain from mentioning the matter again.' He beckoned to a waiter and asked him to send out for chairs to convey them home: Ash to his bachelor apartments in Lincoln's Inn Fields and Harry to Portman House in Berkeley Square.

Ash laughed. 'Twas but a thought, but I've a mind to take a stroll in the park tomorrow afternoon for amusement's sake. I will call for you. You may come or not, as you please.'

Harry did not please and he went home to a lonely dinner of sirloin of beef, partridge, capon and fruit tartlets and two whole bottles of Rhenish wine. He had friends a-plenty and enough work to keep him occupied and could always find diversions, but Ash had unsettled him and he found himself admitting that he was sometimes lonely. He began to wonder what Chalmers's sister was like. An antidote, he did not doubt, outspoken if her brother was to be believed, and if she was as healthy as he maintained, she was probably big and muscular. Mannish was a word that came to mind.

Impatient with himself, he went to his chamber, where he threw off his wig, changed from his finery into a brown stuff coat, fustian breeches, wool stockings, which had once been decorated with vivid red clocks, but were now faded to a dusky pink, and a black waistcoat, so old and worn it was turning green. Jack Sylvester, his valet, declined to help him don this strange attire, and busied himself tidying away the discarded garments, and then watched as his master tied a spotted neckerchief about his neck, put on a tousled scratch wig and set a three-cornered hat on it. Then he rubbed brown make-up over his face and hands and filled his beautifully manicured nails with it. Lastly he pulled on a down-at-heel pair of shoes. 'I am going out, Jack. I do not know when I shall be back, but you do not need to wait up for me.'

He did not hear Jack's reply, but he could guess it, and clattered down the stairs and said the same thing to the footman, locking the front door behind him and putting the key into his pocket against his return. Then he strode out for the Nag's Head. Harry Portman, the mincing macaroni, had become Gus Housman, an altogether more shady character, one that Sir Ashley Saunders would hardly recognise.

Chapter Two

'Mr O'Keefe, never heard of him.'

The man standing in the tap room of the Nag's Head, his portly middle wrapped in a greasy apron which covered his equally greasy breeches, looked at Rosamund with a mixture of contempt and admiration. Contempt because she was so obviously a lady in spite of her shabby clothes and he had no time for those who considered themselves a cut above the likes of him, and admiration for the fact that she dared to venture inside his premises at all. And unaccompanied at that. But if she thought he would risk life and limb to tell her where Mick O'Keefe could be found, then she was way out.

'Then what about the Barnstaple Mining Company?' Rosamund persisted. 'I believe it sometimes does business here.'

He laughed raucously. 'Mining, lady? Where's

the mine about here? Under the cobbles, is it? I could do with one o' them. Mayhap I could mine myself a little gold and I wouldn't have to stand here answering tomfool questions.'

'Gold,' she said, her breath catching in her throat. 'Why did you say gold?'

'Well, ain't that what everyone wants?' he countered, thinking quickly. 'A pot o' gold to make me rich enough to get outa here?'

'Oh, so the Barnstaple Mining Company is not a gold-mining company.'

He shrugged. 'How should I know? I never heard of it. Get you gone, lady, before some of my customers start getting inquisitive. Rough lot some of em.'

She looked about her. The low-ceilinged, dingy room had been empty apart from the tavern keeper when she entered, but now one or two others had come in and were eyeing her with open curiosity. Realising she was getting nowhere, she beat a hasty retreat. Mr O'Keefe and his business, which she was convinced was bogus, had disappeared. It had been foolish to hope that she would be able to track him down and sell those worthless shares back to him, but she had had to try, not only for her father's sake, but for her own. A few guineas might have helped her out of the dilemma she was in. As it was, there was nothing for her to do now but go back to Holles Street and finish selling the furniture and clearing the house.

All that was left was the kitchen equipment, her bed and clothes chest in her bedchamber and in the drawing room a sofa and the little escritoire she had inherited from her mother. All these would go too, as soon as she knew where she herself was going: companion to Aunt Jessica's friend or unpaid nursery nurse at her brother's? Was that the only choice she had? Could she find work for herself? What could she do? Housekeeping came immediately to mind, but surely there was something else? She considered writing a book on household management, but that had been done before and in any case she could not do it in time to solve her problems, which were pressing and immediate.

Aunt Jessica was waiting for her when she returned, sitting on the sofa in her black-and-white-striped gown. 'Where have you been, Rosamund?' she demanded. 'And in that shabby garb. You look like a street seller.'

As that was the look Rosamund had hoped to achieve when she set out for Covent Garden, she did not comment. 'I had business to see to,' she said, throwing her hat on the stool by the escritoire. 'The furniture has to be sold, you know.'

'Yes, I do know and I am glad to see you are getting on with it.'

'I have no choice, have I?'

'No. I have spoken to Lady Bonhaven. She is willing to give you a trial and I have arranged for you and me to go and see her tomorrow.'

'Aunt, you are beforehand. I have not said that I wish to be the lady's companion.'

'Wish!' exclaimed the good lady. 'Wishes do not come into it, do they? We could wish for the moon, but that does not mean we should have it. Beggars cannot be choosers.'

The barb hurt, but she would not let her aunt see that it did. 'What happened to her ladyship's previous companion?'

'I believe she proved untrustworthy. I do not know the details. No doubt we shall learn them when we visit.'

There being nothing to stay for, the lady left, in the sure knowledge that her niece would comply. Rosamund flung herself on the sofa and forced herself to consider the prospect. She would have to go and see the lady because her aunt had arranged it, but that did not mean she would agree. She sighed heavily as Janet came into the room to tell her nuncheon was ready on the kitchen table. She rose and followed the maid, giving a wry smile to think of what her father would say to her taking her meals in the kitchen with the only two remaining servants. She had certainly come down in the world since her mother's death. Once they had had a house full of servants, a carriage and horses, riding horses, grooms and stable boys. And friends, a great many friends. They were always visiting and being visited.

It was a great pity her father had not been able to deal with the loss of his wife and discouraged callers so that in the end they ceased to come. He had withdrawn into himself, spent most of his time at gambling and drinking clubs and only came home to sleep, treating Rosamund like the housekeeper she soon became. She had worried about him, even nagged him a little, but that only made him angry for daring to criticise him, but she still loved him, remembering the happy, loving father he had once been and making excuses for him. His sudden and violent death had been a great blow to her. But she could not mourn him as she ought because her own situation kept getting in the way.

All three ate their frugal meal in silence. There was nothing to say. Janet and Cook had been given notice and were as worried as she was. She felt guilty about them too, but there was nothing she could do to help them. She could not even help herself.

Afterwards she went back to the household accounts. She was sitting at her desk, trying to make sense of her father's muddled papers when her brother arrived. He was dressed in his black-and-silver mourning suit, which had obviously been crafted by one of London's best tailors, and a powdered white wig. He swept off his tricorne hat and advanced into the room.

'You are just the person to help me sort these out,' she said, indicating a pile of bills. 'I must put them in order of priority, in case there is not enough to pay them all.'

'Gambling debts first and foremost,' he said at once. 'They are debts of honour and must be paid. You can leave the tailor's bills; Father will not need his services again. Likewise the farrier, since I have sold his riding horse.'

'What have you done with the money from that?'

'Paid the funeral expenses.'

'Oh. And the bag of counterfeit guineas? Have you handed it in?'

'No, I told you that would be risky. I have hidden

it.' He took the papers out of her hand and laid them on the desk. 'Come on, leave those, I will deal with them later. Let us go for a stroll.'

'A stroll?' she queried in surprise.

'Yes, you have been indoors too long, you are looking pale. A little exercise and fresh air will be good for you.'

'You have never taken me out walking before. And surely if you want to have a walk you should take Charlotte and the children?'

'Charlotte has taken them to picnic in Hampstead.'

'Why did you not go with them?'

'Because I had business in town and I was concerned for you. Now, put on your hat and let us go to Green Park. That is where you like to walk, is it not?'

Mystified by a sudden interest in her welfare, which was not typical of him, she rose and went up to her room to throw a light shawl over her shoulders and put a hat on her own curls. She did not change her dress, having only one black gown, which would have to do until she could afford to buy another. She hated black; it ill became her, but short of defying protocol she was stuck with it.

They set off across the Oxford Road and down Tyburn Lane towards Green Park, which was not so crowded as Hyde Park and had some pleasant paths and little copses of trees. 'Have you decided to take up Lady Bonhaven's offer?' he asked her, as they walked.

'Not yet. I am expected to visit her tomorrow with Aunt Jessica, but I wish there were an alternative. Her ladyship is known as a difficult employer. I have discovered from Janet that she has had three companions in as many years. I am unlikely to please her for long.'

'Far be it from me to shirk my duty to my sister and I would see you settled. If you cannot bear to accept her ladyship's offer, you may live with Charlotte and me, but I cannot afford more than a little pin money.'

'I know,' she said, wondering how much his suit and wig had cost. And the mourning gown Charlotte had been wearing when she last saw her had at least fifteen yards of silk in it and was heavily embroidered with mother-of-pearl. He did not stint on their wardrobes.

'Would you marry if you could?' he asked.

'Now you are being silly.'

They entered the park and were strolling along the path which led to The Mall, when they met two gentlemen walking towards them. One was rugged looking in a dark blue coat and white small clothes, the other, clearly a fop, was in a suit of peach-and-cream satin, a peach brocade waistcoat and cream small clothes. Rosamund would have passed them, but they were evidently known to Max, because he stopped and swept them an elegant bow. 'Gentlemen, your obedient. May I present my sister, Miss Rosamund Chalmers. Rosie, this is Lord Portman and Sir Ashley Saunders.' He indicated each in turn.

They swept off their hats and bowed to her. 'Madam, your obedient.'

She curtsied. 'Gentlemen.'

'May I offer condolences on your bereavement?' Ash said.

'Thank you.'

'We are out for a stroll,' Max said. 'Shall we walk together?'

The two turned and Ash contrived to skip around so that she was walking between him and Harry.

Harry had made up his mind not to indulge Ash, but his friend had turned up on his doorstep and persuaded him that no harm could come from a short perambulation and a surreptitious peep at the lady. 'You must be a little curious as to why her brother feels it necessary to sell her off like a horse,' he had said.

'Perhaps she looks like one.'

'Well, shall we go and see?'

Harry took the opportunity while she chatted to Ash to study the young lady and came to the conclusion her brother had done her an injustice. Her unmade-up face was very pale and she was no beauty in the accepted sense, but she was far from plain; she had good bone structure, high cheeks and a determined chin. Her hair was a light brown and twisted up into a knot beneath her hat, but a few stray curls sat upon her forehead and two ringlets fell over her ears. He could not, walking beside her as he was, see her eyes and mouth, and for some reason he could not explain, he wished he could.

'I believe you looked after your father before he died,' he said.

She turned towards him to answer and he was faced with grey eyes beneath winged brows, which clearly told of sorrow and worry, but behind that was a hint of humour and determination. He wondered how he had managed to read so much in a pair of eyes, but he knew he was right. And there was a slight upward tilt to her mouth. How much would it take to make her laugh? he wondered.

'Yes, my mother died over seven years ago.'

'My condolences.'

'Thank you.'

'You have never married?'

'No.' Her answer was clipped.

'And now you are alone?'

'I have Max.'

'Yes, indeed. I understand he has a wife and family.'

'Yes.'

'Will you make your home with them?'

He saw the slight shudder of her shoulders, which told him more than words that she did not view the prospect with any pleasure. 'It is one possibility. I have yet to decide.'

'There are others?'

'I believe so.'

'Then I wish you well.'

'Thank you.'

'My sister is considering a post as a lady's companion,' Max put in, making Rosamund give him a furious look. He appeared oblivious to it and went on, 'But I am not sure it would suit her.'

'I am sure it would not,' Harry murmured.

'It is not too late for her to marry,' Max continued. 'But being in mourning, she cannot go to balls and routs and places where she might meet eligible gentlemen, so we are at an impasse.'

'Max!' Rosamund rounded on him. 'I am sure

his lordship and Sir Ashley are not interested in my problems.'

'On the contrary,' Ash said. 'I, for one, am interested. It seems to me that it is a very unjust world that condemns women to a life of dependence and when that dependence is withdrawn, to find themselves in sorry straits. I marvel at their fortitude and resilience to make what they can of their circumstances. Miss Chalmers, you have my sympathy. Do you not say so, Harry?'

Harry was as furious with Ash as Rosamund was with Max, but he could only answer politely. 'Indeed, yes.'

Rosamund opened her mouth to make a sharp retort and shut it again. She began to walk very fast, head up and shoulders back and hoped that would be enough to show them how displeased she was. She was convinced that her brother had brought her out on purpose to meet these two: the rugged naval type with the easy manner and the exquisite popinjay who seemed to be able to keep up with her in spite of his high heels.

Sir Ashley was a pleasant gentleman, but he seemed to be in collusion with her brother, but what of Lord Portman? His vanity was palpable. It was plain he spent a great deal of money with his tailor, his wigmaker and his shoemaker and he seemed to be well known for, even in Green Park, he bowed frequently to others out for a stroll. He could hardly enjoy being seen in company with her, and yet he had not fallen behind as Ash and Max had done.

'Have you done quizzing me, my lord?' she asked.

'Lud! I have not meant to quiz you, ma'am. I have simply been making polite conversation. If you do not care for it, I shall remain silent.'

'No, for you may answer my questions now.'

'With pleasure, ma'am.'

'How long have you known my brother?'

'I have had the honour of his acquaintance since yesterday afternoon, though I believe Sir Ashley has known him longer.'

'And in that time you have become familiar with my affairs. I wonder at Max being so forward.'

'It came about when Ash offered his condolences on the demise of Sir Joshua and Sir Maximilian explained how you had been left.'

'Which he had no business to do.'

'No doubt he feels responsible for you, since your father has not provided for you.'

'I suppose he told you that too?'

'Why, yes. I assume, being concerned, he was in a mood for confidences.'

'And who suggested we should meet this afternoon?'

He wondered whether to deny anyone had, but realised she was too astute to believe it. 'Why, I do not exactly recall. It might have been your brother, but it might have been Sir Ashley…'

'Not you?'

'No, certainly not me.'

'Out of uninterest?'

'Now, how am I to answer that? To say yes would not be chivalrous, would it? And to say no would imply a certain curiosity and that, too, would not be chivalrous. I beg you excuse me from answering.'

He was gratified to see her lips twitch into a smile. 'You are excused.'

'Your brother said you would like to marry.'

'That was his idea, not mine.'

'Why not? Do you prefer to be single?'

'My lord, that is a foolish question and I will not answer it. And I thought we had decided you would cease your questions and answer mine.'

'I beg your pardon.'

'Are you married?'

'No.'

'There, you see! You prefer to be single. Why is it different for men? They can boast of being bachelors, but women must be ashamed of being spinsters.'

He gave an elaborate sigh. 'It is an unfair world, Miss Chalmers; however, I am not a bachelor, but a widower.'

She turned towards him and realised the rather languid look had changed and his eyes had darkened at some remembered pain. 'Oh, then I beg your pardon.'

'Granted. I have been in that sorry state for six years now.'

'Six years? Surely you could marry again if you chose?'

'An' I could, if I could find someone to suit me.' His brow had cleared again and he was once more ready to treat the world lightly.

'Are you so particular?'

'I fear I must be.' Again that sigh, but it was accompanied by a smile.

She did break into a laugh then, understanding what her brother and Sir Ashley were concocting and he, hearing that laugh, knew she had realised what was afoot. 'My lord,' she said, a twinkle in those grey eyes, 'shall we play a little game with them?'

He stopped to give her an exaggerated bow, took her hand and lifted the back of it to his lips. 'It will be my pleasure.' He offered her his arm and she took it, still smiling. Not that there was anything to smile at; she was no nearer a solution to her dilemma and really Max was an idiot.

They continued in this way, heads close together, pretending to be absorbed in each other's conversation, though it was nothing but polite trivialities, until they had circumnavigated the park and were approaching their entry point, when she stopped to wait for Max and Ash to catch up with them.

The little party left the park and here they parted, the men bowing and Rosamund dropping a curtsy. She could not wait to tell Max exactly what she thought of his antics and turned on him as soon as the other two were out of earshot. 'Maximilian Chalmers, I am thoroughly displeased with you. Do you know Lord Portman guessed what you and his friend were up to and he was highly entertained by it? I, on the other hand, was mortified.'

'I see you took his arm when it was offered and went on your way, heads together in a most intimate fashion.'

'What could I do, but treat it as a jest? I assume it was a jest.'

'Not entirely. His lordship is looking for a wife.'

'So he might be, but he told me he was very particular. He is a macaroni, so vain that I wonder he does not carry a mirror about with him, and you were trying to throw him at me. He can surely find himself a pretty young wife who will overlook his strange mannerisms.'

'I believe that when you come to know him, you will appreciate his qualities.'

'Come to know him! Max, how am I to come to know him? You are surely not intending to continue with this farce?'

'It is no farce. The man needs a wife and you need a husband, if you are not to go to Lady Bonhaven. It cannot hurt to meet him again.'

'You mean you have made the arrangements?'

'Not exactly, but I have hinted we shall be at the fireworks in Ranelagh Gardens on Saturday evening.'

'I have no intention of going. And I doubt Lord Portman will go either. He has no use for me and I have none for him. Do you think I am so desperate?'

'But you are, are you not?'

'No,' she lied. 'I would rather be a companion to Lady Bonhaven. And why, in heaven's name, would Lord Portman even consider me?' She paused, as a new thought came to her. 'Unless you have offered an inducement?'

'What inducement could I offer a man like him? He is rich as Croesus. No, he simply wants a wife who will not outshine him.'

That hit home and hurt badly, but she endeavoured to turn it against the gentleman in question. 'Oh, I should certainly not do that! I never met such a shining example of a coxcomb.'

'That is all put on. He fancies himself an actor.'

'Worse and worse. I beg you to say no more on the matter.'

He fell silent and she fumed the rest of the way back to Holles Street, where he took his leave. She went into the almost empty house and stood looking about her. It had been her home for most of her life, but it was home no longer. And tomorrow she must go with her aunt to be interviewed by the elderly Lady Bonhaven and accept whatever she was offered. 'Oh, Papa,' she murmured. 'Did you know what a pickle you were going to leave me in?'

She climbed the stairs to her room to take off her hat. The chamber was empty of all but the bare necessities. A trunk, standing on the floor at the foot of the bed, was half-filled with clothes Janet had begun to pack. How much would Lady Bonhaven expect her to take with her? And what about her books and her escritoire? Would she be allowed those?

She sat on the side of the bed, from which the hangings had already been removed for cleaning before being sold, and contemplated her future. That led to thoughts of her brother. He had offered her a home, but had made it abundantly clear he did not want her. He was doing his best to marry her off. And to that macaroni! But even as she derided Lord Portman, she realised there was more to him than met the eye. When they were alone and talking seriously, he had suddenly stopped his mincing gait and matched her stride with his and that high effeminate tone of voice dropped to a more masculine level. What sort of a man was he? Why could he not find himself a bride in the conventional way?

Harry was ringing a peal over Ash, but his friend was unrepentant. 'No harm was done,' he said, as they made their way slowly along Piccadilly towards the City.

'A great deal of harm was done. She guessed what her brother was about and passed it off as a jest, but I knew she was mortified. I felt very sorry for her.'

'So did I. Poor thing, she is like to drown in deep

water unless someone throws her a lifeline.' Ash was an ex-naval man and his conversation was littered with nautical phrases. 'And you must admit she is not the antidote we had been led to expect. Not a beauty, I grant you, but strong and healthy enough to bear children. She could be the mother of your heir with no trouble.'

'I wish to God I had never told you about Beth. I don't know why I did. I never told anyone before.'

'That was because you have been dwelling on the problem and hoping to find a solution. I have given you one. You could at least think about it.'

'I would rather not.'

'Why not?' Ash persisted. 'She is not ugly, or stupid, or idiotish. Marry her, install her at Bishop's Court, make her with child and then get on with your work for the Club and forget her.'

'How callous you are. I am not at all surprised no woman has ever wanted to marry you.'

'Oh, I could have married a dozen times over, an' I so chose. And do not change the subject.'

'I wish to change it.'

'Very well. Do you go to Ranelagh on Saturday? I hear the fireworks are to be especially fine in honour of the royal wedding and coronation. We could patrol the crowds and keep an eye out for pickpockets. And what better place to winkle out people passing counterfeit coins?'

This was true and reminded Harry of the counterfeit guinea he had taken home the day before. He ought to be doing something about that, not bothering himself about women and marriage. 'Very well, I will go.'

Satisfied with the success of his ruse, Ash spotted a couple of chairmen plying for hire and called them over. The two men took their leave of each other and were conveyed on their separate ways.

Once home, in an effort to put Miss Chalmers and her problems out of his mind, Harry went to the safe box he had had installed under the floor of his library and took out two counterfeit guineas, one the wine merchant had given him and the other he had brought home from the card game the day before. He weighed them carefully in his hand, deciding they weighed about the same, which was a fraction less than a genuine guinea. Then he studied them through a strong lens he took from a drawer in his desk, examining the milled edges carefully. He would swear that they had been done by the same hand with the same instrument. He was sure he had two coins by the same coiner, but they had come to him in very different circumstances and there were undoubtedly many more circulating about the capital.

Anyone who wanted to buy wine could have passed the one to the vintner, but which of the card players had put the guinea in the pot? Benedict was certainly too drunk and too foolish to bother his head about the size of the coins he had in his purse. Max Chalmers was a wily bird, but it was unlikely he would knowingly pass bad coins in White's for fear of being excluded very publicly from its portals. Even Ash could have picked it up somewhere else and unknowingly put it down as part of his stake. It could have been done by any of the three, more interested in the game than in the weight of their coins. They would not be looking for bad money, which was something the counterfeiters relied on, more often than not successfully. The question was: if all three were innocent, who had passed them in the first place?

He locked them carefully away again and sat contemplating his next move. The trouble was that a pair of grey eyes kept coming between him and his deliberations. They were a redeeming feature in an otherwise unremarkable face. He imagined her as a companion to some demanding old lady and knew, without doubt, she would hate it. He wished he could help her. It was a pity he did not need a housekeeper; Mrs Rivers had kept house at Bishop's Court for more years than he cared to remember and was entirely satisfactory. And in town, all he needed was his cook and the usual complement of other servants. Besides, Miss Chalmers with her straight back, firm chin and independent mind, not to mention her lineage, was certainly not servant material. If he could not love again, could he bring himself to marry without it? At her age and in her circumstances the lady would not expect it, would she?

He shrugged his thoughts impatiently from him. He must be going mad even to contemplate such a thing. What he needed was a little diversion, something to take his mind off that walk in the park. He sent a footman out for a chair and instructed the chairmen to take him to the Baltic Coffee House in Threadneedle Street. It was the favourite haunt of traders and he might pick up some useful information, perhaps find another bad guinea. He would do the rounds of the coffee and chocolate houses and when they closed for the night, he would move on to the gentlemen's clubs. That should keep him occupied until the early hours and he could go home to his lonely bed.

* * *

Mrs Bullivant arrived at Holles Street at noon the following day, which showed how determined she was; she hardly ever rose from her bed before that hour. Rosamund, who had given up hoping for anything else to save her, put a short jacket over her mourning gown, sat a black bonnet right at the back of her coiffure and tied it on with wide black ribbons. Picking up her reticule, she announced herself ready to go.

Her aunt had brought her carriage and they were conveyed in some comfort to Brook Street, though they could easily have walked or taken chairs. 'I do not want her to think we are beggars,' her aunt said. 'You must comport yourself with some pride, after all.' Her aunt was nothing if not conscious of her rank in society.

'She is unlikely to employ me if I am too top-lofty,' Rosamund said, half-wishing the lady would turn her down.

'There is a middle road. Be polite, a little subservient perhaps, but not too much. Keep your head up and do not mumble.'

'I am not in the habit of mumbling, Aunt.'

The lady ignored that. 'It's that or go to Max. Can you rely on him to treat you with compassion? If ever there was a chip off the old block, it is he, and besides that, he is truly under the cat's paw.'

'I know that, Aunt.'

They drew up at the door of Lady Bonhaven's substantial house and were admitted by a footman. He bade them wait while he ascertained that her ladyship was at home and then led them upstairs to a boudoir that looked out over the busy street. Her ladyship was sitting by the window, so she must have seen the carriage arrive. She was extremely fat and with her padded black skirt and petticoat she left little room for anyone else on the sofa. She wore a black cap tied beneath her chin with a narrow ribbon and her tiny feet rested on a footstool. Beside her, on a small table, stood a half-empty glass of negus, a box of sugar plums, a hartshorn and a little silver bell, all readily to hand.

'Come in, Jessie,' she said, lifting her quizzing glass to examine Rosamund from to top to toe. 'You have brought the girl, I see.'

'Indeed I have, Clarissa. This is my niece, Rosamund Chalmers.'

Rosamund dipped a curtsy. 'My lady.'

'She is taller than I thought. And older. You did not tell me how old she was.'

'I am six and twenty, my lady,' Rosamund answered before her aunt could do so.

'Past the age of being giddy for marriage,' Jessica put in.

'That is a point in her favour.' She waved them into chairs, then addressed Rosamund. 'What accomplishments do you have, miss?'

'I have been educated…'

'Pah! I did not mean that. Your education is of no interest to me so long as you do not flaunt it when I am in conversation with my friends. If I take you on, you will be my shadow, not my mouthpiece. I shall expect you to accompany me when I go out, to make sure I have everything for my comfort, to fetch and carry and keep your tongue between your teeth. Is that understood?'

'Perfectly, my lady.' Rosamund understood only too well. The idea of being at the beck and call of this autocratic lady filled her with misgivings.

'I am a little chilly,' the lady went on. 'Fetch my shawl. You will find it in the cupboard in my bedchamber.' She indicated a door to an adjoining room. 'The lilac-and-cream one.'

Rosamund went to obey, murmuring to herself that her ladyship obviously did not adhere to the rule that, however high one's rank, it was courteous to say please when giving an order. She found the

shawl easily and returned with it, only to be casti-
gated for bringing the wrong one. 'I said lilac and
cream,' the lady said. 'That is mauve and white.
Can you not tell the difference?'

Rosamund, who was tempted to argue the
colours, instead begged her pardon and went in
search of the right one, knowing the old lady had
deliberately set a trap for her. When she returned
with the correct shawl, she was instructed to put it
about her ladyship's shoulders and that also met
with criticism. When at last her ladyship was settled, she said, 'Well, I am not sure you will suit.
You have not been brought up in a way that fills
me with confidence.'

'I was not brought up to be a paid companion,
my lady.'

'My niece means no disrespect,' Aunt Jessica
put in quickly. 'But she will soon learn what is
expected of her.'

'Let us hope so,' her ladyship said. 'I shall give
you a month's trial, Miss Chalmers. Without pay,
naturally. You may start at the beginning of next
week, that will give you time to sort out your affairs. Now, you must excuse me, I am expecting
callers at any moment.' She picked up the bell
from the table and shook it vigorously. When the

footman answered the summons, she directed him to escort the ladies to the door.

As they crossed the pavement towards the carriage, they found themselves face to face with Lord Portman, who was on his way to a meeting of the Gentleman's Club. Today he was in blue and white, elegant as ever. He swept off his sugarloaf hat and executed a graceful leg. 'Good morning, Miss Chalmers. A fine day, is it not?'

Rosamund curtsied. 'Yes, indeed, very fine.' She turned to her aunt. 'Aunt, may I present Lord Portman. My lord, my aunt, Mrs Jessica Bullivant.'

He bowed. 'Ma'am, your obedient.'

She inclined her head in acknowledgement. 'Lord Portman.'

He hurried to open the carriage door for her and handed her in and then turned to do the same courtesy for Rosamund. He closed the door and ordered the coachman to proceed, then watched as the carriage drew away. Then he went on his way, mincing a little and twirling his cane, looking thoughtful.

'When did you meet that gentleman?' Jessica demanded, jerking her head backwards towards Harry.

'Yesterday in the park. Max introduced us and we walked together for a little.'

'I had no idea Maximilian knew his lordship,' her aunt said, evidently aware of Lord Portman's consequence.

'I think they met at White's.'

'I am surprised that Max can afford to game with someone as prodigious rich as he is.'

'How do you know he is rich?' Rosamund asked. 'Just because he evidently spends a fortune on his clothes does not mean he is wealthy. He could be in debt to his tailor.'

'Oh, undoubtedly he is. What gentleman of his rank is not? But I have heard he inherited forty thousand a year besides Bishop's Court in Middlesex and a hunting box in Leicestershire. Every unmarried girl for miles around would like to catch his eye.'

'He told me had been married, but his wife died six years ago and he had found no one since to suit him.'

'Did he now? That is a very personal disclosure for so new an acquaintance.'

'Yes, but I asked him.'

'Rosamund! How could you be so forward?'

'It was done in self-defence; he was asking me about my marriage prospects and it annoyed me.'

'What did you tell him?'

'Nothing that he did not know already,' Rosamund said gloomily. 'His lordship was not the only one revealing personal details. Max was particularly forthcoming. He told him about Papa not providing for me and the fact that I was contemplating being a lady's companion. He even said I would like to marry to avoid that. I was exceedingly cross with him.'

'Whatever was Max thinking of?'

'I think he and his lordship's friend, Sir Ashley Saunders, were trying to throw us together. Lord Portman certainly thought so...'

'And?'

'He treated it as a jest.'

'Yes, I can see he would—why would he consider you when he could have the pick of London's débutantes?'

This scathing comment did nothing to bolster Rosamund's self-esteem and she fell silent. But she was not so much humiliated as furious. It was a mood that stayed with her the rest of the day and stopped her thinking about her future with Lady Bonhaven. She went back to her father's papers, determined to go through them with a fine-tooth comb to see if there was any way the lawyer could have been mistaken and there was some small bequest for her.

'There is a clever coiner passing guineas in London,' Harry told the rest of the group. 'I have picked up two myself.' He took the two fake guineas from his pocket and laid them on the table. 'I'd be obliged if you would look out for guineas like these.'

Jonathan pulled out his purse and tipped the contents on to the table. 'I do not think there are any bad ones here,' he said, picking his coins up one at a time and returning them to his purse.

The others followed suit and Ash was found to have one in his money. 'Well, I'll be damned!' he said. 'Where did that come from?'

'It would help if you could remember,' Harry said, taking possession of the coin.

'I've bought nothing that needed change in guineas,' Ash said.

'A debt repaid?' Harry prompted. 'Or a win at cards? I ask because one of these…' he indicated the two he had brought with him, then put all three in his pocket '…was in the pot when we played at White's the day before yesterday.'

'You think I put it in?'

'Anyone could have done so. You, Stafford or Chalmers. Inadvertently, of course.'

'Even you,' Ash said, with a grin.

'No, for I have handled too many of them to be taken in. Examine all your winnings in future, will you?'

'Certainly I will.'

'Have you any idea who the counterfeiters might be?' James asked.

'No, but I am looking and listening. If I can find out who they are, then I must also find out where it is being done in order to produce evidence. Possession of a single guinea is not evidence; anyone could have innocently accepted and tried to pass on a fake coin. But I wish you all to be on your guard.'

'We will all do that,' James said, and with that the meeting broke up.

'It was Benedict put most in the pot,' Ash reminded Harry as they left. 'And he did leave somewhat hurriedly.'

'Yes, but that was because he hoped I had forgotten to ask for his voucher. If he had guineas to spare, he would not cry hard up, would he?'

'Chalmers, by his own admission, has pockets to let.'

'That is the tale he tells to unload his sister on

to an unsuspecting bridegroom,' Harry said. 'I do not believe it.'

'Poor woman.'

'Yes, I know you feel sorry for her, Ash. I suggest you marry her yourself.'

'I do not need a bride. On the other hand, you do. For someone who owns a vast estate like Bishop's Court and no direct heir, it is a necessity.'

'I am more concerned with tracking down whoever is passing false guineas and hoping he will lead me to the coiners.'

'Yes, I should like to see them in chains myself. I do not like having my pockets raided…'

'Raided, Ash?'

'Well, you have deprived me of a guinea and put it in your own pocket.'

'You could not have spent it without being an accessory. If the loss of a guinea is so important to you, then I will give you one.'

'No, no, my dear fellow, wouldn't dream of it. Tell you what, I'll take you to the Cocoa Tree and toss you for it.'

Harry raised one quizzical eyebrow at his friend. 'A bad guinea?'

'Good heavens, no! A good one.'

'Very well.'

They repaired to the Cocoa Tree and spent a convivial evening with the dice. Miss Rosamund Chalmers appeared to be forgotten.

Chapter Three

Ranelagh Pleasure Gardens were in Chelsea, next to the Royal Hospital, and were a favourite place of leisure for the more select of London's inhabitants, simply because the admittance was more than that at the New Spring Garden at Vauxhall. The entrance fee of two shillings and sixpence or five shillings on firework nights was beyond the means of the honest poor and they had to content themselves with viewing the show from boats on the river. The price of entrance did not deter robbers, pickpockets and passers of counterfeit money who used the shadows and the letting off of fireworks to ply their trade. But in spite of that, the gardens cultivated an air of respectability and the *haut monde* happily mixed with the middling sort to enjoy a night out.

Rosamund had said all along she would not go. She was in mourning and it was unseemly and the last thing she wanted was for Lord Portman to think she was pursuing him, to all of which Max had an answer. No one knew her, so being in mourning did not signify; she could go in half-mourning, grey or mauve, and if his lordship were to show an interest, then she should be glad and cultivate him in so far as it was in her ability to do so. 'Do you want to work for Lady Bonhaven?' he demanded, when he arrived to escort her and found her unprepared. 'She is an inveterate gabble grinder, out and about everywhere, and you will have to tag along behind her like a pet pug. Worse than that because a pug is not expected to work for his keep.'

'Do you think I do not know all that?'

'Then seize what opportunities are offered.'

She gave a short laugh. 'I doubt I shall be offered an opportunity to seize.'

'Then let us go to enjoy the fireworks.'

'Oh, very well.' She didn't know why she agreed, except that sitting at home alone was something she had been doing so often of late, she felt she needed a little diversion. Perhaps, if she could put her problems to one side for an hour or two, her subconscious might come up with a solution.

She went up to her room to root about in her half-packed trunk for another dress and found a dove-grey silk she had worn when she had gone from mourning to half-mourning after her mother died. It was sadly out of fashion, having a wrap-around bodice, narrow oval hoops and wide, stiffened cuffs to the sleeves, but it was a change from unrelieved black. A white kerchief served to fill the neckline. She scooped her hair up under a wide-brimmed hat she thought might hide her face and returned to her brother.

He looked her up and down. 'Is that the best you can manage?'

'Yes. If you do not care to be seen with me, I beg you to go alone.'

'No. Come along. We shall be late.'

He had hired chairs to take them, so there was no opportunity for conversation until they were set down at the entrance. Max bought two tickets at five shillings each, paying for them with a guinea and receiving four half-crowns and a shilling in change, then he took her arm and hurried her inside.

The gardens were crowded and they were jostled several times as they made their way forwards, heading for the magnificent circular building in the centre of the garden, where the patrons could listen to the orchestra from its many boxes, or parade the central floor, sometimes drowning out the music with their chatter. There were booths selling tea, coffee and chocolate, as well as others containing gaming tables. Some booths were privately hired and here Cyprians and demi-reps and even apparently respectable ladies, would meet their lovers. Max ignored them as he hurried her along.

Rosamund supposed he was in a rush to meet Lord Portman and wished she had not agreed to come. What, in heaven's name, could she say to the man? Half of her hoped he would not come, the other half began to look forward to seeing him again and wondering if her first impression of him as a strange mixture of the empty-headed exquisite and the perspicacious man about town would still hold good.

As they neared the Rotunda, Max slowed his pace and they walked more sedately. 'There they are,' he said suddenly. 'Do put on a smile, Rosie. I never saw such a Friday face in my life.'

Harry had not expected to see her there and was at first surprised, but then he saw Ash's grin and knew he had been hoaxed. There was nothing for it but to greet the lady with his usual gallantry. 'Miss Chalmers, how do you do?' His hand, holding his hat, swept forwards over his foot as he bowed to her.

She noticed his burgundy silk coat, pink waistcoat and pink small clothes as she bent her knee and bowed her head in acknowledgement. He was nothing if not colourful. She straightened herself to meet cool blue eyes regarding her with amusement. She felt herself blush at his scrutiny. Was he, like her brother, deprecating her gown? 'I am well,' she said, taking a firm grip on herself to answer him. 'And you?'

'All the better for seeing you, ma'am.'

She laughed at this preposterous lie. 'Then you must have been feeling singularly out of sorts before that. Has your friend been roasting you again?' She turned to Ash and dropped him a small curtsy. 'Sir Ashley, I bid you good evening.'

'It is a very good evening now you have arrived,' he said, bowing to her.

'I do not know which of you is worse,' she said. 'Pray do not try your flummery on me, sir. I am immune to it.'

'Then you are the first lady I have met who is,' Harry said, looking at her through his quizzing glass. It was an affectation; his eyesight was perfect. He saw that she had changed out of the dreadful black silk, but the grey she wore was only marginally better. It was a great pity because he felt sure she would repay a little spent on a wardrobe, even in mourning. 'Surely you are not averse to being told your company is a pleasure?'

'Not if it is true, but I suspect the contrary. I vow you had no idea you would meet me tonight.'

'That does not signify. Shall we walk a little?' He abandoned the idea of catching anyone passing counterfeit coins and instead offered her his arm and she laid her fingers on his silk sleeve. The path was so crowded all four could not walk abreast and Max and Ash fell behind.

'I came to view the fireworks,' Rosamund said, feeling she ought to have a reason for her presence.

'I did too, so we can view them together.'

'My lord, please do not feel you have to entertain me or even be polite to me. I am well aware of what my brother is up to and if I were you I would pay neither him nor me any heed and go about your business.'

'It is not in my nature to be impolite,' he said. 'And what do you suppose Sir Maximilian is up to?'

'Would you put me to the blush by asking me to speak of it when you could not help but know what he is about?'

'I beg your pardon. I was not sure you perfectly understood.'

'To be sure, I understand. He does not wish to give me house room himself and yet he is averse to his sister lowering herself to go to work, especially as Lady Bonhaven's companion. He has other ideas, which are even more embarrassing.'

That was what she had been doing in Brook Street when he had met her and her aunt; he had guessed as much. Poor thing, he would not recommend Lady Bonhaven as an employer to anyone. Her ladyship had been a friend of his late mother and he knew her to be a tyrant to her servants. 'And do you think you will like working for her ladyship?'

'I know I should hate it.' There was no point in trying to hide her dilemma from him, since her brother had already been more than frank. 'If I could find congenial work or set up a business, do something useful that will earn me enough to live on, I would not need to.'

'What could you do?'

'I do not know. I have been educated. I could teach. Or help someone catalogue a library, or write book on household management. Or do fine embroidery.'

'Ugh!' he said with a shudder. 'It would ruin your eyes. And such lovely eyes too.'

She ignored the compliment. 'It is all very well for you to belittle such occupations, but you are not in my shoes.'

'I do not think they would fit, my dear,' he said, lifting up one elegantly shod foot and regarding it complacently. His balance on one foot was perfectly steady.

'I wish I had never said anything to you at all, if you are going to treat it as a jest,' she said angrily, noting his muscular calf in its pink silk stocking; there was no need for padding there. In fact, his whole physique belied the idle fop. She shook such irrelevant thoughts from her. 'As for my brother's outlandish scheming, that is certainly not to be taken seriously...'

'Then you are at an impasse.'

'It would seem so. But do not mistake me, I am not done yet.'

'No, of course you are not.' He looked sideways at her, wondering how much of the last half-hour had been carefully planned to trap him, how much of an actress she was. He gave a little chuckle. 'You have forgot one calling open to impecunious ladies.'

She turned to stare at him. 'How dare you! I had

thought you were a gentleman, my lord. I see now how mistaken I was.' Angrily, she began to walk on very fast, but he soon caught her up.

'You misunderstand me, ma'am,' he said, taking her arm and forcing her to stop. 'Such a thing never entered my head. I was thinking of the stage.'

She pulled herself out of his grasp. 'An actress! That is nearly as bad.'

'It need not be. The stage is becoming re-spectable, you know. I am acquainted with several actresses who are as staid as nuns.'

'How disappointing for you!'

'Ouch! Perhaps I deserved that. Shall we call a truce? I so dislike being at outs with anyone.'

'Very well,' she conceded. 'But I cannot act, and it does not appeal to me.'

'But do you like to watch a play?'

'I used to, when Papa was…' She paused. 'I have not been lately.'

'Then we should remedy that at once. I have a box at the Theatre Royal. It will be my pleasure to escort you.'

'Why?' she demanded.

'In order to make amends for my serious blun-der just now.'

'There is no need for that. I have forgiven you.'

He stopped and bowed to her. 'I am indeed

relieved.' He took his place beside her again and they continued their walk. 'But what about a visit to the theatre?'

'Lord Portman, you forget I am in mourning for one thing and on Monday I am to begin work at Lady Bonhaven's. I will have no opportunity to see a play, unless she chooses to go and I accompany her.'

'She won't do that. I know the lady and she abhors all such entertainment as the height of depravity. A more strait-laced matron it would be hard to imagine.'

'Then I am sorry, I shall have to forgo the pleasure.'

'I am sorry too. Look, we are at the end of the path. Shall we turn about and go back to the Rotunda or make our way to the field for the fireworks?'

She turned, looking for her brother and Sir Ashley in the milling crowds, but they seemed to have disappeared. She suspected they were deliberately throwing her into a compromising situation. 'Oh, it is too bad of Max. Where has he got to? I must go at once and look for him.'

'He will find us if we go to the fireworks. If not, I will undertake to see you safely home.'

'How could he?' she stormed. 'How could he?'

It was not a question to which she expected a reply, but he chose to answer it. 'I think he is hoping that I will be chivalrous enough to make you an offer, as I am sure you are aware.'

'Then he has been wasting his time. You are not going to, are you?'

'You are nothing if not outspoken,' he said. 'And you have put me in a predicament, as you did when we first conversed three days ago: to agree would certainly not be gallant and to disagree would mean that I must make the offer.'

'Oh, be done with your jests! I cannot abide any more of them.'

'Then by all means let us be serious.' He drew her to one side of the crowded path, where a Grecian statue stood on a plinth in a little arbour. Here it was quiet and they would not be disturbed. She knew she ought to protest, but there was something about him that was hard to resist. He pulled her down beside him on to the plinth, which was at the right height to make a seat. 'We could play their little game out for them.'

'You refer to my brother and Sir Ashley?'

'Yes. Both are convinced we should make a match of it.'

'I know Max's reasons, but what are Sir Ashley's?'

'He knows I must marry again in order to beget

an heir to my estate.' He paused, wondering whether to explain about Beth, but decided not to; he wished he had never told Ash. 'Sir Ashley has chosen you for the role of my bride.'

His use of the word role made her wonder if he saw it all as a play and they were each acting out their parts. 'Why?'

'Do you know, I have no idea? Perhaps he appreciates your qualities.'

'I do not see how he can know them. Whenever we have met, he has seen fit to disappear with my brother, leaving us together.'

'Your brother is not a very diligent escort.' He was rapidly coming to appreciate her qualities himself. She was not cowed or overawed and had a ready wit. She was also, as Ash had pointed out, not tiny as Beth had been, but strong and healthy. She was not beautiful, but she was certainly not repulsive. Those divine eyes made up for a great deal. Supposing she were to bear his children— would they have eyes like hers? He tried to imagine them and the picture was not at all unpleasant. She needed to earn a living and he could offer her something a great deal better than working for Lady Bonhaven. Could it work? According to Ash, no woman would turn down the chance to be mistress of Bishop's Court.

'Let us ignore Sir Ashley and your brother and decide for ourselves what is to be done.' She opened her mouth to speak, but he put a finger over her mouth to stop her. 'I will say my say, then you may say yours. Agreed?'

She nodded, aware of the dry warmth of his finger on her slightly parted lips and had to take a firm hold on herself not to nip it with her teeth.

'Good.' With the marble Venus smiling down on them, he took both her hands in his. 'Let us consider the pros and cons. One, I need an heir and to beget an heir I need a wife. Two, I am not disposed to fall in love again, but any wife I choose must be up to the task of being mistress of my household and being a good mother to my children.' He stopped, realising there was an important question he had not asked. 'You do wish for children, I assume?'

Too bemused to speak, she nodded again

'Good. Where was I? Oh, yes, point three. Health and looks.' He regarded her face gravely as if sizing these up. 'I am told you have never been ill in your life.'

'Max,' she said ruefully. 'I'll wager he did not commend my looks.'

'I can judge those for myself.'

'He said you required a wife that would not

outshine you.' It was said as a put-down, but it only served to make him throw back his head and laugh. It was a laugh very different from that of the macaroni. He was forever surprising her.

'There is that, of course. I am indebted to your brother for that point. Now what number were we up to? Four, was it?'

'Five if you take account of the one my brother furnished.' The conversation was so preposterous, she felt herself playing the game out of amusement and curiosity.

'Five, then. You must find a home and a way of making a living which, I understand, has become urgent. Is that so?'

She nodded again, knowing she ought to stand up and walk away, but finding it impossible to do so.

'We come to six. You do not care to be a companion and there is no time to develop your other ideas. Housekeeper. A wife keeps house, does she not? Embroidery. I am persuaded every lady, wife or not, does that. As for cataloguing books, if you really wish to do that, I have a library of tomes at Bishop's Court in urgent need of arranging into some sort of order. What else was there? Oh, yes, writing a book. I have no especial dislike of that idea. You may occupy yourself in that fashion whenever you are not busy at any of the others.'

'Lord Portman,' she managed at last, 'just what are you saying?'

'Why, I am listing the advantages to be had from joining our two selves in holy matrimony. You did not think I was offering *carte blanche,* did you?'

'I was not sure.'

'My dear Miss Chalmers, if you go back to point one, you will recall I said I needed an heir and by that I meant a legitimate one.'

'You are not jesting, are you?' she said, regarding him frankly.

'No, I am not jesting. Now you may, if you wish, list the disadvantages.'

She said the first thing that came into her head. 'We hardly know each other.'

'True, but that can be remedied.'

'I am in mourning.'

'I think, under the circumstances, that can be overlooked. I am sure your brother, as the head of the house, would agree with that. It is a pity they have done away with Fleet marriages, but the ceremony can be a quiet one in the country.'

'I am too independent and outspoken.'

'That could be construed as a disadvantage, it is true,' he admitted. 'I will mark that one up.'

'I am six and twenty.'

'Then you will not be giddy and requiring my undivided attention every minute of the day. I could not abide that. Of course we should not delay too long before beginning our family...'

'And if I should turn out to be barren?'

'Is there any reason why you should be?'

'None at all, but one can never be sure.'

'True. Perhaps we ought to mark that one up too.'

'I am told you already have a daughter.'

'Yes.' His bantering tone left him suddenly. 'I see little of her. She is with foster parents.'

'But she would not be, if you had a wife, would she? Supposing she does not take to me?'

'She will do as she is told.' It was said flatly.

'You cannot make her love me. Love is not something you can command.'

'How did we come to be talking of love?' he demanded, somewhat put out. 'I have not mentioned it. I hope you were not expecting me to fall into raptures and declare my undying devotion.'

She laughed, endeavouring to lighten the atmosphere again. 'That, my lord, would be expecting too much.'

'Then I make it six to two.'

'Six to two what?'

'Six points in favour, two against. Rather good odds, I should think.'

'You, I collect, are a gambler, my lord. I, on the other hand, am not.'

'You will not be gambling. I shall provide you with a good portion, ample pin money, clothes, jewels, a carriage, the freedom to order the household as you will, and a title. What have you to lose?'

'My independence.'

'How much is that worth at the moment?' He paused to look into her face. 'Remember Lady Bonhaven.'

She did not want to remember the lady. 'My lord, if all that was a proposal of marriage, it is the strangest I ever heard.'

'You have had so many?' he queried, smiling at her, his head on one side.

'That would be telling.' Honesty made her add, 'But that is neither here nor there.'

'So, shall we wed?'

'I am afraid I cannot view the prospect of a marriage of convenience with equanimity. How do I know we should not quarrel?'

'I am not usually quarrelsome,' he said. 'Quarrelling indicates a lack of restraint, don't you think? Are you like to quarrel with me?'

'With the life you have promised me? It would be singularly ungrateful in me to do that. But is gratitude a substitute for that tender feeling a husband and wife should have towards each other?'

'Only you can answer that. But you need not feel grateful. The bargain will not be all one-sided. You will be expected to play your part.'

She gave a dry laugh. 'So, it is an actress you would make of me after all. I doubt I could match you in that. I have never met a man of so many parts.'

He laughed. *'Touché.* But what do you say?'

'I need to think about it.'

'By all means. But do remember points one to six.' He stood up and held out his hand to help her to rise, just as a whistle and bang heralded the first of the fireworks. 'Let us go and view the fireworks and perhaps we shall come across your brother and Sir Ashley.'

They left the shelter of the arbour and made their way towards the river, where cheers and more bangs, followed by brilliant colours of red, green, yellow and blue shooting high into the sky showed the fireworks were well under way. They stood close together to watch the entertainment, a most incongruous couple, the fop and the anti-dote, and though she was aware of it, he seemed unperturbed. A strange and unaccountable man, she decided. Could she marry him? It would not be the marriage she had dreamed of as a young girl, but she could not expect that, could she? What would it be like to share a bed with him? To see that muscular body without any clothes? To be touched by him in intimate places? Feeling the warmth rush into her face, she dismissed such erotic questions from her mind and tried to concentrate on the fireworks.

It was a splendid display and after the last one had died away, he turned towards her. 'Before I knew I would meet you here, I ordered supper to be served in one of the booths near the Rotunda and no doubt we shall find Sir Ashley there with your brother.'

They joined the crowds leaving the arena and made their way back to the centre of the garden. It was now quite dark, although the lamps strung along the paths made a ribbon of light converging on the Rotunda. Harry took Rosamund's arm and guided her unerringly and, sure enough, they found the two missing men already sitting in the booth, waiting for them.

'There you are,' Ash said. 'We had quite given you up for lost.'

Rosamund opened her mouth to a scathing retort

and shut it quickly when Harry said, 'My dear Ash, it was you and Sir Max who were lost. We have simply been perambulating and watching the fireworks.' He pulled a chair out from the table as he spoke. 'Miss Chalmers, please be seated. I shall have refreshment brought at once.'

Rosamund looked at Max. He was smiling like a cat who had got at the cream and it made her want to hit him. Taking the offered seat, she refused to look him in the eye.

Now they were once again in company, his lordship resumed his role of tulip, flicking at his cuffs, picking up his quizzing glass and surveying the people passing by the booth and making humorous comments on their appearance. Max laughed hilariously at his jokes, Ash looked at him in disapproval and Rosamund was simply too bemused to react at all. Their recent conversation was going over and over in her mind… Had he really proposed marriage to her? Had he really promised her ample pin money, clothes, jewels, a carriage, the freedom to order the household, all in exchange for giving him an heir?

A baby. A little human being, not a pugdog, not a doll, but a real live human being who needed both parents, not only for a few days and weeks, but for a lifetime of growing up. Supposing the marriage was so awful it had to be ended? What would become of any child then, especially if she had become excessively fond of it? Why had she not brought that up as a point for consideration? No, she decided, he had been jesting.

She realised he had not been jesting the following afternoon when he called on her at Holles Street. She was in her black gown again and had done nothing to her hair except brush it back and tie it with a ribbon while she sat at the escritoire, writing notes. Janet, agog at the sight of him, forgot to ask if she were at home and showed him straight in. Flustered, she rose to receive him. 'My lord, I did not expect you.'

He swept her a bow. 'Did you not, madam? I fancied we had unfinished business.' He looked about at the bare room. There was a sofa, besides the chair she was using at the desk, but that was all. And Janet had disappeared.

'Oh. Are we still acting our parts?' she queried, making light of her confusion. 'I had fancied the curtain had come down on that particular play.'

'No, that was simply the first act. Was it not left with you saying you wished to think over my proposal?'

'Did I?' she queried vaguely. 'Perhaps I did not

wish to offend you by giving you an immediate answer.'

'Ah, I see. You were the one who was offended.'

'No, my lord, but I could not help but think you did not mean it and were only doing it to appease Sir Ashley in the certain knowledge I would not take it seriously.'

'Now I *am* offended!'

'Why?"

'That you should think I am so in awe of Ash that I must do as he bids. He is a good friend, but he does not rule my life. The reasons for my wanting to marry, which I expounded to you last evening, were my own, not his, and the choice of a bride is mine, not his. And I would hope your answer would be your own, not your brother's.'

'That you may rely on. If you were in earnest, my lord, then I am flattered by the honour you do me, but I cannot agree to become your wife.'

'Why not? Do you hold me in aversion? If you do, I shall retire and that is the last you shall hear of marriage from me, but if not…'

'No, my lord, you have been altogether agreeable, but I am constrained to wonder what it would be like to live with you day by day, when all you want me for is a breeding machine.'

'Good God! You do not pull your punches, do you, Miss Chalmers?'

'It is as well to be perfectly frank with each other.'

'True.' Her reluctance to commit herself, in some perverse way, made him all the keener to break down her resistance. 'But I think your sensibilities are too nice. I hope you have not fallen into the notion that we shall be living in each other's pockets. You will have your life and I will have mine, but in public and when we are with our children, we will, to all intents, be a happy and united family.'

'You assume the children.'

'That is the whole point. If there are none, then I am sure the marriage can be brought to a discreet end. You will be no worse off. In fact, you will be a great deal better off because I will make sure you are well provided for and will not need to resort to the likes of Lady Bonhaven. She is already boasting to her friends that you are brought so low she has felt obliged to take you in out of pity.'

'Oh, no!' She was aghast.

'Miss Chalmers, surely what I am offering is better than that?'

'Yes, but I am asking myself if it is the only alternative.'

She turned as the door opened and her brother came in. He smiled broadly on seeing Harry alone with his sister. Such unconventional behaviour could only mean one thing and he congratulated himself on contriving it. Not only would he not be obliged to give his sister a home, but he would be related to one of the wealthiest men in the country and that could do him nothing but good. He smiled broadly. 'Portman, I did not know you were here.'

Harry bowed to him. 'As you see. I am about to leave.' He turned to Rosamund. 'Your obedient, ma'am. If you change your mind, send me word and I will attend you again.' And with another flourishing bow, he took his leave.

Max watched him go, consternation writ all over his face. 'Rosie, do not tell me you have rejected him.' He threw himself on to the sofa and looked up at her, standing exactly as she had been all through her interview with Harry, stiffly straight with her hands clasped in front of her. 'Are you run mad?'

She sighed and sank back on to the chair by her escritoire. 'You know why he was here?'

'Of course. No gentleman would compromise a

lady by being alone with her if he were not going to make an offer of marriage. It is the most marvellous thing. You will be the envy of the *ton*.'

'I will not, for I have not accepted him.'

'Oh, that does not signify. He expects you to change your mind.'

'I cannot help thinking you have contrived the whole affair and I find it humiliating in the extreme.'

'Fustian! If our father had arranged it, you would think nothing of it and as I am the head of the family, it behooves me to do what I can. All I have done is make you known to each other. Is there anything wrong in that? You do not think, for a moment, I could influence Lord Portman to do something he does not want to do, do you?'

'No, I certainly do not think that.'

It seemed she was to get no peace, for Mrs Bullivant arrived at that point. Max rose to bow to her. She brushed past him, panniers swaying, the plumes in her hat waving. 'Is all ready?' she asked Rosamund. 'I thought you might need help with conveying your trunk tomorrow and came to tell you that I will put my coach at your disposal. I shall come with you and see you safely installed...'

'Why, Aunt, did you suppose I would abscond?' Rosamund queried.

'She might very well do so, for she has butterflies in her attic,' Max told her. 'She has rejected an offer of marriage.'

'Marriage?' queried the lady, much astonished. 'To whom?'

'To none other than Lord Portman,' Max told her.

'Portman!' The old lady sat down heavily on the sofa vacated by Max. 'You mean the Lord Portman I met outside Lady Bonhaven's three days ago?'

'Yes,' Rosamund said. 'He requires a wife and a mother for his children and apparently I have been selected.'

'Good heavens!'

'As you say, good heavens,' Max said. 'He is the answer to Rosamund's prayers. She will have the rank and consequence of a fine lady, not to mention a generous portion and a home at Bishop's Court. That is his estate near Isleworth, you know. I believe he has others.'

'I know that,' the lady snapped. 'I had it from Lady Bonhaven herself, who used to be a bosom bow of his late mother.'

'Oh, Aunt,' Rosamund said. 'You surely did not quiz her ladyship about him.'

'Oh, not in that way. I simply said I had met him and found him very agreeable. I cannot believe someone of his consequence has offered for Rosamund. Why, she is—'

'Past marriageable age,' Rosamund put in with a wry smile. 'But do you know, he said it did not signify, that it meant I should not be giddy and demanding.'

'Quite right.'

'Nor am I a beauty.'

'Did he say that?'

'He did not need to. I know it. I am to be a brood mare and give him an heir.'

'So what's to say about that?' her aunt demanded. 'Though I could wish you had phrased it a little more delicately.'

'She rejected him,' Max said gloomily.

'Oh, you do not say so. Rosamund, whatever were you thinking of? To be sure, I arranged for you to go to my dear Clarissa, but only because I could see no other course open to you. You must accept. Just think what it will be like being Lady Portman. You will be invited everywhere. Why, I do not doubt you will receive an invitation to the coronation, if not the Royal wedding. How can you even thinking of turning his lordship down?'

Max grunted. 'He hopes she will change her mind.'

'Then of course she will.'

Rosamund let them rattle on, giving her one reason after another why it would be the height of folly to reject his lordship and outlining the many advantages, all of which she already knew. By the time they had drunk the tea she had ordered and eaten the last of the cake in the house, she was almost convinced. But not enough to admit it.

The following morning Cook left for a new post as under-cook at a large estate in Hertfordshire and Janet took herself off to her sister, where she intended to stay until she found a new position. Left alone in the empty house, Rosamund sat on her trunk in the hall with a portmanteau beside her to await her aunt's arrival, contemplating her life as Lady Bonhaven's companion and trying to compare it with what Lord Portman had offered. She came to the conclusion she had been a fool to turn him down.

Her aunt arrived, bustling into the house and surveying her niece and her luggage with a critical eye. 'I really should have taken you to shop for a new mourning gown,' she said. 'That one is far too shabby. Her ladyship will not wish you to dress *à la mode*, but she will certainly expect you to look respectable. I wonder if it is too late. We could see if we can find a ready-made gown at one of the shops.'

'No, Aunt, it is not necessary,' Rosamund said firmly. 'I am not going to Lady Bonhaven's. Will you please convey to her my regrets and apologies for the short notice.'

The old lady's face lit up. 'You are going to accept Lord Portman?'

'Yes, I think I must. If he will still have me.'

'Of course he will. No gentleman would go back on an offer once made.'

Rosamund gave a wry smile. 'Let us go and put it to the test, shall we?'

'My dear girl, you cannot call on a single gentleman, do show some sense. Come home with me and I will invite him to call. We must do this properly.'

She looked startled when her niece burst into laughter. Keyed up to almost breaking point, she laughed until the tears ran down her face. 'Oh, Aunt, how can you talk of propriety in a situation like this?' she said, wiping her streaming eyes on her handkerchief. She became serious as her aunt requested her to get up off the trunk and let her footmen carry it out to the coach. While this was being done, Rosamund checked that all doors and windows were secure, refusing to give way to nostalgia over the task, and then followed her aunt out to her coach.

Chapter Four

Harry was in the library of his home, writing up notes for the Gentleman's Club, a requirement for all the members when on a case, when a letter was brought to him from Mrs Bullivant, requesting him to call on her at Chandos Street that afternoon. It was a minute or two before he could place the lady and then he remembered being presented to her by Miss Chalmers. He allowed himself a faint smile and calmly continued with his writing. He finished it just before noon and went into the dining room to eat a leisurely luncheon, after which he ordered his landau to be brought to the door, then went to his bedroom and began stripping off the riding coat he had been wearing. 'I think the lilac coat and the flowered satin waistcoat and white small clothes.'

'Yes, my lord.' Jack had long ago given up trying to understand his master's whims where clothes were concerned. He was just as likely to dress as a street porter as a macaroni and when he donned those clothes, his character changed to match. He could be a porter, a macaroni or a Corinthian with equal ease. Today, it appeared, he was to be a Corinthian, beautifully, but not outrageously, attired.

The valet fetched out the suit and helped him change into it. 'Shoes, my lord?' he queried.

'Not the red heels, definitely not those,' he answered, frowning at the pair Jack had produced. 'The black with the silver buckles.'

A tall white wig was fetched after these were donned, but was waved away. 'The small toupee with the side curls,' he said, looking in the mirror and meditating on where to put a patch and then deciding not to bother.

He topped the outfit with a three-cornered hat and, picking up his cane, declared himself ready. Jack watched him go with some satisfaction. He liked to see his master well dressed and today he looked extremely fine. Ten to one there was a lady behind it.

Harry smiled a little as his coach carried him to Chandos Street. He could be wrong, of course, but he would lay a guinea to a sixpence, Miss

Chalmers had changed her mind, or been persuaded to, and Mrs Bullivant had determined to do the thing properly. This play was rapidly becoming a farce.

He was admitted by a liveried footman and conducted to the drawing room, where he found Mrs Bullivant and Sir Max waiting to receive him, but no sign of Miss Chalmers. So, he was to be interviewed by her family before being allowed a few minutes alone with her. Considering their conversation in the Ranelagh Gardens, it was laughable. But he kept a straight face as he bowed to them and Mrs Bullivant bade him be seated and ordered refreshments.

While these were being prepared, they conversed about the warm weather, which Mrs Bullivant found very wearying, and the crowds who were already flocking to London for the celebrations. At a time when the *haut monde* would normally all be leaving the capital for their country homes, they were choosing to stay. 'It is particularly tiresome for those of us who live here all the year round,' the lady said. 'When we can hope for a little peace and quiet, it is noisier and busier than ever. And not a chair to be had when one needs one.'

'Yes, ma'am,' he said.

'I collect you have a country estate in Middlesex, I believe.'

'Yes, ma'am. Bishop's Court. It is between Isleworth and Hounslow, conveniently near town and yet far enough out to escape the smoke and fog and noisome streets of the capital.'

The conversation was brought to an end by the arrival of the refreshments and Mrs Bullivant busied herself making and pouring tea and offering little cakes. There was silence for a moment as they drank and ate. Harry waited patiently for them to come to the purpose of the summons. He wished he and Rosamund could have arranged everything together without this charade, but it would not be polite to hurry them along.

At last, Mrs Bullivant put down her cup. 'My lord,' she said. 'My niece tells me you have offered her marriage.'

'So I did. She declined.'

'Perhaps because the manner of making it was…' she hesitated, searching for a way of telling him politely that he had gone the wrong way about it '…not quite proper,' she added lamely.

He only just refrained from laughing. 'I stand corrected.'

'I think if you were to ask her again, you might

have a different answer,' the lady said. 'Do you wish to ask her again?'

'Naturally, I do.'

She picked up a little bell from the table at her side and rang it vigorously. When a maid came in answer to the summons she was despatched to fetch Miss Chalmers.

Rosamund was as amused by her aunt's antics as Harry was, but she entered the room demurely and curtsied to him, as he rose to bow to her. 'My lord.'

'Your obedient, Miss Chalmers. Are you well?' This was not simply a polite enquiry; he had noticed how pale she was. Was the prospect of being married to him so daunting?

'Perfectly well, my lord.'

'Rosamund,' said her aunt, 'Lord Portman has something to say to you, so we will retire and you may have a few minutes alone with him.' And with that, she rose and majestically left the room, followed by Max.

As soon as the door had closed on them, Rosamund burst out laughing. 'Oh, my lord, I am sorry for that, indeed I am, but my aunt would not countenance me approaching you myself.'

He was laughing himself, glad to see she had not lost her sense of humour and was not, as he had supposed, cast down by the situation. 'Oh, no, that would never do. And I have been reproached for proposing to you in a manner that was bound to draw a rejection on account of its being not quite proper.'

'Did she really say that?' she asked in surprise.

'Indeed she did.'

'Then I am sorry for it.'

'No matter.' He drew her down on to the sofa beside him. 'Did you turn me down on those grounds?'

'No. That is absurd. I...I was not sure...'

'And now you are?'

She nodded without speaking, afraid her voice would give away the fact that she still had enormous doubts, but his proposal was preferable to the alternative.

'Then, Miss Chalmers, will you do me the inestimable honour of becoming my wife?'

'On the conditions you outlined on Saturday evening?'

'If they are acceptable to you, ma'am.'

'I accept,' she said solemnly.

His memory suddenly furnished him with a picture of Beth when he proposed to her. She had been shy at first and then her face had lit up and she had literally thrown herself into his arms. That had not been proper behaviour either, but it had delighted him. This was very different. Miss Chalmers was not just out of the schoolroom, as Beth had been. It was, he reminded himself, one of the reasons he had chosen the lady. All the same he ought to display some sign of his pleasure. He picked up her hand and kissed the back of it, before placing it gently back in her lap. 'Thank you, my dear. I must arrange to have the banns read. When and where would it be convenient to you to have the ceremony?'

'I am afraid it has been taken out of my hands, my lord. My aunt and my brother are vying with each other to make all the arrangements to see me off. I know it is not what you had planned—a quiet wedding in the country, you said—so perhaps you can persuade them not to make a great to-do about it.'

He smiled wryly. The brother and aunt had not even wanted to give her house room before he proposed. Now, he supposed, having realised their plain Jane had netted a fairly big fish, they intended to make the most of it. He squashed his inclination to insist on a quiet ceremony, knowing it would cause more gossip when the news did get out and that would not be fair on his bride. 'My dear, I shall not even try, unless you wish it,' he said. 'A lady ought to be able to puff herself up on her wedding day, if no other. And as far as the *haut monde* is concerned, there is to be nothing havey-cavey about this wedding.'

'You are very kind.'

'I hope I may always be kind, Rosamund.' It was spoken quietly and went some way to stilling her doubts.

There was a scratching at the door and Mrs Bullivant put her head round it. 'May we come in?'

'Yes, of course,' Rosamund answered.

They came into the room, Mrs Bullivant all eagerness, Max a little more sedately. 'Are we to offer felicitations?' the old lady asked.

Harry bowed to her. 'You may. Miss Chalmers has agreed to wed me.'

'Oh, happy, happy day!' she exclaimed as if it were the first time she had heard of it.

'Congratulations, Portman,' Max said, offering his hand. Harry took it, noting how clammy it was.

'When is it to be?' Mrs Bullivant demanded. 'I think, under the circumstances, we may shorten the period of mourning. We can say Joshua knew what was in the wind and asked especially that Rosamund should not regard it.'

'I was not acquainted with Sir Joshua,' Harry pointed out, inwardly laughing at the old lady's imaginative fabrication.

'My brother knew everyone and everyone knew him,' Jessica maintained. 'I cannot think how you can say such a thing. Why, he was a member of all the clubs, as I am sure you are.'

'Of course,' Harry said, deciding to go along with her. 'I met him several times, played cards and drank with him, only natural he should speak of his daughter and make us known to each other. Long-standing acquaintanceship, goes back to my own father. Why, he even recommended the union of our two families.' Catching sight of Rosamund's expression, he frowned at her to stop her laughing aloud.

'Then we can arrange the wedding for a month from now, if that is convenient to you, my lord.'

'Perfectly convenient. I will leave the arrangements to you, ma'am.'

'My niece may stay with me until then and be married from here. I will see to everything concerning the wedding. Max, as head of the family, must arrange financial matters.'

'Yes, shall we do that now?' Max suggested. 'We could go into the book room and leave the ladies to their discussions on ribbons and gowns and suchlike.'

Harry bowed and followed Max from the room, leaving a triumphant Mrs Bullivant to face her niece. 'There!' she said. 'You may count yourself very fortunate indeed.'

'I do, Aunt, but about the wedding…'

'What about it?'

'I am not in the first flush of youth and I do not want to be puffed up as though I were. I wish for a quiet wedding. After all, I am still in mourning. Besides, I have nothing to wear.'

'That will all be taken care of. We shall go shopping for a gown and wedding clothes. We must make lists…' She went on to enumerate the many lists, guests, food, wine, flowers, but Rosamund had ceased to listen. She was too busy wondering just what she had done. What would the *haut monde* make of it? An unknown, unimportant, impoverished spinster catching a baron of immense wealth and consequence—how had she managed it? She could imagine the tongues wagging and wished it were all over and she was safely in the country, away from the gossips, trying to adjust to her new life.

'You do understand, there can be no question of a dowry,' Max was saying to Harry. 'I explained our situation at the start, did I not?'

'Oh, explicitly,' Harry said. 'It is of no moment.'

'But I do not want Rosie to know that. It would hurt her feelings. Could you perhaps pretend you have received a small dowry?'

'With all the pleasure in the world, my dear fellow. I will do nothing to hurt her feelings.'

'And the wedding. My aunt is determined on some sort of show, and given your standing in society, it is to be expected, but I find myself unable to—' He stopped. 'You see how it is?'

'Perfectly. Will five hundred pounds suffice?'

'You are very generous, my lord,' Max said, deciding two hundred would amply cover a quiet wedding, as long as Rosie did not find out the true amount. 'But—'

'But I should not tell Miss Chalmers about that either,' Harry finished for him. 'I understand. It would look as though I were buying her.'

'I would not go so far as to say that,' Max said, breathing a sigh of relief.

'No, I hope you would not. I will have a draft made out to you and sent round to your address.'

Max bowed. 'Thank you.'

There being nothing else to say, they returned to the ladies, to hear what they had arranged and soon after that Harry bowed his way out. Rosamund went to the door with him. 'My lord,' she began, 'if my aunt's arrangements displease you, you must say so.'

'It is not I who has to be pleased, my dear,' he said gently, 'but you. Do as you wish. I shall fall in with your plans. And after the ceremony, we will repair to Bishop's Court. I am sure you will like it there.'

He bowed to her, put his hat on and went back to his carriage, musing as he went. It had been the strangest week of his life and he hoped sincerely he was not going to regret what he had done.

As soon as he arrived home, he sent for his lawyer and arranged the money order for Sir Max and then sent a note to the *London Journal*, announcing his betrothal. After that he changed his suit for something a little less colourful and set off for a meeting of the Piccadilly Gentleman's Club where he was able to report he had been given a name that might lead him to a new gang of coiners. While out in his disguise, he had met a man called Mick O'Keefe passing not one, but two fake guineas. He had not apprehended him, but engaged him in conversation. Although he had not learned a great deal, he would continue to further his acquaintance and perhaps gain his trust.

'By the bye,' he said, at the end of his report, 'you may congratulate me. I am to be married.'

'You did it!' Ash exclaimed. 'I never thought you would.'

'You sly old fox!' Jonathan said. 'Who is she?'

'Her name is Miss Rosamund Chalmers. She has recently lost her father and is living with her aunt, Mrs Bullivant, in Chandos Street. We are to be wed next month in St George's Church. I shall ask Mrs Bullivant to include you all in the invitations.'

'How did you meet her?' James asked. He had known Harry several years. Harry had been a protégé of his mother-in-law, the actress, Sophie Charron, in the days when the young man aspired to be an actor before he came into his inheritance. 'You have never mentioned her before.'

Harry shot a meaningful look at Ash before answering. 'Our fathers were friends. I have known her for some time, but only recently renewed the acquaintanceship.'

Everyone congratulated him, slapping him on the back and calling for more wine to celebrate.

It was late when the meeting broke up and he and Ash repaired to the Crown and Anchor in the Strand to dine.

'Didn't think you would do it,' Ash said, grinning at him. 'What made you?'

'I admire the lady greatly.'

'Fustian! You cannot mean it.'

'Indeed I do. She has a lively mind and a delight-ful sense of humour. We shall deal well together, I think.'

'You have never fallen in love?'

'No, of course not. Neither has she, but I would not for the world have it put about that we are not sincerely attached. For the lady's sake, you under-stand?'

'Perfectly, my friend. The circumstances of your meeting will never pass my lips, I promise you.'

'Thank you.'

'Lud! This will take the *ton* by storm, when it gets out.' Ash was chuckling.

'Which will be tomorrow when the *Journal* comes out.'

They passed into the tavern and, having dined, spent the evening in a convivial game of piquet.

Harry was not at all surprised the next morning to have his breakfast interrupted by his cousin, Francis, carrying a copy of the *London Journal*. He dazzled the eye with a pink silk coat with enor-mous silver buttons, a short waistcoat in a sickly raspberry colour embroidered all over in leaves and flowers, yellow-and-white-striped breeches with ribands at the knee and a huge bow in place of a cravat. His silly little hat topped a tall wig with three rows of buckles on each side.

Harry looked up at him and grimaced, knowing Francis considered himself in the first stare of fashion. 'Good morning, Frank,' he said cheerfully. 'What has befallen to have you out of your bed at so early an hour? Nothing more dreadful than the departure of your valet, I hope.'

'Departure of Villiers? Why would he leave? I pay him well and he has always given satisfaction, if you discount a tendency to liking plain colours.'

'I can quite see that you would object to that,' Harry said, looking his young cousin up and down. 'But had you considered he might be right?'

'Of course he is not right. Plain colours are a bore. And I did not come here to discuss my wardrobe.'

'No? Then you must have come for breakfast. Do sit down and I will order some fresh coffee and more hot rolls.'

'Didn't come for breakfast either.' Nevertheless he sat down at the table and helped himself to coddled eggs and ham. 'Came about this.' He tapped the newspaper which he had put down beside his plate.

'The *Journal*?' Harry enjoyed teasing his cousin. 'So, what is in it to fetch you out at...' he glanced at the ormolu clock on the mantelshelf '...nine in the morning? Why, the streets are hardly aired. It must be something dire.'

'It is. Someone has been playing a joke on you, Coz. Knew you would not see it yourself, so came at once.'

'Oh, dear, you have me in quake. Please do enlighten me.'

Francis abandoned his breakfast to pick up the paper and find the page containing the announcements of births, deaths, marriages and betrothals. He folded it so that Harry's announcement was uppermost and tapped it with his finger. 'This. I enjoy a joke as much as the next man, but this is beyond everything. You must insist on a disclaimer.'

'Must I?' Harry murmured, taking the paper from him and scanning the notice, which had faithfully reproduced his words. 'Why?'

'But you cannot have everyone believing you are going to marry this...this...' He paused to take the paper back and refer to it for the name. 'Miss Rosamund Chalmers, whoever she might be. Ten to one she doesn't exist.'

'Then you would lose your money, Cousin, because she undoubtedly does exist. A most charming lady.'

Francis stared at him, his mouth open. 'You do not mean… You cannot mean…'

'Oh, but I do. You may felicitate me.'

'Well, of all the sly, mean, underhand things to do.'

'I do not quite understand you,' Harry said, though he understood only too well. 'What is sly and mean about it?'

'You always maintained you would not marry again. You as good as swore it.'

'I do not remember swearing to it. That would have been an exceedingly foolish thing to have done. And if I expressed a reluctance to remarry, it was perhaps because I did not think I should find a lady to suit me. But now I have and she has consented to become my wife.'

'Without a word to me.'

'But why should I consult you, Frank?'

'I am your heir.'

'So you are,' Harry said calmly. 'What is that to the point?'

'You might have children.'

'I hope I may.'

'I do believe you have done it to spite me.'

'Now, Frank, why on earth would I harbour spite? You know that is not in my nature. Besides, you have never done anything to harm me, have you?' He paused and smiled. 'Unless it be to hurt my eyes with your dazzling coats.'

'Well, I hope you do not come to regret it, that's all I can say.'

'Is it? I had hoped for a word or two of congratulation.'

'Oh, as to that, yes, my felicitations.' It was said grudgingly, but it had to be said because he was a little pinched in the pocket and he dare not slay the goose that laid the golden eggs.

'Thank you,' Harry said, as solemnly as he could manage.

'There's something else I meant to ask while I was here, but perhaps it's not the time.'

'The time is as good as any. In deep, are you?'

The younger man looked startled for a moment, then grinned. 'Yes, I am a touch.'

'How much?'

'Five hundred would settle my most pressing debts. The rest can wait.'

'On the contrary, I do not wish to be dunned for your debts, which will undoubtedly happen if you do not pay them, especially now when your creditors will know I am about to wed again, so I will have a list of the whole, if you please.'

'I ain't exactly sure...'

'Come now, Frank, a figure if you please.'

'Five thousand should do it.'

'Five thousand!' Harry was accustomed to his cousin's profligacy, but even he was surprised at the amount. 'How did that come about?'

'Don't rightly know. Things just mount up, you know.'

'Very well.' Harry rose and left the room and returned a few minutes later with a bill of exchange made out and signed for five thousand guineas. He laid it on the table beside his cousin. 'I hope that will suffice.' He sat down again and refilled his coffee cup.

'My eternal gratitude, Harry.'

'I know you think you are only spending what will one day be yours, Frank, but I give you notice that should I have any more demands of this nature, I shall have nothing to do but refuse. Contrary to your belief, my purse is not bottomless. Try, at least, to curb the gambling and give your tailor the bag. He is not worth the money you lay out on him. I can recommend one who will serve you better.'

'I am perfectly content with my tailor, thank

you. And you can't expect a fellow to give up gambling, now can you? You do it yourself.'

'So I do, but not to excess and I can afford to. You cannot.'

Francis had no answer to this and, having got what he came for, he bowed his way out, the bill safely tucked into his capacious coat pocket.

Harry watched him go, with some amusement, then sallied out to the mews to have his stallion, Hector, saddled and took himself off to his own tailor to bespoke himself a wedding outfit.

Learning that Lord Portman had furnished Max with two hundred pounds with which to deck herself out for her wedding, Rosamund was overcome with his generosity, though Aunt Jessica did not agree. 'With all the riches he has, he could afford more than that,' she grumbled. 'Does he not know how much it costs to finance a society wedding?'

'I do not suppose he does,' Rosamund said mildly.

'Then Max should have pointed it out to him.'

'I do not suppose Max knew either,' Rosamund said reasonably. 'Men don't, do they? And I am perfectly content. We can buy a fine gown and everything to go with it and bespoke a wedding breakfast easily with that.' She gave a wry smile, which her aunt did not understand. 'I do not wish to outshine my groom. And I beg you, Aunt, not to refer to it as a society wedding.'

'If you think you are going to get away with a hole-and-corner affair, you are mistaken, miss. Lord Portman is a man of consequence and his wedding will be talked about. You will become the centre of attention and to try to hide from it will cause more gossip. Now let us go shopping. I have sent for my carriage.'

There was nothing for it, but to follow her aunt on a round of shopping, which was exhausting. The most important item was the wedding dress itself, which Mrs Bullivant's mantua maker would make up for her. After a great deal of argument over what colour would be proper given her state of mourning and Mrs Bullivant's determination she should shine, a pale dove-grey silk was chosen. The material was heavily embroidered with swirls of leaves and flowers in silver. The pattern chosen was a sack-back, with a square neckline and narrow sleeves to the elbow, finished in a froth of lace. The stomacher was of white quilted satin, which was laced with silk cord and came to a point below the waist. It was to be worn over a panniered petticoat. Having settled that all-important issue they moved on to order underclothes, shoes, hats, shawls and jackets, which ate up more than half the money his lordship had provided. They would have been furious with Max if they had known the true extent of Lord Portman's generosity, but they had no reason to doubt his honesty.

'It is a month to the wedding day,' Aunt Jessica reminded Rosamund as if she needed reminding. 'His lordship will want to take you out and about, so we must have day gowns and walking-out gowns.'

'Surely those I have will do. I cannot come out of mourning before the day of my wedding.'

'Mourning clothes can be attractive, child. It is all in the quality and cut of the material. Come, let us see what we can find.'

Rosamund sighed and followed her aunt, who was enjoying herself even if Rosamund was not. But she could not help becoming caught up in the excitement and for a little while tried to forget the strange manner of her betrothal and pretend that she really was a bride going to the altar to marry the man she loved. It did not hurt to dream. Contrary to her aunt's conviction, she wondered if she would see her groom again before the wedding day and came to the conclusion that it was unlikely.

In this she was wrong because he called the next

afternoon, at a time when Aunt Jessica was entertaining a crowd of her bosom bows who had seen the announcement in the newspaper and were curious to discover what there was about her niece to capture the likes of Lord Portman. They found a mature young lady, dressed simply in a black taffeta sack gown trimmed with white lace, who wore her own hair simply dressed with a few curls and ringlets. Not a beauty, they decided; she was too tall for one thing and too thin, and, without powder and patch, her face was too highly coloured when the fashion was to be pale.

The old lady was in raptures over Harry's arrival and twittered about presenting all the ladies to him and it was some minutes before he was able to greet and talk to Rosamund. 'You are overwhelmed, I see,' he said, indicating the crowded room, after bowing to her and kissing her hand.

'It pleases my aunt. Please do not feel you must stay beyond what politeness dictates.'

'You do not wish to see me?' he asked, his voice so low only she could hear it..

'Oh, I did not mean that. I…' She floundered. 'Naturally I am glad to see you.'

'And I you, my dear. We should take every opportunity to get to know each other, don't you think? Then we shall not have any unpleasant surprises later.'

She wondered what he meant by that. Did he think she had unpleasant habits or inherent faults? Did he have secret vices? No doubt he drank and gambled, but what man didn't? 'I hope there may not be,' she said. 'I am as you see me.'

'I do not doubt it. I was thinking of myself. You must wish to know more about me. And to that end, I came to ask if you would like to come for a drive. I have my phaeton outside.'

'I can hardly abandon my aunt and her friends.'

'I do not see why not.' He turned to address Mrs Bullivant. 'You will forgive me, dear lady, if I carry off your niece. I have a fancy to drive a little way into the country and would have her company.'

'As to that, I can have no objection,' Mrs Bullivant said. 'But who is to chaperon her? I cannot leave my guests.'

'I had to part with my maid, when I left Holles Street,' Rosamund explained. 'It was one thing I meant to ask, if you would allow me to ask her to serve me.'

'Why, my dear, you do not need to ask. By all means, fetch her back. Where can she be found?'

'She has gone to stay with her sister in Hampstead until she can find a new position.'

'Then send for her at once. Better still, let us go and fetch her.'

'My lord,' Aunt Jessica objected, 'Should you—'

'Oh, no doubt I should,' he said airily. 'I cannot have my bride-to-be without a maid, not even for an instant. I do hope you can accommodate her for the short time Miss Chalmers will be staying with you.'

'Yes, of course.' She could hardly say anything else with all her friends present.

'Good.' He turned to Rosamund. 'Come, my love, we shall not be overlong. I am sure these good ladies will excuse us.' He bowed all round, took Rosamund's hand and fairly dragged her out of the door, leaving behind six open mouths and six pairs of eyes agog.

'My lord,' she protested as he led her out to his carriage. 'You have shocked those dear ladies.'

'Oh, they will forgive me and will no doubt put it down to the great affection I have for you and my impatience to have you to myself.'

'You are taking this play acting too far,' she said, as he helped her into the carriage, climbed in beside her and took up the reins.

'Nonsense. If they are going to be shocked and amused, then it shall be with me and not you.'

She was silent, unable to make up her mind if

this handsome, very rich nobleman was making fun of her or not. Surely he could not make the *ton* believe he had fallen in love with her? And why would he want to? Marriages of convenience were not rare. While still being in complete control of his horses, he had turned to look at her and was studying her face so closely she began to wonder what there was about it that absorbed him so. She knew she was not a beauty, but neither was she ugly. 'You must be the first gentleman I have met who is indifferent to the opinion of the *haut monde*,' she said.

He laughed. 'I can afford to be. They call it eccentricity.'

'Eccentric enough to take a nobody for a wife.'

'Please disabuse yourself of the notion you are a nobody. According to your aunt your family can trace its lineage back to Tudor times.'

'No doubt she is busy this very minute telling that to her friends to explain away your *eccentricity.*'

'And your eligibility.' He paused to negotiate a turn, which he did to a nicety. 'Shall we agree we are well matched and leave it at that? Tell me about the wedding arrangements. Do they go well?'

'Yes, and I have you to thank for that.'

'Forget that too. I have. Have you sent out the invitations?'

'Not yet. My aunt is busy drawing up a list.'

'I have one or two names I should like to add, if you would be so kind. My Aunt Portman, my father's sister, and my cousin Francis and a few close associates.'

'Of course. Please give my aunt their directions. I assume Sir Ashley is one of their number?'

'Yes, but you need not fear he will betray us. He is the soul of discretion. As far as the world is concerned we have contracted a perfectly conventional marriage.'

'Is it my pride or yours you are protecting?' she demanded.

Not for the first time he was taken back by her perceptiveness and her outspokenness. 'Both, my dear. Now we are arrived in Hampstead, be so good as to direct me to your maid's address.'

Janet was overjoyed to find she was going to back to Rosamund, whom she had known since she was a child, and as a lady's maid, which was a big step up for her. And Miss Rosamund was to become Lady Portman, which was a source of even greater delight. 'You deserve some happiness, after looking after your papa for so long,' she told Rosamund, while Harry looked on with amused tolerance. 'And I wish it for you with all my heart.' Her sister was out and she needed time to pack her few belongings and so Harry said he would send a carriage for her the following day; having arranged a time, they left.

'I cannot believe this is happening to me,' Rosamund told Harry as they set off back to town. 'I sincerely hope you may not regret it.'

'I cannot think why I should,' he said calmly. 'We have each set out our stall and there can be no room for misunderstanding, can there?'

'None at all,' she said. His words put a damper on her feeling of euphoria and brought her back to reality with a painful bump, and for the remainder of the journey, they talked about the weather, speculated on what the Royal bride would be like because she had not yet arrived in the country, and commented on *The Jealous Wife*, the latest play at Drury Lane, which had been heralded as one of the finest comedies of its time—everything except their coming nuptials.

When they arrived at Chandos Street, Harry accompanied her to the door, but declined an invitation to come in for refreshment. 'I will call again, if I may,' he said, taking her hand and bowing over it. 'To bring my friends' directions. And we can arrange an evening for our visit to the Theatre Royal. I will introduce you to some of the cast afterwards and perhaps we can have supper with them. That is if you would like it.'

'Certainly I would, my lord.'

The footman had opened the door and she passed inside, leaving him to go back to his carriage.

Her aunt was alone in the drawing room and all agog to know what had happened, to which she replied, 'Why nothing, Aunt. We saw Janet and she is to come here tomorrow.'

'I cannot think why you mentioned her to his lordship. She has not been trained as a lady's maid.'

'After Mama died, she always maided me when I needed it and I shall be glad to have someone familiar by me when I move to Bishop's Court. Lord Portman has relations and friends he would like invited to the wedding. He is going to call with their directions. And he is going to take me to the theatre.'

'Oh, Rosamund, what a gentleman he is! You have certainly fallen on your feet and will be the envy of the whole *ton*.'

In the four weeks before the wedding, she was frequently seen out and about in Lord Portman's company. Although they could not go to balls and routs on account of her mourning, they could, and did, attend musical concerts, went for walks and rides in his lordship's phaeton, visited Vauxhall Gardens, called on Viscount Leinster and his charming wife, Louise, saw the play at the Theatre Royal, where she met Lady Sophie Charron, the famous actress and mother-in-law to Lord Drymore. In public Harry was always the sumptuously dressed macaroni, with the affected high-pitched voice and mincing gait, but in private he dropped the pretension and became a very different man: strong, kind and careful of her. She was tempted to ask why he did it, but decided she did not know him well enough.

Not a word of adverse gossip reached her ears and she put it down to the story he insisted on telling that their fathers knew about the match and heartily approved. She realised as the days passed that it would be all too easy to fall in love with the real man, the one beneath the pose, and that was something she must guard against at all costs.

Every time she began to think what her future life would be like as Lady Portman, she felt a deep knot of guilt inside her, which would not go away, knowing she was using his lordship to escape from Lady Bonhaven or having to live with her brother and his wife. Her search through her father's papers had revealed nothing and she was no nearer discovering why he had been hoarding a bag of counterfeit gold coins, nor anything about the Barnstaple Mining Company. She was rapidly coming to the conclusion it did not exist, had never existed and was therefore untraceable. Max had told her to mind her own business and to leave it all to him, but he did not seem to be doing anything about it. The last person she could speak to about it was her husband-to-be.

Chapter Five

Rosamund woke early on the morning of her wedding day and lay in bed listening to the birds twittering outside her window and the barking of a stray dog in the street and asked herself what had possessed her to agree to this travesty of a marriage. She had sold her independence, her identity, even the kind of person she was, for what? To be done with debt. To escape from penury. To find and bring to justice the men who had cheated her father—already that quest had proved abortive and she did not know where to look next. Was it worth it? According to Lord Portman, they would lead their own lives after the ceremony, but he would expect her to adhere to certain rules, rules she might find irksome. She had a feeling that she was going to be lonely. Thank heaven for Janet!

As if thinking about her maid had conjured her up, the door opened and Janet came in, bearing a cup of hot chocolate. 'Good morning, Miss Rosamund,' she said cheerfully, setting the chocolate down on the little table by the bed. 'It is a lovely day for it. Not a cloud in the sky.' As if to prove her point she drew the curtains, flooding the room with sunshine.

Rosamund sat up and sipped her chocolate, watching Janet flit about fetching out her underclothes, her petticoats, hose and shoes, laying them out ready for her to don, then going to the door to admit a maid with jugs of hot water to fill the hip bath, which already stood in the middle of the floor. It was all going on around her, this hustling and bustling, but she was strangely lethargic. It was a dream, a fantasy. She was not going to marry the most eligible man in town; she was not going to wear that lovely dress which was hanging on the door of her wardrobe, she was not going to live in a stately home and have any number of servants at her beck and call.

'Come, Miss Rosie,' Janet said, calling her by the name she had used as a child. 'It is time for you to bestir yourself. It will take at least three hours to have you ready.'

Three hours to dress! Whatever were they going to do to her in that time? Still in a dreamlike state, she left her bed and allowed Janet and the other maid to bath her, using scented oils. Then they arrayed her in her underclothes, padded petticoats and stockings before putting her into an undress robe to have her hair arranged. This was to be done by a French gentleman her aunt had engaged on the advice of one of her bosom bows.

While they waited for the *coiffeur* to arrive, breakfast was brought up on a tray, but Rosamund could not eat. Her throat was dry and swallowing difficult. Janet coaxed in vain. 'But I will have a cup of coffee,' she told the maid. Perhaps that would revive her and make her aware of what was happening around her.

Her aunt brought the hairdresser up and there followed a heated argument about what should be done to Rosamund's locks. The young man, thin almost to the point of being skeletal, wanted to pile it up over a padded cage, powder it heavily and fill it with flowers and ornaments. Rosamund would have none of it. 'No padding,' she said.

'But, *mademoiselle*, I cannot make de creation widout de padding,' he said in a heavy accent. 'De flowers and leaves and beads and de leetle fan and yellow flutterby will not stay in.'

'I do not wish to make a garden of my head,' Rosamund said, smiling at his mangling of the

English language. 'Give me curls and a little ribbon to match my gown. I shall wear a big hat.'

He gave in with a sigh, but the finished arrangement was, she had to admit, very becoming, especially when she took off the dressing gown and the wedding gown was put on, the stomacher laced and the hat set at an angle on her head and tied with silver ribbon. She put a heart-shaped patch beside her left eye, slipped into her shoes and looped her fan on her wrist.

'Oh, miss, you look beautiful,' Janet said, her eyes wide in wonder.

She went downstairs where a gargantuan feast was being laid out for their guests. There was roast beef and baked ham and a whole suckling pig, not to mention pies and pastries and exotic fruits. Her aunt had spared no expense. Rosamund was sure there was nothing left from the money his lordship had so kindly donated. Even Max, caught up in the excitement, had offered to buy the wine and cognac and hired four beautiful white horses to draw her carriage to the church, saying he did not want it said that he could not give his sister a good send off.

'Why, you look comely,' Max said, looking her up and down in undisguised surprise, before escorting her out the carriage. 'Lord Portman can have no complaints that you are not a fitting match for him.' Which was praise indeed from a brother who was always stinting in his approbation.

Harry, resplendent in oyster satin coat and waist-coat delicately embroidered in the same colour and cream small clothes and stockings, watched her come up the aisle towards him and was almost open-mouthed. She was heart-stoppingly lovely! Why had he not seen that before, why had he accepted her brother's description of her without question and not seen what was under his nose? He should have looked beneath the unmade-up face, the plain clothes, the unpowdered hair and seen what was beneath. It put a whole new complexion on their bargain. He had thought he was doing an antidote a favour by marrying her and saving her from a lonely spinsterhood; instead he was depriving a lovely young lady of the opportunity of finding a loving husband. He was half-inclined to stop the ceremony before it began. But how could he do that? What reason could he give that would not humiliate her and make him look an utter fool?

'My God!' Ash whispered beside him. 'She is transformed. You've made a good bargain there, my friend, if her children turn out to be as fetching as she is.'

Harry did not like to be reminded of what he expected of her; it made the whole thing seem sordid. He saw, as she approached him, that she was pale and nervous, and smiled to put her at her ease as he offered her his arm, though he felt far from at ease himself. She laid a hand on his sleeve and together they faced the parson. 'Dearly beloved,' he began.

If anyone witnessing the marriage of Harry, Lord Portman, to Miss Rosamund Chalmers had wondered at what seemed a strange alliance, they revised their opinion and sighed indulgently at what appeared to be a genuine love match. Apart from Sir Ashley, who would never have breathed a word, the only people to doubt the truth of that was Francis Portman and his mother, to whom that young man confided everything.

Rosamund did not meet him until the day of the wedding and she had no opportunity to speak to him until it was all over and they found themselves face to face at Chandos Street afterwards where everyone gathered for the wedding breakfast. The young man, who could only recently have reached his majority, astonished her with his outlandish attire and extravagant manners. She had thought Harry dressed flamboyantly, but his cousin outdid him by a mile. He wore a coat of sky-blue velvet with huge silver buttons, embroidered with silver-and-gold leaves and flowers. His breeches were striped blue and white and fastened at the knee with bright blue-and-yellow ribands. His white stockings had gold clocks and his shoes enormously high heels. As for his wig, she wondered it did not topple off his head, it was so high at the front with three enormous curls over each ear. It was all she could do not to laugh at him, as he executed a flourishing leg in front of her.

'My felicitations, my lady,' he said, the first person so to address her, which made her realise that the deed was done and that, for good or ill, she was now married to Lord Portman. She had gone through the whole ceremony in a dream, as if she were acting out the role in a play whose words she implicitly knew, and she supposed that was the truth of it. But this play was to last the whole of her life, unless, of course, she turned out to be barren and his lordship divorced her. He was wealthy enough to afford to do that.

'Thank you,' she said.

'I was never more surprised than when Harry told me he was to wed,' he went on, shaking down the lace that flowed out from under the wide cuffs of his coat sleeves. 'Always swore he never would. Couldn't get over Beth's death, you see.'

'Yes, he told me.'

'Did he?' he said in surprise. 'He don't usually spout about it to strangers.'

'Mr Portman, I am not a stranger.'

'No, didn't mean that, but you see, you ain't ever going to convince me you and Harry have known each other above a month. Can't think what got into him, getting himself leg-shackled in such a hurry. Took me by surprise, it did.'

'Are you close to your cousin then?' she asked sweetly.

'Course I am. I am his heir, though I doubt he told you that.'

'I recollect that he did,' she said, unwilling to admit that her husband-to-be had neglected to tell her that fact.

'His daughter can't inherit, all entailed,' he said, moving closer to her and making her take a step back. 'You did know he had a daughter?'

'Of course I did. I am looking forward to meeting her.'

'Not likely to meet her at Bishop's Court. He won't have her there. Can't stand the sight of her.'

The temptation to ask why ever not was cut off before she could utter it. 'I do not suppose it is easy for a man without a wife to bring up a small child,' she said, as haughtily as she could manage. 'That does not mean he dislikes her and I think it disloyal in you to suggest it.'

'Best you know the truth, my lady. Daughters he won't have at any price. Let us hope you do not give him a girl child, or you might find yourself cast out along with her.'

'Mr Portman, I think you have said enough.'

'I beg your pardon. Thought you ought to know.' He swept her a bow and wandered off. She stood looking after him, knowing she had unconsciously made an enemy and wondering how much truth there was in what he had told her.

'What has he been saying to you?'

She turned to find Harry at her side. 'He was only felicitating me,' she said, her heart quickening at his nearness.

'Is that all? I would expect him to catalogue the wrongs I have done him.'

'Why? Have you wronged him?'

'Not in the least, unless it be to marry you. He always fancied himself as the owner of Bishop's Court. It will be a great disappointment to him an' he is not. Now, let us forget that coxcomb and show ourselves to our guests before we set off for home.'

He put his hand under her elbow and they perambulated round the room, receiving congratulations and well wishes and then they bade everyone goodbye and went out to Harry's landau, which someone had bedecked with ribbons. He handed her in and then climbed in beside her, and with everyone standing at the door waving handkerchiefs, the newly wed pair set off for their new life together. His valet and Janet had gone on ahead in a separate carriage with all the luggage in order to have everything prepared for their arrival.

The carriage was luxurious and the equipage boasted a coachman, a postillion and two grooms riding alongside. Rosamund leaned back on the blue-velvet upholstery and shut her eyes. She was exhausted.

'It has been a trial for you,' he said quietly. 'But it is over now.'

'Yes.' It was the deceit of it that was tiring, having to pretend it was a love match when it was nothing of the sort. She would as soon have stuck to their original plan of having a quiet wedding followed by her retirement to Bishop's Court out of the public eye.

'Then I will not disturb you with conversation,' he said.

* * *

The journey to Isleworth took an hour and a half and was accomplished smoothly and, for the most part, in silence. Both were brooding on the future. Rosamund was only too aware of the handsome man at her side, her husband now, though she found that difficult to believe. Ahead of her was Bishop's Court, where she was to make her home for as long as she remained Harry's wife, but more worrying even than that was the prospect of the fast-approaching wedding night.

Giving his lordship an heir was the major part of the bargain on her side and no doubt he would wish that to be accomplished as soon as possible. The anticipation of that was sending her into a dreadful quake. She wanted a child, more than one if possible. Children would be company for her, would perhaps give her the love her husband could not. But the begetting of them! Oh, she knew what happened between a man and a woman from reading and listening to the servants, but she had no idea what it felt like. And for her, without love, cold-bloodedly, as a matter of duty, how could she bear that? Her thoughts were making her uncomfortably hot and she felt her cheeks burning. What, in heaven's name, had she let herself in for?

Harry, too, was wondering what he had done.

Why had he listened to Ash? And Max Chalmers. He did not like the man. Rosamund's brother had turned up at the wedding in a pure white suit of clothes embroidered in silver, and a white wig, all of which must have cost at least fifty guineas. For someone pleading poverty he did not stint on his wardrobe. Chalmers had sold his sister and, like a fool, he had bought her! He was never so remorseful in his life.

But the deed was done and could not be undone and it behooved him to make her life as comfortable for her as he could while he went about his business. Thinking about the coiners helped to stop him dwelling on the bargain he had made. Counterfeit guineas were turning up all over the place. If they were coming from the same source, the operation must be a large one. The vintner had given him several more only the day before, though he did not know the man who had bought the wine.

'I never saw him before,' he had told Harry. 'He was a big man in a fustian coat and leather breeches, not the sort I would expect to be buying fine wine. I fancy he had been sent by someone else because he did not seem interested when I asked him if he wished to sample a glass. He appeared anxious and kept looking about him. I did not realise he had paid with false coin until after he had gone. Now I have lost both wine and money.'

'Did he give you an address to deliver the wine to?'

'No, he took it in a carriage. Old-fashioned town chariot, it was. I fancy there was someone sitting in it, but I could not be sure.'

Harry had recompensed him and taken the coins home to be compared with those he already had. They had been tampered with in exactly the same way. As soon as his bride was settled in her new home, he would have to return to London to unearth the villains. He turned to look at her. She was looking straight ahead, her back upright, her chin up and the rather fetching hat awry. But she looked sad. Sad on her wedding day! It should have been the happiest day of her life. He resisted the temptation to take her hand to console her; better to keep his distance.

'Bishop's Green,' he told her, as the carriage turned off the road into a narrow lane. 'We are nearly there. Bishop's Court is only a quarter of a mile distant now.'

'Which bishop is it named for?'

'Not a bishop, Rosamund, a man whose name was Bishop. Robert Bishop. He built the house a century ago, when Charles II was restored to the throne after the Commonwealth failed. He was awarded the land and money to build the house for services rendered to the Royalist cause. The village of Bishop's Green grew up around it.'

The hamlet was a collection of small cottages, a church, a rectory and a few small businesses that depended on the estate to thrive, including a tavern. All seemed well built and well tended. The carriage turned in at some wide-open gates and continued up a gravel drive lined with trees until the house came into view. It was four storeys high, standing on a stone terrace with a row of shallow steps up to the front door, before which was a wide circular carriage sweep in the middle of which was a statue of a man on a huge muscular horse with two great deerhounds beside him.

'My great-grandfather,' Harry said, noticing her looking at it. 'He was a great huntsman.'

The carriage came to a stop and the grooms dismounted. One came and opened the door and let down the step for Rosamund to alight. She stood on the gravel looking up at the great mansion with its rows of deep windows either side of a two-storey portico, and felt overwhelmed by its size and the terrifying thought that she was to be mistress of it. It was a ridiculous notion. The house and its owner were way above her touch. She must have been mad to agree to that preposterous proposal. It was a dream, a nightmare, a cruel jest and soon she would wake up and find herself back in Holles Street waiting for her father to return from whichever gambling house he had decided to favour with his custom that night. But her father was dead, had died in violent circumstances and he had left behind nothing but some worthless shares and a bag of false coins. What had Max done with those?

She felt a light touch under her elbow which, for all its gentleness, startled her. She jumped and stiffened. 'Come, my lady,' Harry said, letting go of her as if he had been stung. 'The servants are waiting to receive you.'

Without touching her again, he ushered her up the steps and into the cool hall where a double line of servants waited, beginning with Conrad, the butler, and Mrs Rivers, the housekeeper, and working downwards through footmen, cook and maids to scullery maids and boot boy. Harry greeted each by name as he presented them to her. They bowed and curtsied, and though the lower ones seemed overawed, most smiled a welcome. Rosamund smiled back and had a word for each one, though she could not afterwards remember what she said.

'Has her ladyship's maid arrived?' Harry asked Mrs Rivers.

'Yes, my lord. She is upstairs unpacking and waiting for her ladyship.'

Harry turned to Rosamund. 'I am sure you are fatigued, my dear,' he said. 'Mrs Rivers will show you up to your rooms. I shall see you at supper.'

And with that the servants were dismissed to go about their normal duties and Rosamund was handed over to the housekeeper. Harry strode off down the corridor, leaving Rosamund feeling abandoned. She told herself that she ought not to have expected anything else. The public show was over; he was going about his business and she was to settle down as best she may.

'This way, my lady.'

She followed the housekeeper up a wide, curving staircase, which took them to the first floor. Here there was a landing with corridors going to left and right. The housekeeper ignored those and continued up to the next floor and along another corridor, leading her past several doors before stopping at one. 'Your boudoir, my lady.' She opened a door and stood aside for Rosamund to enter.

It was a large room, comfortably furnished with sofas and chairs, little tables, bookcases and shelves. There was an adjoining door, which she thought might lead to Harry's rooms, but she was disabused of that idea when Janet came through it, a beaming smile on her face. 'Miss Rosie—' She stopped suddenly. 'I beg your pardon, my lady.'

'Never mind, Janet,' Rosamund said. 'We must both become used to my new title, must we not?'

'I will have hot water and refreshment sent up,' Mrs Rivers said. 'If there is anything you would like to ask me…'

'Not at present,' Rosamund told her. 'No doubt I shall think of a great many questions later. Perhaps we can meet tomorrow, after breakfast?'

Tomorrow, she thought, tomorrow was another day. She had yet to survive the night. Better not think of it, or, if she could not help thinking of it, she must consider it a painful duty which must be done and not dream of being in the arms of a loving husband who wanted her for her own sake. It would be all too easy to do that; Harry Portman would fit the role to perfection.

'Certainly, my lady. The bell will be rung in the hall half an hour before supper and again at five minutes to. Your maid will show you the way to the small dining room.' With that she bobbed her knee and disappeared, closing the door behind her.

Rosamund flung herself on one of the sofas. 'Janet, Janet, what have I done?' she cried.

Janet smiled. 'Got yourself wed to the finest man in the kingdom. You should hear what the servants say about him. "Never was there a better lord and master, so considerate, so generous, so polite." That's what they say, miss...I mean, my lady. The only word said against him and that not really a criticism is that he is so rarely at home and he never sees his daughter, but they hope that now he is married again, that will change.'

Rosamund wondered about that, but she did not say so. She sprang to her feet and went to the window. It looked out over a courtyard on the far side of which was a wall and beyond the wall, some outbuildings she guessed were stables, and beyond that the beginnings of a park. A belt of trees in the distance shielded the grounds from the village, but she could see the church spire, rising above them.

She turned to Janet and pointed to the inner door. 'What is through there?'

'Your bedchamber and dressing room, my lady. I have unpacked your trunks and laid out a dress for you to change into. Shall you want to explore the house before supper?'

'No, that will do tomorrow.' She walked across

the room and into her bedchamber, wondering if it had been the bedroom of the first Lady Portman and if his lordship had come to her there. She hurriedly thrust the thought from her.

The window of this room faced the same direction as the sitting room, but was beyond the courtyard and she could see the end of the stable yard and the coach house. Harry was talking to Travers, his head groom, engrossed in whatever he was saying to him, pointing and gesticulating. She was struck all over again by his muscular figure, his strong thighs and broad shoulders and the way his hair curled naturally about his shoulders. He disturbed her in a way she could not understand.

Their hurried travesty of a courtship had left no time to get to know him properly, to discover his faults and well as his virtues, to find out what pleased him and what made him angry. She remembered his cousin saying he would not have his daughter to live with him. *'Daughters he won't have at any price,'* he had said and that seemed to be borne out by what Janet had learned. *'Let us hope you do not give him a girl child, or you might find yourself cast out along with her.'* It had been said maliciously, but was it true? She left the window as servants brought hot water and a tray of refreshments. They put them down in silence and just as silently left.

Janet helped her off with her wedding clothes and into something a little less ostentatious, a sack gown of grey taffeta trimmed with white lace. By the time the coiffure's creation had been dismantled and her hair had been arranged in natural ringlets and held in place with combs, the half-hour bell had sounded.

Out in the yard Harry heard the bell, finished talking to Travers about the horses, instructed him to find a suitable mount for Lady Portman and turned to go back into the house, glancing up as he did so. He fancied he saw Rosamund at the window, but if it was, she had quickly moved away. He hoped she approved of the rooms. They were the ones his mother had used, not Beth's, and he had had them done up and modernised for her. Beth's rooms were at the further end of the corridor and he never went anywhere near them if he could help it.

He climbed the stairs and paused outside Rosamund's boudoir, half-inclined to go in and see if she was happy with her accommodation, but decided against it. Those three rooms were her refuge and he would not invade them unless invited. He laughed at himself as he moved on. How then was he to claim her part of their bargain from her, the most important part? He went on to his own rooms, washed and changed and, hearing the five-minute bell, made his way along the corridor towards the stairs. Rosamund was coming out of her room as he reached it. 'My lady.' He bowed and offered her his arm. Together they went down to the dining room and sat down, one at each end of a long refectory table.

The meal was a stilted affair; while the footmen hovered round to serve them intimate conversation was impossible. Rosamund supposed that was how it would always be. She was glad when it was time for her to rise and leave him to his cognac. A footman conducted her to a small parlour, where the tea things—kettle, teapot, caddy and cups—were arranged on a small table. She had just brewed the tea, when Harry joined her, folding his long frame on to a sofa opposite her.

'No sense in sitting in two rooms on our own, is there?' he said.

'No sense at all, my lord.'

'Besides, I wanted to ask you if your rooms were satisfactory. If you want to change anything, then let Mrs Rivers know. I want you to be comfortable.'

'The rooms are very comfortable, thank you, my lord.'

It was not the rooms he meant, but he let it go. 'It is late tonight, but tomorrow I will show you the house and perhaps we can ride round the estate and explore the countryside. You do ride?'

'I used to as a child when I stayed with my grandparents in the country, but that was a long time ago. I have not been on a horse for years.'

'Travers will find you a quiet mount. You do have a habit?'

'Yes, my aunt insisted on buying one.'

'Good. And there is a gig in the coach house you might like to drive out when I am away from home.'

'I cannot drive, my lord.'

'Then it will be my pleasure to teach you.' He paused, stood up and offered her his hand. 'Come, it is late. Time for bed.'

She was trembling as she took his hand and allowed him to raise her. The time had come. She tried a smile, but all she could manage was a travesty of one. He tucked her hand beneath his elbow and escorted her from the room, along a corridor to the hall and up the stairs. She tried to calm her shaking nerves by looking about her at the portraits that lined the staircase, some very old, some more recent. Could one of those be his first wife? She could not bring herself to ask.

They reached the second floor and her bedchamber door where they halted and he turned towards her. 'Rosamund, I…' Whatever he was going to say died on his lips. She waited, hardly daring to breathe. Then he lifted his hand and touched her cheek with the back of his finger and then gently stroked it down her face to her chin. She felt the heat flare in her face and, as he raised her face to his, it spread right through her until she felt as if her whole body were on fire. He looked down at her, his glance moving from eyes to mouth and back again, as if he were trying to read her thoughts. She did not dare blink, the moment was so fraught with tension.

He bent his head and put his lips to hers. It was not a proper kiss, it was over too soon, but it was as if he were testing the ocean with his toe before plunging in. Was he waiting for a sign from her that she had not forgotten their agreement? That she was still willing? She put her arms about his neck and kissed him back. He seemed to respond and pulled her closer against him, pressing his lips to hers, making her shiver with delighted anticipation.

And then suddenly drew back, took her hands

from around his neck and gently put her from him. 'Goodnight, my lady,' he said, and then he was gone, striding down the corridor to his own quarters, leaving her staring after him in disbelief.

She moved at last and went into her bedchamber where Janet waited for her. The maid made no comment as she helped her undress and into the fine cambric nightrail, with its delicate embroidery which her aunt had insisted on buying and which no doubt Lord Portman had indirectly paid for. And he didn't want to know! Janet left her to go to her own room and she climbed into bed where she lay wide awake, staring at the ornately carved ceiling by the flickering light of a candle, trying not to cry, trying to make sense of Lord Portman's behaviour.

Had he changed his mind about the bargain they had made? It was surely a little late to have second thoughts. Did she mind? She was shocked to discover she minded very much indeed. Had she expected him to be a conventional husband? But she had known from the beginning he would not be that, so why was she so disappointed? Was it because he had not referred to their agreement at all since the wedding and she had hoped they might come to a deeper understanding of each other, especially as he was so courteous and careful of her?

And just now, as they stood outside her door, he had kissed her and her heart had leapt inside her, wanting him to go further, wanting him to come into her room and really make her his wife. It was what they had agreed. Instead, he had left her standing. She felt humiliated and betrayed and very, very lonely. He had bought her. He could do with her as he wished and if it amused him to keep her on tenterhooks, then she would have to endure it. Oh, how muddled she was!

It had been a long, tiring day and even her tumbled thoughts could not fight sleep all night. At last her eyelids flickered and closed and she drifted into fitful slumber.

Harry, in his own room, had sent Jack away and now sat looking out of the window at the moonlit landscape, wondering what madness had got into him, to make him propose to her. It was all very well to blame Ash and Max Chalmers, but he was his own man, able to make up his own mind what to do, especially about something as important as his marriage. Was he so desperate for a son he was prepared to take a stranger to his bed? But she was no longer a stranger; in the short time he had been trying to court her in the conventional way, he had come to know her a little and in doing that had realised she was too beautiful, too courageous, too altogether admirable to be used as he had intended to use her.

Standing with her outside her room, he had only intended a chaste kiss of goodnight, had not expected such a powerful physical response to leap up in him when his lips met hers, and when she had returned his kiss, he had wanted nothing so much as to pick her up and carry her to bed. He might have done, too, if he had not been visited by a sudden vision of Beth and the manner of her death. The same thing could so easily happen again. He smiled ruefully at himself; it had never occurred to him that his plan to beget an heir from someone he did not care for would stumble because he had come to like his new wife a little too much.

He left the window, undressed and climbed into bed, where he lay wide awake, debating what he should do. The sensible thing to do would be to annul the marriage. He could make sure she had sufficient funds to keep her comfortably for the rest of her life, or at least until she found a husband who could love her as he could not. But she would be hurt by what would appear to be rejection and she had done nothing to deserve that. And at the moment, still feeling the pressure of her lips on his and her hands wound about his neck, he was not feeling at all sensible.

He drifted into sleep but his dreams were filled with visions of Beth writhing in agony and cursing him and then the figure was Rosamund's, not Beth's at all, and he woke in a cold sweat. It was dawn and there was nothing to be gained by lying in bed. He rose and dressed and went out for a long ride, but he had decided nothing by the time he returned for breakfast.

Rosamund declined breakfast in her room that morning, dressed and went downstairs. Harry was at the table eating ham, eggs, a steak and toast. Slightly taken aback, he rose when she entered. 'My lady, I did not expect you to rise so early.'

'I am used to rising early,' she said. 'And it is a fine day for exploring.'

'So it is, but sit down and eat first.'

Instead of taking the chair at the foot of the table she walked the length of it to sit beside him. A footman drew it out for her and then offered her the dishes. She indicated she would have a coddled egg and a slice of bread and butter. Harry dismissed the footman and poured coffee for her. 'Did you sleep well, my lady?'

'Yes, thank you,' she lied.

'Good.' He paused, opened his mouth to speak and shut it again. Dressed in a blue-and-white striped-gingham round gown with only a minimum padding of the hips, she seemed so bright and cheerful he could not bring himself to refer to the night before and broach the subject of an annulment. Or their bargain. 'Which would you like to do first?' he asked. 'Shall I conduct you round the house or shall we go riding? It will take but a moment to have the horses saddled.'

'I have arranged to speak to Mrs Rivers this morning,' she said.

'Why?' he demanded.

'Why?' she repeated, puzzled. 'She is the house-keeper and I would learn from her how things are done in your household, what her duties are and what she expects of me. If we are to work together...' Seeing him frown, she stopped suddenly. 'Is something wrong?'

'You do not need to trouble yourself with the housekeeping, my lady. Mrs Rivers is perfectly capable.'

'Oh, I am sure she is. I will not interfere with her, but she will wish to know that I am mistress of the house now and that she is to come to me if she has a problem or needs a decision. And I need to see the accounts.'

He laughed suddenly. 'Your brother was right. He said if you went to live with him, you would want to take over the housekeeping. Now I know what he meant.'

'And a more chaotic house than his is hard to imagine,' she said defensively. 'But we are not talking about my brother's house, but this one. Are you telling me you do not wish me to take an interest in the running of it? It is part of a wife's duties to manage her husband's home, is it not? And did you not specifically mention it when we made our pact?'

He did not like to be reminded of that. Instead he stood up and went to open the door. The footman was standing impassively beside it. 'Johnson, ask Mrs Rivers to join us,' he said, then returned to his seat and poured himself more coffee. Neither spoke. Rosamund felt as though she had transgressed, that she was a wrongdoer awaiting punishment. She waited with baited breath for the arrival of the housekeeper.

Mrs Rivers entered silently and bobbed to them both. 'You sent for me, my lord?'

'Yes, Mrs Rivers. I believe my lady arranged

to speak to you this morning about the house-keeping?'

'Yes, my lord.'

'I am afraid the interview will have to be post-poned. Her ladyship will spend the morning with me.'

'As you wish, my lord.'

'In the meantime, carry on as usual. Lady Portman will no doubt see you later and make her wishes known.'

'Yes, my lord.' She inclined her head and turned to go.

Rosamund could not let her go like that. There was resentment in every line of her figure. 'Mrs Rivers,' she said, causing the woman to stop and half-turn, a questioning look on her face. Rosamund took a deep breath. 'I do not wish to change any-thing in the running of the house, ma'am. I am sure it runs like clockwork. It is simply that I would like to know what you expect of me. I am very ignorant, you see.' It was said with a winning smile.

An answering smile creased Mrs Rivers's face. 'I understand, my lady. If there is anything you want to know, you only have to ask.' She bobbed again and was gone. Rosamund turned back to Harry to discover he was laughing.

'What do you find so amusing, my lord?'

'You pleading ignorance,' he said. 'Forgive me if I do not believe it.'

'I did not want to start out at odds with her,' she said. 'And the way you spoke to her was bound to make her think I was going to take over.'

'I will speak to her as I please.'

'So you may, but not on my behalf.'

Once again he was taken aback by her forth-rightness. This was a side of her he had not bar-gained for. 'Madam, you are my wife,' he said sharply, forgetting he had almost decided to have the marriage annulled. 'I expect you to be of the same mind as I am. I do not expect you to have opinions of your own.'

'Then I am sorry to disappoint you, my lord. I am no schoolroom miss to be moulded into an echo of my husband. I have lived too long and seen too much for that. However, I shall endeavour not to embarrass you by expressing my opinions before the servants or your friends.' It was said with all the hauteur she could manage.

Instead of continuing the argument, he laughed. 'Oh, I do not think this marriage of ours will be dull,' he said. 'Come, let us go on a tour of inspec-tion and you may tell me your honest opinion of your new home.'

The house was very large and very grand. The ground floor was given over to public reception rooms, a vast dining hall, a ballroom, the estate office and the gunroom, besides the usual offices of kitchen, dairy, pantry and staff dining room. On the first floor there was a library and several small sitting rooms. The bedrooms with their dressing rooms and adjoining sitting rooms were above that and higher still the servants' quarters, divided into male and female, each with their own staircase.

Some of the furnishings, especially in the public rooms, were light and airy, but some were dark and gloomy. 'We do not use those rooms,' Harry told her. 'It is a long time since the house was full.'

Rosamund found herself wondering about his first wife. Had she filled the house with guests? What was she like? According to Mr Portman, his lordship had never got over her death. Had he loved her so much he could not abide the infant who had been the cause of her death? Her heart went out to the child. She was tempted to ask about her, but did not want to spoil his good humour, which he had recovered remarkably quickly.

'What do you think of it?' he asked, as they returned to the ground floor.

'It is very grand. I am not sure I shall be able to find my way about it.'

'You will soon learn. Now shall we look at the garden?' He offered his arm and she took it.

The garden she fell in love with on the spot. It was beautifully tended with terraces, lawns and shrubbery and flower beds. The park was criss-crossed with paths and dotted with mature trees under which horses grazed. One path led through a belt of trees to a lake, bright with yellow pond lilies and flag, and the tall brown spikes of bul-rushes. There was a boat house and a small boat riding on the ripples, moored to a stake. 'Oh, it is so beautiful and so peaceful. I do not know how you can leave it for the smoke and dirt of London,' she said.

'Sometimes I must,' he said. 'In fact, I must return to the capital tomorrow. There is business I have to attend to.'

'So soon?'

'I am afraid so. I am sure you will be able to amuse yourself while I am gone.'

'I expect so,' she said. 'But if your business is so pressing I wonder we did not stay in town after the wedding until it was done.'

'You would have been bored, my dear, and I wanted to see you settled here.'

Out of sight, out of mind, she thought. *He expected to impregnate me and leave me. So why did he leave me alone last night?*

'How long will you be gone?'

'I do not know. If you wish to make calls or go shopping, you may use the landau until I have taught you to drive the gig. Travers will assign a groom to drive it for you. He will take you wherever you wish to go.'

'Thank you.'

It was time for nuncheon, which was served in the small dining room and afterwards, while Rosamund went up to change into her habit, the horses were saddled ready for their ride.

The little mare was called Honey, because that was her colour. She had a temperament to match, being docile and obedient. Rosamund soon discovered she had not forgotten how to ride, as they walked their horses across the park and out of a gate on the far side of the house, which gave on to a lane. The hedgerows were heavily perfumed with cow parsley, interspersed with honeysuckle and wild roses. Trees grew in arches over them, so that they rode in dappled shade. It was peaceful and Rosamund did not want to spoil it by speaking.

They took a turn and she recognised the road on

which they had approached Bishop's Green the evening before and soon a few cottages came in view and then the village green with its stocks and its well, at which a group of women were gossiping. When they saw Harry, they bobbed curtsies and looked surreptitiously towards Rosamund.

'How are your boys, Mrs Ballard?' he enquired of one of them.

'Doing well, my lord, thank you for asking,' the woman answered with a bob.

'And your father-in-law, Mrs Dalton?'

'As contrary as ever,' a toothless woman replied with a grin.

He spoke to each in turn and then he said. 'Ladies, this is my wife, Lady Portman. No doubt she will make herself known to you all in due course.'

They curtsied and Harry and Rosamund rode on, leaving a twitter of comment behind them. 'You have set the tongues wagging,' he told her with a smile. 'But they all seemed happy to meet you. It will please me if you would get to know them and take an interest in their welfare.'

'I shall be glad to do so.'

Their next call was at the blacksmith's where Harry spoke about a horse that needed shoeing and the repair to a gate on the estate. They passed the tavern without going in and that took them to the far side of the green and the church. 'Shall we go inside?' he asked.

'I should like that.'

They dismounted and left Hector and Honey tethered by the lych gate and made their way into the cool interior. It was a small, plain church; the only decoration seemed to be the memorials to the Portman family and one or two other notables. They sat a moment in the family pew in quiet contemplation and then returned to the horses.

Harry took them by a different route back. The road wound upwards on to a heath and here he asked her if she would like to canter. She wondered if the docile Honey would respond, but she lengthened her stride when asked and the gentle canter soon became a gallop. Rosamund let her have her head and felt the breeze in her face and the freedom only a good gallop could give. She could hear Harry alongside her, matching her speed, and felt this was how it ought to be: she and the man she loved happily riding in unison. She could almost imagine that was how it really was. When she drew up she was laughing.

'You have deceived me, madam,' he said, reining in beside her. 'You said you had not ridden for years.'

'Nor have I. I suppose it is something you do not forget.'

'We have a great deal to learn about each other,' he said.

'Yes, I suppose we have.'

'When I come back…' He started, then stopped. He did not want to get to know her any better, he did not want to come to like and admire her any more than he already did. To do so would put their pact and his peace of mind in jeopardy. 'Come, let us go back, it must be nearly dinner time.'

As they turned for home, she wondered what he had been going to say. Whatever it was, he had thought better of it.

Chapter Six

Harry left next morning, taking his town chaise, accompanied by Jack Sylvester. He was not in a good mood. He knew he was supposed to have made love to Rosamund before he left in the hope that she might become pregnant at once, but he could not make himself go to her room, especially after what had happened the night before. Whether she was relieved, disappointed or annoyed he had no way of knowing. She was clever enough not to show her feelings.

She had joined him for breakfast again, smiled, bade him good morning and sat down to talk to him, just as if there were not this dreadful barrier between them. She must surely have wondered why he had stayed away from her bed a second night. He could not believe she was so ignorant that she did not realise there was something wrong. But perhaps she was simply enjoying her reprieve.

Was the prospect of consummating their marriage so repugnant to her?

'My lord,' she had said, as she buttered toast. 'I have been thinking…'

'Oh, what about?' he asked warily.

'Your daughter, my lord. What is her name?'

'Annabelle. It was my late wife's choice. It was to be Annabelle for a girl and Henry for a boy.'

'Annabelle,' she repeated. 'A pretty name.'

'Yes.'

'Where is she?'

'With foster parents. I believe I told you that.'

'Yes, but where? Is it far? I should like to make her acquaintance.'

'I do not think that is a good idea, Rosamund.'

'Why not? I am her stepmother, and you did say, when we made that bargain, that you wanted me to be a mother to your children, and I assumed that meant *all* your children.'

'She is happy where she is and wants for nothing.'

She deplored the practice among some aristocrats of sending very young children to foster parents until they were five or six. 'Yes, but do her foster parents love her as a real parent would? Surely they must have realised that some day she would return to you.'

'It was never discussed.'

'When did you last see her?'

'Madam, leave off your quizzing, if you please. My daughter's welfare has been taken care of.'

'With money, I do not doubt.' She knew she was treading on very infirm ground, but she could not help herself. Her heart had gone out to the child. 'But what about her father's love and attention? Do you visit her regularly? Do you have her here for visits?'

'No. It would only unsettle her.'

'My lord, I cannot help thinking that it is not the way your late wife would have wanted it.'

'You know nothing of my wife,' he said angrily. 'And I did not bring you to Bishop's Court to lecture me.'

'I did not mean to. I beg your forgiveness.'

'You are forgiven because I am persuaded you do not understand.' He stood up. 'Now, I must go. I do not know when I shall return, but no doubt you will be able to occupy yourself.' He bowed to her and left.

And now he was being conveyed back to London, leaving behind unsolved problems which seemed to have no solution. Rosamund's probing questions had made him feel more guilty than at any time since he had sent Annabelle away. It had been done because he could not look at her without seeing a vision of Beth's dead body and all those bloody sheets. None of the servants would have dared question him as his new wife had done. He had gone along for years, leaving everything as it was because it was easier that way, sending money and assuming all was well with the child. For a man who prided himself on never shirking his duty, he had failed in the matter of his daughter, and he did not like being reminded of it.

Rosamund finished her breakfast, musing on his reaction to the questions she had asked. She had only intended to enquire if she might meet his daughter and it had developed into a full-scale criticism. which had angered him. Was it simply that he did not like girls, as his cousin had said, or was it that the child reminded him of his late and beloved wife? But surely that should make him treasure her all the more, not cast her from him? She wondered if there was something wrong with the child. Was she deformed? Or an imbecile?

Going up to her room to don her riding habit ready for a ride out, she found Janet tidying her room, moving quietly and efficiently, humming a little tune to herself. Someone was happy even if she were not. 'Janet,' she began, sitting on the stool against her escritoire, which Harry had arranged to be brought to Bishop's Court for her. 'You talk to the other servants, do you not?'

'Yes, Miss Ro…my lady.'

'When they talked about his lordship not seeing his daughter, did they say where she was?'

'No, I do not think so. It was only said in passing and I did not ask questions. It is not my concern.'

'No, but I think it is mine.'

'Have you not asked his lordship?'

'We talked about Annabelle, but he was in a hurry to leave and he did not say where she lived…' She paused. 'I am too impatient to wait until he comes home again—do you think you could find out without letting anyone know that I want to know? It would seem strange to servants that I am ignorant of where the little girl is.'

'Oh, Miss Rosie, it will seem like spying.'

'I do not want you to spy. You can bring the subject up in conversation, in a roundabout way.'

'I could try, but if I find out, what will you do?'

'If she lives nearby, I intend to visit her…'

'But, Miss Rosie, ought you not to wait until his lordship takes you, or sends for the child?

'Janet, you are my friend as well as my maid, but that does not mean you may tell me what I ought to do. His lordship asked me to get to know all the villagers and help them if they need it, and that I intend to do, and if it means I come across his daughter while doing it, so be it. I shall be discreet, you may depend upon it. So will you try to find her direction?'

'Very well, but it might be a long way off.'

'Then I shall not be able to visit her, shall I? Now help me out of this gown and into my habit. I am going riding.'

Half an hour later she was trotting down the drive and out of the big gates, bent on obeying her husband and making the acquaintance of some of the villagers.

Harry went straight to Portman House where he changed into his well-worn clothes, dirtied his face and hands with stage make-up and set out on foot for the Nag's Head. He knew that if the coiners, who were part of the tavern's clientele, were to discover his true identity, they would not hesitate to kill him. But his disguise was good, his acting ability even better and he knew enough about clipping coins to deceive the real coiners into thinking he was one of them. It was a challenge he enjoyed and today it would serve to take his mind off Rosamund and his daughter.

He had discovered the names of some of

O'Keefe's associates, simply by sitting in a corner of the tavern and listening to them talking to each other. Besides O'Keefe, there was a blacksmith called Bert Ironside, Thomas Quinn, a die maker once employed in the Royal Mint, and Job Smithall, whose job it was to pass off the fake coins. He was more expensively dressed than the others, as he would have to be if he were to pass himself off as a man who regularly paid for things with guineas. They had also mentioned a farm, which Harry surmised was where they had their workshop. Although O'Keefe appeared to be their leader, Harry was sure there was someone else behind the gang, the real brains, and he was anxious to uncover him before moving against the rest.

Thomas Quinn, Bert Ironside and Job Smithall were in the tavern, but not O'Keefe, which was disappointing. Nevertheless, he joined them. 'Good day to ye, gen'lemen,' he said, signalling the waiter to refill everyone's tankard and bring one for him.

They grunted a reply. When the drinks arrived, he pulled a counterfeit shilling from his pocket to pay for it. The tavern keeper weighed it in his hand, ran his thumb over the milling and slapped it back on the table. 'If you think I was born in a cabbage patch, you think wrong, my friend. That's not good money.'

'Beg pardon, my mistake.' Harry pretended to be overcome by confusion and began rooting about in his dirty coat pocket for a genuine coin. He found a sixpence, enough to buy four pints of beer, and offered that. The man went off satisfied.

Smithall had picked up the shilling and was studying it. 'Where did you get this?'

Harry shrugged. 'I dunno, do I? There's so many of 'em about these days, it's 'ard to tell.'

'I reckon you was 'oping to pass it off and get a good sixpence in change,' Bert Ironside said.

'So what if I was? A man 'as to live, don't 'e?' Harry wiped beer froth from his mouth with the side of his sleeve.

Smithall laughed. 'You won't get much profit from shillings and sixpences.'

'It's better than naught. Now, if I was to come across a guinea or even a half-guinea…' He paused and shrugged. 'I wouldn't say no to having one or two o' them.'

'What for?'

'What for, he asks?' Harry laughed raucously. 'What for do you think? I could make good use of 'em.'

'I ha' no doubt you could, but yeller boys are hard to come by hereabouts.' This from Quinn.

'Your friend Micky O'Keefe had a couple of 'em when I met 'im in 'ere the other day. I reckon they were clipped.'

'How do you know they were clipped?'

Harry tapped the side of his nose with a dirty finger. 'I seen some. Done some too. Up north. The gang got bust by the Excise. Only just got away with me life.'

They looked at each other and it was Job Smithall who spoke. 'Supposin' you was to be given a yeller boy or two and supposin' you was to pass 'em off for good money, would you fetch the change back here and keep your mouth shut?'

Harry knew that good 'passers-off' were always needed. 'What would I get out of it?'

'A percentage. Mind, we would have to talk to Micky about it. He's the one to say yea or nay.'

'Where is he today?' Harry asked.

'In the country somewhere,' Job said. 'He don't have to tell us where he is all the time.'

Harry knew they would not tell him any more than that, though he had hoped to find out the locality of the farm. 'How many pieces can you get?' he asked.

'Now there's a question,' the smith said. 'How many d'you want?'

'You mean you can get a lot?' Harry pretended greedy eagerness.

'Could do. Depends on the supply of good coins, you understand. We can't work without gold. Now if you was to come up with a few genuine guineas, we might consider countin' you in.'

'I might.'

'How?'

Harry shrugged again and finished off his beer. The man he was supposed to be would not have guineas honestly obtained. 'There's always the highway lay.'

'Where and when?'

'Don' know yet. Hounslow Heath, perhaps. It's near town and plenty of coaches to choose from.' He gave a grunt of a laugh to cover the fact that he was thinking fast. 'There's always that fop, Lord Portman. 'E goes back and forth regular and not like to put up a fight.'

They laughed. 'You bring us good guineas to work with,' Bert Ironside told him, 'and we might trust you with a few coins to pass off. Tha's if Micky agrees.'

Harry took his leave of them unhurriedly. Once outside he set off in the opposite direction from

Berkeley Square, knowing that one of them would be sent to follow him. Without appearing to look back, he made his way to St Giles, where he lost his pursuer in the maze of dirty street and warrens, and from there he made his roundabout way home, being careful that no one saw him enter the house.

His valet was disgusted with the state of him and wanted to burn his dreadful clothes, but he would not allow it. 'I shall need them again,' he said. 'The dirtier the better.'

'I thought with you being newly married and going to Bishop's Court with Lady Portman, you'd give up your rackety ways,' Jack said, aggrieved. 'What would her ladyship say if she could see you now?'

'But she cannot see me, can she?' he answered reasonably. For the last two hours he had managed to put Rosamund from his mind and he wished Jack had not reminded him of her. 'And I trust you to say nothing.'

'I'm not like to admit I send you out dressed like a chimney sweep, am I?' he said. 'Especially to your lady wife.'

'You do not send me, I go.' He did not know why valets always wanted to boast about how they 'sent out' their masters or why they should take it personally when the master wore something not to their liking. 'Now I am going out again, so I shall require a bath and a change of raiment.'

Jack went off grumbling to order the bath and hot water. Harry suspected it was not so much the old clothes as the fact that he was kept in the dark about the reason for wearing them that peeved his valet.

An hour later, freshly attired in dove grey and white and with his hair neatly arranged in a queue, he arrived at the headquarters of the Piccadilly Gentleman's Club to report progress.

'Harry, we did not expect to see you today,' James commented as he took his place at the table. 'Surely you are not tired of your new wife so soon?'

'Not at all, but there was unfinished business in town and my lady is busy getting to know the staff and exploring her surroundings.' He noticed Ash grinning at him and quickly turned away. Ash might find the situation amusing, but he did not. 'I wanted to strike while the iron was hot. Counterfeit coins of all denominations are turning up all over London: at Vauxhall and Ranelagh Gardens; at tailors and vintners: at coffee shops and gaming houses. It is no good simply arresting those who pass them on, we need to nab the coiners themselves. Unless they are caught and stopped they could destabilise the economy of the country.'

'What can you tell us?' James wanted to know.

'I have discovered a gang of them. I do not suppose it is the only one, but I have reason to believe it is one of the most prolific.' He went on to name and describe the men and what he had learned about them. 'I must prove my worth by producing some real guineas for them to mutilate before they will admit me to their ranks.'

'Why not simply put the Excise men on to them?'

'Because I want to grab their leader and I do not yet know who he is. I need them to trust me and I need proof that cannot be disputed.'

'So, you can spare a few guineas, can't you?' Jonathan said.

'To be sure I can, but they will want to know how a man in my desperate condition came to have them, so I have said I will hold up a coach.'

'Hold up a coach!' James exclaimed. 'I will not sanction that, no matter how worthy the cause.'

Harry grinned at him. 'Not even if it is my own coach?'

'Explain.'

'They do not know my true identity, so I want one of you, preferably you, Ash, since you are about the same size and shape as me, to dress in my rough clothes and hold up my coach and relieve me of a purse full of guineas.'

'Can't you tell them you held up a coach without actually staging it?' Ash asked.

'I could, but I need newspaper reports and gossip about it to convince the gang it really happened. And I cannot ask anyone to hold up a real coach, so it has to be mine. Afterwards we will meet for you to change into your own clothes and give me my clothes and purse back.'

'I'll do it,' Ash said enthusiastically. 'When and where?'

'On my way home to Bishop's Court tomorrow. I will take the road across the Heath. If you can spare the time to come to Portman House with me now, I will give you my clothes.' He chuckled suddenly. 'You are not going to like them, Ash. They stink. But I can promise you a bath and a good meal at Bishop's Court afterwards.'

'And shall I renew my acquaintance with Lady Portman?'

'Naturally she will be there.'

The rest of the Society business was dealt with. Harry and Ash walked to Berkeley Square together. 'How is married life?' Ash asked him.

'If you are asking what I think you are asking,' Harry said morosely, 'it isn't. I could not do it.'

Ash stopped in mid-stride and turned to his friend in astonishment. 'Why not?'

'I don't know. I wish I could dislike her. I wish she were not so attractive. And so innocent. I am sure she has no idea...'

'Good God, man! Surely that is not holding you back?' Ash resumed walking. 'Take her, she will soon find out.'

'It would seem like rape.'

'A man cannot rape his own wife, Harry.'

'She doesn't feel like my wife. She is a stranger.'

'But I thought that was the whole idea, to impregnate a stranger.'

'It isn't going to work, Ash. I wish I had never listened to you and that muckworm of a brother of hers.'

'I'm sorry. I thought only to help you out of your dilemma. And to be truthful, it began as a jest and I did not expect you to do it. You must have seen some merit in the idea.'

'There is a huge chasm between an idea and the execution of it,' Harry said. 'I do not know what came over me in Ranelagh Gardens. I must have run mad.'

'The balmy night, the music, the fireworks, all very romantic,' Ash murmured.

'She knew what her brother was about and I felt sorry for her. And once the offer was made…' He shrugged. 'In the cold light of day I could not retract, could I?'

'So what are you going to do?'

'I do not know. I can have the marriage annulled, I suppose.'

'To do that you will either have to blame her for refusing to consummate it, which will be a blow to your pride, or make yourself look a fool for not being able to.'

'I know. I cannot do either.'

'Then you must make the best of the situation. Make her your wife.'

'I keep asking myself if I want to. She is outspoken to a degree that is bound to make the sparks fly. I am not used to being questioned about what I do.'

'Not about the Piccadilly Gentlemen?'

'No, she knows nothing of my involvement with the Society, but before I left she was asking me when I last saw my daughter.'

'And when was that?'

'The day she was born.'

'Did you tell her that, Harry?'

'No.'

'Did you tell her anything about your first wife?'

'Only that I was widowed six years ago. And before you say anything, I have no intention of telling her what really happened.'

They had arrived in Berkeley Square and he hurried up the steps and into the house with Ash behind him and the subject of Rosamund and his marriage was dropped. 'Will you dine with me?' he asked as they sat in the drawing room enjoying a glass of cognac. 'We can talk over our plans for the robbery while we eat.'

The meal was a simple one of only five courses, and though it was superbly prepared, neither man noticed much of what he was eating, so absorbed were they in their plans.

'For God's sake do not mistake anyone else's coach for mine,' Harry said. 'And it would be best if there were no other vehicles nearby at the time. I do not want some gallant with more stomach than brains to try to come to my rescue. Someone might be hurt.'

'It is a busy road, the timing might not be easy.'

'As long as no one is near enough to intervene, that ought to suffice. A distant witness would be a help, though. It should only take a minute to stop me, take my purse and gallop away.'

'You do not want me to injure you, I hope?'

'No need.' Harry laughed. 'Lord Portman is known for his lavish dress and foppish ways, not his bravery. I will be terrified and put up no resistance. Afterwards I will make a great song and dance about losing my money.'

'What if your coachman decides to act the hero...?'

'He won't. He has instructions that if we are ever held up, he is to remain passive and not risk his life for a few guineas, which is all I usually carry. When the deed is done, make your way to Bishop's Court. You cannot come up to the house in disguise, so go to the boat house down by the lake. You can wash the make-up off in the water and change there. If you give me a suit of your clothes in a bag, I will have it on the seat of the coach and you can take that along with my purse. Bundle up the purse and the disguise and bring them up to the house in the bag. Go back to the lane and ride up openly as if you are paying a call.'

'I understand. Tell me about your other self, the man I am supposed to be impersonating.'

'Gus Housman is a most disreputable character, up to every sort of rig short of murder, filthy,

uncombed and unshaven, not the sort to have guineas honestly come by. After we have eaten I will
give you his clothes and show you how to make
up your face and hands. You can bring me your
clothes before I set out in the morning.'

'No wonder they say you had a promising career
as an actor in your green days if you can convince
the criminal fraternity you are one of them. Shall
you put out a warrant for my arrest?'

'I shall have to, shan't I? It will look smoky an'
I do not, but as the blackguard who did the deed
does not exist, he will never be apprehended, will
he?'

'I have just thought of something,' Ash said,
taking a mouthful of wine. 'Won't the Piccadilly
Gentlemen be expected to investigate the crime,
especially as it is one of their number who has
suffered?'

'So? They can give the task to you. 'Tis a pity
you will have to fail, but you cannot succeed every
time.'

And they both laughed and opened another
bottle of wine.

Travers had assigned a spotty youth called Ben
to drive Rosamund. She was glad the head groom
had gone with his master because he might well

question why she wanted the gig to visit Feltham Farm. If he did not ask her directly, he would certainly speak of it to Harry. And she would rather tell her husband herself.

It had not been necessary for Janet to question the staff about Annabelle's whereabouts after all. Mrs Rivers told her what she wanted to know without being asked. 'I shall not be available to go over the linen with you this afternoon, my lady,' she had said. 'I visit his lordship's daughter's foster parents on the first day of every other month to take money and little gifts for the child. And today is the first of July.'

'She is not far away, then?'

'No, at Feltham Farm. It's on the other side of the Heath, nearer Hounslow than here. I usually get one of the grooms to drive me over in the gig.'

'I could go for you, Mrs Rivers. I have nothing to do this afternoon and you must be busy.'

'I don't know,' the woman said doubtfully. 'It has always been my task.'

'But that was when there was no mistress at Bishop's Court. I am here now and I should like to meet the little girl. I am her stepmother, after all.'

'What do you think his lordship will say?' The housekeeper was still doubtful.

'Leave his lordship to me. I think some things need to change, don't you?'

Mrs Rivers's brow cleared and she smiled. 'Yes, my lady, I do.'

So here she was, bowling over the Heath towards Feltham Farm with no clear idea what she would do and say when she arrived. Not wishing to over-awe the child she had dressed in a simple gingham gown, open from the waist to reveal a plain padded petticoat. She wore a large hat with a feather over her own curls which shaded her face from the sun, for it was a warm day. In her reticule was a purse containing five guineas and beside her on the seat was a little toy monkey on a stick, which could be made to dance by pulling a cord up and down. The foster parents were a Mr and Mrs Chappell who ran the farm with Mr Chappell's brother, so Mrs Rivers had informed her.

They had almost reached the other side of the Heath where the character of the landscape changed. Here was farmland, with hedges and trees and cultivated fields where the wheat was tall and almost ripe. After a little while Ben turned the gig down a rutted farm track. It was a mile or two before she saw any buildings because they were shielded by woodland, but after they had left the trees, they saw the farm ahead of them, nestling in a hollow. It was so well hidden that unless you knew of it, you would never guess it was there. Ben drove into the yard and drew to a halt. A huge dog barked ferociously, straining on the chain that held it. Rosamund was disinclined to leave the gig for fear it might free itself and attack her.

A woman came out of the house, wiping her hands on a grubby apron. She was followed by a gaggle of children, boys and girls. Rosamund counted six of them. She wondered how many were the woman's own or if they were all fostered. She looked from one to the other, wondering which was Annabelle. Some were too old, others too young. There was one that might have been six years old, but she could not see a likeness to Harry. They all seemed well fed, though dirty and ill clothed.

The woman evidently recognised the gig. 'Where's Mrs Rivers?' she demanded, coming up to where Rosamund sat. 'She ain't left, hev she?'

'Mrs Rivers is still housekeeper at Bishop's Court,' Rosamund told her. 'I come in her place. I am Lady Portman.'

'Lady Portman!' the woman exclaimed in astonishment. 'You don' say his lordship hev wed ag'in?'

'Yes.'

'I can't believe it…'

'Oh, you may believe it.' She turned to the young groom who had driven her. 'Ben, tell Mrs Chappell who I am.' And to the woman, 'I assume you are Mrs Chappell.'

'Course I am.'

'She's her ladyship, all right,' Ben told her. 'Lord Portman's new wife. And you'd best do as she says.'

The woman shrugged. 'So be it. You'll be wanting to come in.' She stepped aside so that Rosamund could get down. The dog continued to bark. 'Shut up!' She rounded on it and gave it a vicious kick which sent it yelping and sprawling in the dust. Then she led the way into the house. Rosamund followed her, with the children, some silent, some chattering excitedly, close behind.

'Sit you down. I'll make some tea.'

Rosamund stood and looked about her. She was in a large kitchen with a stone-flagged floor that was so grimy it could not have seen a mop in years. The table was strewn with the remains of a meal, which a black cat was enjoying. Mrs Chappell knocked it off. It squealed and fled.

'No tea, thank you, Mrs Chappell,' Rosamund said, sitting gingerly on the edge of a chair. 'Which of the children is Annabelle?'

'Oh, she ain't one o' these. These are all my own.'

'Where is she then? I would like to see her.' Already she was determined to take the child away from this filthy place.

'In her bed. She ain't bin too well.'

'What is wrong with her?'

'Belly ache. She ate some sour crab apples off a tree down the lane. I ha' told her not to often enough. I give 'er some physic. She'll soon pick up.'

'Have you informed Lord Portman?'

'No, 'e don't want to know. He've never bin to see 'er, not once, in all her life. I was expectin' Mrs Rivers to come with her keep money, then I can buy her some more physic. The bottle I had is done.'

'Take me to her.'

'Oh, you don' want to be goin' up there, m'lady. What with her heavin' her guts up and havin' the flux an' all…' She did not elaborate, leaving the state of the child to Rosamund's imagination.

'Nevertheless I wish to see her.'

One of the older boys began to giggle, but stopped when his mother lifted a hand to him. 'Very well, m'lady. But don' say I didn' warn you.'

Rosamund followed her up a flight of narrow stairs, which led on to a landing. There were four rooms on that floor. Mrs Chappell opened the door of one and Rosamund almost recoiled at the stench. There were three beds in the room, a big four-poster, another a little smaller and a tiny truckle bed and it was on this the child was lying, covered by a stinking rag of a blanket.

'Annie, you got a visitor,' Mrs Chappell announced.

The child hardly stirred. Her face was white as paper and her hair was plastered to her scalp. She was wearing what looked like an old shirt of one of the boys. 'Oh, you poor, poor dear,' Rosamund said, dropping to her knees to stroke the hair from her forehead. 'Mrs Chappell, she is burning with fever. Have you sent for a doctor?'

'No. She'll get over it. She's already better'n she was. Another good dose of physic and she'll be right as ninepence.'

'She needs a doctor. I am going to take her home with me, where she will be looked after.' She stood up and bent over the bed to gather the child into her arms. She was too weak even to cry.

'You can't do that. This is her home...'

'No longer, Mrs Chappell.' She carried the child downstairs, followed by Mrs Chappell protesting in the strongest terms that she was taking away her livelihood . The rest of the children were still in the kitchen, their mouths open in curiosity. Rosamund marched straight past them and out into the yard, where the dog began barking again. She ignored it and climbed back into the gig with the child still in her arms. For a six-year-old she was very light. Ben sniffed. 'My lady, she stinks like a pigsty.'

'It cannot be helped, Ben. We have to get her away from here.'

Mrs Chappell hurried out behind them. 'Hey, what about my money? Five guineas is owed to me.'

Rosamund flung the purse at her and instructed Ben to drive on. He wheeled the gig round and they left the dreadful place behind them. She half-expected someone to give chase, but no one did, and once they were back on the road and crossing the heath, she set about talking to the little girl, trying to soothe her, telling her she was going to a nice new home where she would have a bath and clean clothes and a soft bed and a doctor would make her better.

Her quiet voice belied how she was feeling. Inside she was seething. Had no one checked on the welfare of the poor child? Had anyone taken the trouble to make sure the money meant for her keep was spent on her? Did no one care? Why had Mrs Rivers, who visited regularly, not seen what was happening and reported it to Lord Portman? Why had he never taken the trouble to visit her himself? Now he would have to take some notice of her. Not even he could ignore the child's plight.

'My lady.' Ben's voice held a note of alarm. 'There's trouble ahead.'

Rosamund looked up to see a coach stopped by the side of the road and a man on horseback pointing a gun at the occupant. Even from a distance she recognised the equipage. 'It's Lord Portman,' she cried, as her imagination pictured his lordship lying across the seat, broken and bleeding. Her anger with him was forgotten. 'Quick, Ben, we must go to him. He might be hurt.'

'My lady, the man has a gun.'

'Gun or no, we cannot stand by and do nothing. Whip up the horse. We might scare him off.'

Ben obeyed, making the little gig bounce about on the uneven road. Annabelle whimpered and Rosamund was occupied in trying to calm her and shield her from the worst of the bumping. The highwayman, still brandishing his gun, looked up and saw the gig bearing down on them. He appeared to say something, grabbed a bag from inside the coach and galloped away.

Ben, much relieved to see the back of him, drew up alongside the big coach, but before Rosamund could extricate herself from the burden of Annabelle and go to her husband, Harry was out and striding over to her. She was the last person he had expected to see and the last one he wanted as a witness to the hold-up. 'Madam, what are you doing here?'

She ignored his question. 'Are you hurt, my lord? What did he take?'

'Nothing but a few paltry guineas, and, no, I am not hurt.' He put his hand on the side of the gig and saw the child in her lap. 'Good God! What have you there?'

'This, my lord, is your daughter.'

He looked from her to the child and back again. 'Nonsense. She's filthy and she stinks.'

'So she is and so she does. Nevertheless, she is your daughter. She is ill and needs a doctor and I am taking her home to look after her, for clearly her foster mother has not been doing so.' She pulled the filthy blanket from about the child's face so that he could see her, while Ben stared straight ahead, trying to pretend he could not hear what was going on. 'Mrs Chappell has six more children at home, all well fed on your guineas, my lord, whereas this poor mite is so hungry she has been eating unripe crab apples.' That was only a guess, but it served to shock him to the core.

He took another look at the child. She was painfully thin; her fair hair was lank and her blue eyes were bright with fever. He could not believe, did not want to believe, that this disgusting object was the product of his loins, the tiny infant his wife had died to bring into the world. And yet... And yet, there was something about her that touched a chord. She reminded him of his young sister who had died of fever when she was six. He had only been eight at the time, but her illness and death was something that had stayed in his memory. He reached out and touched the child's cheek and in that moment he felt the first faint stirrings of fatherhood.

He hesitated to lift the child from Rosamund's arms in case he frightened her. 'Take her home,' he said, abruptly. 'I will follow.' And with that he returned to his coach and climbed in.

Ben drove the gig past the stationary coach and set the horse to a trot.

Half an hour later they were turning in at the gates. 'Pull up at the kitchen door,' Rosamund said.

As soon as they stopped, he jumped down and took the child from her, while she scrambled down, just as the coach pulled up behind them. Harry was out before the wheels had stopped turning and took the child from the young coachman. 'Go and fetch Dr Marshall, Ben,' he said. 'Tell him it is urgent.' Rosamund opened the door for him and he marched into the kitchen where the kitchen staff gaped in astonishment. 'A bath, hot water, clean clothes,' he ordered. 'Take them to...'

'My dressing room,' Rosamund said.

'Her ladyship's dressing room,' he confirmed, and took his burden through to the front of the house and up the stairs, followed by Rosamund. She opened her door for him to precede her into the room. Janet came rushing forward. 'My lady—' She stopped to stare.

Harry looked about him. There was a sofa in the room and he put Annabelle on that. 'Clean her up and put her to bed,' he instructed Rosamund. 'We will discuss this later.' With a last look at the child, who had no strength even to cry, he left them to do what needed to be done and went to his own room, where Jack helped him to change his clothes. Then he went downstairs to the library, shut himself in and began pacing back and forth.

His first reaction on seeing his wife with the child had been cold fury: fury that she was on the road at all, fury that she had meddled in his arrangements for his daughter, fury that she had gone to the farm and seen fit to abduct the child from her foster parents, even after he had said it was not a good idea. This changed to fury with Mrs Chappell for her neglect of the child and for not informing him she was ill and fury with Mrs Rivers for not realising and not reporting that she was being neglected. But none of that disguised the fact that above all he was angry with himself.

How could he have assumed that because he paid handsomely for Annabelle to be looked after, that was all he needed to do? What had Rosamund said? *What about her father's love and attention? Do you visit her regularly? Do you have her here for visits?* And when he answered, coldly because he did not like being questioned, she had added, *I cannot help thinking that it is not the way your late wife would have wanted it.* Her barbs had hit home and they hit deep, more so since he had seen the child. The arrival of Rosamund Chalmers into his life and into his household had certainly caused a stir and shaken him out of his complacency.

He looked up as she came into the room. She had changed her clothes and tidied her hair and they faced each other in open hostility. 'Madam, I require an explanation,' he said, still angry.

'I have given you one,' she answered calmly. 'I am sure you do not need me to repeat it. I came to tell you the doctor is with Annabelle now. I assume you would wish to speak to him.'

He brushed past her and hurried up the stairs with Rosamund behind him. The doctor had just finished his examination and was closing his bag. Annabelle, who had been bathed and put into a clean nightgown that was several sizes too big for her, lay very still with her eyes closed and Harry thought for one dreadful moment she had died. His memory conjured up a picture of Beth lying so still and pale in death and he turned his face away.

'A bad case of colic,' Dr Marshall told him, before he could disgrace himself with tears. 'Made worse because the child is so badly nourished. What she needs is a wholesome diet and plenty of rest.'

'She shall have it. And a nurse.'

'I will nurse her,' Rosamund said, ashamed to see him turn away from the child. The poor little thing could not help being born, nor being ill. 'I have already asked for a bed to be brought in here for her.'

'There is no need—' Harry began

'Oh, indeed there is. The child needs a little loving attention; however good the servants are, they cannot give her that. It will be my pleasure to care for her and it will give us the opportunity to get to know each other.' She reached out and put a hand on his arm. Why she did it she did not know, except that she wanted to take the anger out of him.

He looked at her hand with its long capable fingers and was torn between brushing it off and taking it in his own and lifting it to his lips. She had that effect on him. It was impossible to remain angry with her. He knew then, that whatever else happened, he could never annul the marriage. Annabelle needed her even if he did not. He picked her hand off his sleeve and squeezed it gently in reassurance before letting it go. 'Very well, my dear, if that is your wish.'

He accompanied the doctor down the stairs. 'I can trust your discretion in this, Doctor?'

'Of course.'

'You know who the child is?'

'I can guess. Was I not here when she was born? Poor Lady Portman, she so wanted the child to be a boy, to please you.' He sighed. 'Alas, we cannot always have what we want.'

'No, but I would like to believe she thought she had given me a son.'

'You are very fortunate in your new wife,' the doctor went on. 'She has shown herself compassionate and practical too. With her care, the little one will thrive.'

'Yes. I had no idea what was happening. Mr and Mrs Chappell will pay dearly for their neglect.'

The doctor paused at the bottom of the stairs and turned towards him. 'And you? Will you keep her here when she has recovered?' It was the nearest he dare go to a criticism and Harry knew it.

'Naturally I will.'

It was as he was seeing the doctor off the premises that Ash rode up. He was relaxed and smiling. He dismounted, took the portmanteau containing the old clothes and the coins off the back of his saddle and came towards Harry, smiling broadly. 'Well, here I am,' he said.

'I had forgotten all about you,' Harry said.

Ash looked taken aback. 'Am I not welcome?'

'Of course you are. Come in. I will have to leave you with Lady Portman. I am afraid I have to go out.' He turned to see Rosamund coming down the stairs. She looked strained, but otherwise calm. 'My dear,' he said. 'Sir Ashley has favoured us with a visit.'

She offered her hand to Ash, who took it and bowed low over it. 'Your obedient, my lady.'

'Will you arrange for him to be given a bedchamber?' Harry told her. 'He will wish to refresh himself and change after his journey. Jack will help him. I have to go out again, but I shall be back in time for dinner.'

'Where are you going?' she asked.

'I am going to Feltham Farm. Those two must be punished.'

'What can you accuse them of, except neglect?' She did not need to add that they were not the only ones guilty of that; he knew it. 'Let them be. They have lost the income you gave them and that will punish them. And you could put yourself in danger.'

'Danger—what are you talking of, Madam?'

'I do not know. It is just that I have a strange feeling about that place, as if there is evil there. As if I were being watched. Please do not go.'

Ash had been standing beside his horse's head, the portmanteau in his hand, looking from one to the other. 'Have I arrived at an inconvenient time?' he asked.

'No, no,' Harry assured him. 'We have had a little upset.'

'Oh.' He waited to be told about the highway robbery, anticipating his expression of surprise, but Harry seemed to have forgotten all about it.

'My daughter has been taken ill.'

'I am indeed sorry to hear that,' Ash said. 'Shall I take myself off and find an inn?'

'No, we have much to discuss,' Harry said. 'Make yourself comfortable. I shall not be long. After I have been to the farm, I will report the highway robbery to the Watch, though what good it will do, I cannot think.'

'You have been robbed?' Ash queried, pretending innocence.

'Yes. Lady Portman will tell you all about it. She was there. I will take your horse for you.' He picked up the reins and led the stallion towards the stables.

Ash turned towards Rosamund. 'Lady Portman, I am sorry to impose myself upon you, but Harry did ask me to call.'

'You are welcome, Sir Ashley,' she said, wishing him anywhere but where he was. With Annabelle to look after, and Harry in the mood he was in, a guest was the last thing she needed. 'Come indoors and I will see about a room for you. You will forgive me for leaving you to be looked after by Mr Sylvester. I need to be with my stepdaughter.'

She sent for Jack Sylvester and when Ash went off with him, she returned to the sick room. She was so busy looking after Annabelle that it was

some time before she realised there was something strange about Sir Ashley's visit. Why had
he ridden from town when Harry had plenty of
room in his carriage? And she could swear that
the portmanteau he carried was the one stolen
from Harry. How had he come by it, unless he had
either been the highwayman himself or had taken
it from the robber? It would have been easier to
believe the latter if she had not been quite so sure
the horse he rode was the one used in the hold-up.
It was a noble animal with distinctly marked nose
and socks. Surely Harry must have noticed that?
Perhaps she ought to warn him that his friend was
not all he purported to be.

Chapter Seven

Harry returned in time for dinner as he had promised, but there was no opportunity for Rosamund to speak to him alone, and after the meal the two men retired to the library where she knew she would not be welcome. She took tea in the drawing room alone and then went to Mrs Rivers's sitting room to talk to her about her visits to the farm.

'Surely you knew there was something wrong?' she asked her. 'The child has been half-starved.'

'I never knew that. I didn't like going there. Mrs Chappell was only interested in the money and she insisted on it being in guineas, which surprised me because she hardly needed gold coin to do the shopping she did. She said she was getting Annabelle special food, which cost dear because the poor wee thing never seemed to thrive. I believed her at first, but later, when I came to question it, she became aggressive and told me to mind my own business. She said if his lordship doubted her capabilities he could come and see for himself. Of course he never did.'

'You did tell him?'

'I tried, but whenever I mentioned his daughter, he shut me out by talking about something else and as I am only the housekeeper, I could not argue with him. I am so glad you went today, my lady. The poor child will do well now she is here with you to look after her. You won't send her back, will you?'

'Certainly not. It is a dreadful place. I cannot imagine how she came to be there.'

'Mrs Chappell was recommended by the wet nurse and, to tell the truth, it was not so bad in the beginning. The woman was clean and did her best. It is only in the last two years she's let every-thing go to pot. I blame her husband, a real tyrant if there ever was one. He frightened me. I would not be surprised if he took most of the money from her.'

'Has his lordship spoken to you today?'

'No, my lady. Everyone has been too busy. And now he has Sir Ashley with him. No doubt he will send for me tomorrow. I am dreading it.'

'Lord Portman is a fair man,' Rosamund said.

'If you tell him what you have told me, I am sure he will not blame you. Now I am going up to my room to sit with Annabelle. I am sure his lordship will not need me any more tonight.'

Harry was sprawled in an armchair, facing Ash. Both were nursing a glass of cognac. 'I was never so taken aback as when I saw my wife with that child,' Harry said. 'And so plainly ill. It gave me a turn I can tell you. The robbery went clean out of my head until you arrived.'

'But you have reported it?'

'Yes. A description of the thief is being circulated. I have offered a reward for information as to his whereabouts.'

Ash chuckled. 'Then no doubt you will be besieged by people knowing where he is to be found and claiming it.'

'Perhaps. More to the point, will the news reach O'Keefe and his gang?' He paused. 'They may have set someone to watch me. I did suggest that Lord Portman might be an easy target.'

'When I go back to town I will spread the word and no doubt it will reach the newspapers. Did you go to the foster parents?'

'Yes, and it is as my wife said. The place was filthy. The woman was deferential, whining that it wasn't her fault the child had not thrived. She had always been sickly. And when I asked her why she had not informed me of that, she said she had supposed Mrs Rivers would tell me and because I had not been near she assumed I did not want to know. Her husband came in then. He threatened me with violence.' He grinned suddenly. 'And as I went there as the macaroni, I had to stay in character and beat a hasty retreat, much as I would have liked to give him a facer.'

'Her ladyship might be right,' Ash said. 'And nothing can be done. You put the child in their hands and they are no worse than hundreds of other foster parents. Just be thankful Lady Portman found her in time.'

Harry digested this without comment. He finished his brandy and refilled both glasses. 'I have to go back to the Nag's Head as soon as I can and hand over those guineas. I am hoping it will lead to my being taken to the farm where the coins are worked on.'

'You could be putting yourself in danger, you know. Let me come with you.'

'Certainly not. You are the enemy, the thief-taker, so be assiduous in that task. I will find some way of letting you know if I need you. Now I'm for my bed.'

They left the room and parted at the top of the stairs, but Harry did not immediately go to his bed, but went to Rosamund's room. He smiled ruefully as he knocked and entered. The day's events had given a whole new meaning to his relationship with his wife, though he could not quite put his finger on what it was.

A little bed had been put up in the adjoining dressing room and Rosamund was sitting on a stool beside it, watching over the child. Annabelle's white gold hair had been washed and was spread over the pillow. One arm was flung out. He was shocked at how skinny it was. But the disturbing vision of Beth did not return as he dropped down on his knees beside Rosamund; he saw only the child. 'How is she?' he whispered.

'The doctor gave her something to end the flux and send her to sleep. She is peaceful. When she wakes she will feel better and we can try to fatten her up a little.'

'Poor little one,' he murmured. 'How I have wronged her. I wonder if she will ever forgive me?'

'I am sure she will.'

He had been gazing at Annabelle, but now turned towards Rosamund and put his hand over hers on the coverlet. 'And will you forgive me?'

The pressure of his hand was having a strange effect on her heart. It was beating so hard it was making her breathless. Was he going to talk about what had happened on their wedding night, perhaps explain himself? She tried to sound calm. 'What is there to forgive?'

'My anger. I should not have taken it out on you. I was angry with myself.' He gave a twisted smile. 'I am like all my sex, I do not like having my faults pointed out to me. But you were right and I was wrong.'

She knew how much of an effort that admission had taken even if it was not what she had hoped for. 'I am often too outspoken,' she admitted.

'I deserved it.'

In his present mellow mood she felt bold enough to continue. 'What I do not understand is why you did not want to bring up your daughter yourself? She is such a pretty little thing. Is she like her mother?'

'A little, but I did not see it then. Babies all look alike, don't they?'

She gave a suppressed chuckle and looked at Annabelle as she stirred in her sleep, but she did not wake. 'That is a typical masculine reply, but she is no longer a baby, my lord. I can see a little of you in her. The eyes and the mouth. I think that could be a stubborn little mouth.'

He turned to look at the sleeping child. 'She reminds me of my sister.'

'I did not know you had a sister, my lord.' There was so much she did not know about this enigmatic man and it seemed today was a day for revelations.

'She died when she was six. The same age as Annabelle is now. I was only eight at the time.'

'An impressionable age.'

'Yes. I did not understand how anyone could be so alive one day and so cold and lifeless the next. It frightened me. It was the same when Beth died.'

She was slowly beginning to understand. He had loved his wife and had been unable to come to terms with her death. 'But this little one is not dead, is she?' she said, refusing to entertain the pang of jealousy that made itself felt.

'No, thank God, but if you had not found her, she might have been.'

'We will not talk of what might have been, my lord, but the future. You will not send her away again, will you?'

'No, with you to watch over her, I would not dare.' It was said with a touch of ironic humour, which made her smile.

'I think I shall enjoy being a mother,' she said.

They both fell silent, reminded of their bargain. No progress had been made in that direction at all. But perhaps now they had established some kind of rapport, the situation might change. She surprised herself with how much she wanted it to.

She slept fitfully that night, her ears attuned to any sound coming from the dressing room, ready to rush in if Annabelle needed her; consequently she woke later than usual and, dressing in a hurry, went into the next room to find Harry sitting on the stool, watching his sleeping daughter. 'She looks so peaceful,' he whispered, standing up. 'We will not waken her.'

He took her elbow and guided her back into her bedroom, where Janet was busy. 'See to the child,' he told her. She scuttled into the dressing room.

'I have to go back to town,' he said after the maid had left. 'I will be as quick as I can and should be back tomorrow. Can you manage?'

She tried not to let her disappointment show. Nothing had changed, after all. 'Of course. What about Sir Ashley?'

'He left on horseback half an hour ago. I shall take the coach.'

'Oh.' She paused, wondering whether to say what

was in her mind. 'Harry, do you trust Sir Ashley?' she asked.

'Entirely, my dear. Why do you ask?'

'I noticed that the portmanteau he carried with him when he arrived yesterday was remarkably like the one the highwayman took from your carriage, and the horse was identical to the one he rides. Its markings are very distinctive.'

Harry silently cursed his oversight. Aloud he said. 'I do not suppose Ash's is the only horse marked like that. And portmanteaux of that design are manufactured in their hundreds. The idea that Ash is a highwayman is ridiculous. Anyway, why would he rob me? He has his own fortune.'

'I am sorry, I did not mean to accuse him, I just thought…' Her voice tailed away; she was not sure what she had thought. 'I meant only to point out what I had noticed.'

'Then I thank you, but you need have no fear. Sir Ashley is my friend. I would trust him with my life.' He bent forwards and kissed her cheek. 'I must go. I will be back tomorrow.' He left her rubbing her cheek where his lips had touched it. Was this all there would ever be, a few kind words, a touching of hands, a chaste kiss on the cheek, when she wanted so much more?

* * *

'My wife is too observant for comfort, Ash,' he said with a wry smile, that evening. They were dining at Portman House because they could talk there without being overheard. 'She recognised your portmanteau and your horse yesterday and came to the conclusion that it was you who had robbed me. I had to explain that your horse is not unique and neither is the bag.'

'Was she satisfied?'

'She seemed to be.'

'Had you thought of telling her the truth?'

'Good God, no! That side of my life is a closed book to everyone but the Piccadilly Gentlemen. It is the only way I can work.'

'Have you made contact with the gang? Did they swallow the story of the hold-up?'

'I think so. O'Keefe said he witnessed it himself. He had followed you and was hiding in some bushes nearby, so I am very glad we worked that ruse.'

'Then he must also have seen Lady Portman.'

'Yes, and that worries me, but as long as he does not connect Lord Portman with Gus Housman, she should be safe enough. It is one reason, and a very compelling one, for not telling her what I am up to.'

'I think I had better dispose of that stallion. It is a pity, he is a good mount, but if her ladyship recognised it, so might others.'

'I am sorry for that,' Harry said. 'If it had not been for Rosamund…'

Ash laughed. 'If it had not been for your dear lady pointing out our mistakes we might never have thought of them and O'Keefe might have twigged what was happening. Now, at least we can take steps to limit the damage.'

It was still early when they finished their meal and by common consent they repaired to White's for a game of cards and to listen to the gossip, most of which centred around who was and who was not going to receive an invitation to the Royal nuptials; where was the best place from which to view the coronation procession; and who had been held up and robbed on his lawful business about the capital. Harry made one or two mental notes for passing on at the meeting of the Piccadilly Gentleman the next day. Then, all being well, he could head back to Rosamund and Annabelle with a clear conscience.

White's had a new proprietor since Mr Arthur had died the previous month. His name was Robert Mackreth. Harry had asked him to be on the lookout for clipped coins, telling him he was making enquiries at the behest of Sir John Fielding without mentioning the Society. People had heard of it, of course, but its purpose and exact membership could only be guessed. He and Ash were enjoying a class of Rhenish wine and settling down to a game of whist, when Mackreth bent to whisper in Harry's ear, 'My lord, I would have a private word with you.'

Harry excused himself and followed him from the room to a small room off the corridor used as an office. 'My lord, you asked me to let you know if I ever received clipped guineas.' He held out two coins. 'I believe these are counterfeit.'

Harry took them, weighed them in his hand one at a time, then examined the milling. 'Yes, these have been clipped. Do you know who gave them to you?'

'No, the wine waiter took them, not realising they were not genuine, but I have made a list of everyone who was on the premises at the time.' He went to a desk and produced a sheet of paper. 'They are all bone-fide members and their guests.'

'Thank you. I will study it later. They may all be innocent victims, but if you receive any more, make another list. If the same names crop up again, we shall be able to narrow down the suspects. I am sure I do not need to tell you that you should say nothing to anyone.'

'You may rely on me.'

Harry reimbursed the man for the clipped coins and pocketed them along with the list, and returned to his game. Whoever was passing the coins was becoming bolder, or perhaps more desperate. He was sure it was not Job Smithall because he had no access to White's. It was not beyond the bounds of possibility that some gentleman member, whose gambling debts were more than he was able to honour, had succumbed to temptation.

In no time Annabelle began to recover and the good food and care she received soon put a little flesh on her bones and roses in her cheeks. Her bed had been removed from Rosamund's dressing room and she had been given a room of her own a little further down the corridor, and she was soon running about and exploring her surroundings, all of which enthralled her. Rosamund had bespoken clothes for her from a seamstress whom Mrs Rivers knew and other items were obtained from shops in Hounslow and Isleworth.

'When are yer goin' to send me 'ome ag'in?' the child asked Rosamund one day when she had been at Bishop's Court nearly three months. She was dressed in a white dimity dress with a wide blue sash, white hose and neat black shoes. She was very proud of the shoes; she had only ever worn boots before and those scuffed and worn and several sizes too big, having been handed down from Mrs Chappell's older children. They had just returned from a walk and Rosamund was removing her bonnet for her.

'Sweetheart, this is your home now. Surely you do not want to go back?'

'No, I like it 'ere, but Mama will be real angry if I'm not there.'

'Why would she be angry?'

'I 'ave to do me chores and 'elp her in the kitchen, or I 'ave to go to bed wivout me supper.'

That Mrs Chappell expected a child so young to work in the kitchen and, what was worse, to be punished by depriving her of food appalled Rosamund. 'Annabelle, there is something you must know.' She paused to gather her thoughts. 'Mrs Chappell is not your real mama. She is what you call a foster mother.'

'Wha's tha'?'

Rosamund explained as gently as she could. 'Lord Portman is your papa. You were sent to Mrs Chappell because your own mother died when you were born and there was no one to look after you.

Now you have me. I am married to your papa and that makes me your stepmama. I will never let you go back there to be ill treated, I promise you.'

'You mean tha'?' Her eyes lit up with pleasure.

'Yes.' She smiled and kissed the child's cheek. 'But you have to learn to be the little lady, so I have arranged for you to have lessons.' She had already established that Annabelle had not begun to learn to read and write, a fact that had angered Harry, who thought some of his guineas had been spent on tuition for her. It just showed how divorced from reality he had been over his daughter.

When he was at home, he saw and talked to Annabelle every day, though she was more than a little in awe of him and he found it difficult to unbend, especially as he found her vulgar way of speaking repugnant. 'Get her some elocution lessons,' he had told Rosamund. 'She sounds like a gutter urchin.' Rosamund, who was beginning to understand his moods, knew the abruptness hid a burgeoning love for his daughter he found difficult to express. He was often away on business, though what that business was she had no idea. He had not seen fit to enlighten her.

Hearing the sound of a coach and horses on the gravel one afternoon, she thought it was Harry returning, but it was her brother. He was dressed in his usual elegant way: black silk with silver embroidery and a black cravat. 'Thought I'd pay you a visit to see how you are going along,' he said, breezing into the small parlour where she was teaching Annabelle her letters.

'Very well,' she said, instructing the footman who had admitted him to send the parlour maid to her.

'And who is this?' He beamed at the child, who was staring at him in curiosity.

'This is Annabelle,' Rosamund said. Then to the child, 'Run along to the kitchen, sweetheart. Cook will find you something to eat, and then you must find Janet. She will look after you.' She watched the child leave the room, then turned to her brother. 'Sit down, Max. Will you drink tea?'

'Tea?' He dropped on to a sofa opposite her. 'Have you nothing stronger?'

'Of course, but as it is early in the afternoon, I thought you might prefer the beverage.'

He sighed. 'Very well, tea will do.'

A maid appeared and Rosamund gave the order, then turned back to Max. 'What brings you here?'

'I told you. I came to see how you are faring.'

'As you see, I am well.'

'Increasing, are you?' he asked bluntly.

'It is early days.'

'You have been married nigh on three months, time enough, I should have thought. I hope you do not disappoint his lordship in that respect. He will have no compunction about divorcing you an' you do. It was his whole reason for marrying you.'

She had no intention of telling him the truth, that if it had been his lordship's reason, he must have changed his mind. Fortunately a maid arrived with the tea tray and saved her the bother of giving Max a put-down. She dismissed the maid and set about making tea.

'How is Charlotte?' she asked before he could resume quizzing her.

'As extravagant as ever.'

'And the children?'

'As demanding as ever. You do not know how lucky you are.'

'Indeed I do,' she said, and meant it. There was only one cloud on her horizon, but she hoped that might be dispelled with a little patience, not that she would have breathed a word of that to anyone, not even to Janet, who knew most things about her; certainly not to her brother.

'Is Portman about?' he asked.

'No, he is in town.' She poured tea and handed him a cup. He took it, then put it on the floor at his side so that he could extract a small flask from his pocket which he emptied into the tea.

'I wish I'd known,' he said. 'It would have saved me a journey.'

'You said you came to see me.'

'So I did. Need to see him too.'

'He may be back this evening. You are welcome to stay.' She sipped her own tea. 'What do you want to see him about?'

'Business.'

'And would the business have anything to do with money?' He looked discomforted and she added. 'How much do you want?'

He brightened. 'Why, do you have any you can spare?'

'I don't always spend my pin money. I can let you have two hundred.'

'Two hundred! Not near enough.'

'Max, you seemed to be well up in the stirrups when Papa died. You and Charlotte were extravagantly dressed and you paid for the wine and the carriage at my wedding.'

'It did not last long.'

'What did not last long? What are you talking about?'

He looked sheepish. 'Father's money.'

'But you said there was none. I had to leave my

home and sell all the furniture and—' She stopped suddenly. 'You are not talking about that bag of counterfeit guineas, are you?' His shamefaced expression gave her his answer. 'Oh, Max...'

'Well, I could not let them go to waste, could I? Father was cheated by whoever gave them to him. They should have been genuine. I did not see why we should be the losers.'

'You said you were going to find out how he came by them. Did you do anything about it? Did you try tracing Mr O'Keefe and the Barnstaple Mining Company?'

'No such man, no such company.'

She knew from his tone he had not even tried. 'So instead you decided to pass counterfeit coins. You are a fool.'

'No one knows who passed them, I was very careful.'

'So you say. What if they are traced to you?'

'They won't be. And even if they are, I can always plead ignorance. It is almost impossible to tell them from genuine ones. You saw them.'

'And now they are all gone, you come here to beg from my husband.'

'He can afford it.' He paused. 'You won't tell him what I have just told you, will you?'

'No, of course not. I do not want to see you

hanged. But I am very glad you do not have any more of them.'

He did not confirm that and in the silence that followed, they heard horses and wheels on the drive, and a few minutes later, Harry came into the room.

He had been looking forward to an evening with his wife, talking to her about her day and the progress Annabelle was making. Whenever he saw Rosamund and his daughter with their heads together, laughing at some game they were playing, his heart ached with regret that he had missed so much of the child's growing and a strange longing to take his wife in his arms and make love to her. Really make love, not simply make her with child. His whole reason for marrying her had been turned on its head. All he wanted to do these days was to do his work for the Piccadilly Gentlemen as thoroughly and quickly as he could and come back to Bishop's Court. He was not altogether pleased to see his brother-in-law, though he made himself sound cheerful. 'You here, Chalmers,' he said.

Max scrambled to his feet to execute a bow, 'In the area. Thought I'd pay a call. Didn't think you would mind.'

'Don't mind at all, my dear fellow,' he said, remembering to be the fop Max believed him to be and returning the bow with even more exaggeration than usual. 'My wife's brother is always welcome at Bishop's Court. Staying, are you?'

'If I may? I have a little matter to put to you.'

'After dinner,' Harry said, taking a cup of freshly brewed tea from Rosamund and smiling at her, as he did so. The hand that offered the cup had been shaking a little and she seemed flustered. He wondered what she and her brother had been talking about to agitate her. He wished he could like the man for her sake, but he found his false joviality irksome. It did not take a genius to guess what he wanted.

He was proved right later that evening. Dinner was over, Rosamund had gone to Annabelle's room to see her into bed and tell her a story, leaving the men to smoke and drink in the library.

'I had no idea Bishop's Court was so large,' Max said. 'It must cost a fortune to keep up.'

'Luckily I have a fortune,' Harry said drily. 'My forebears managed their wealth wisely.'

'And no doubt you are carrying on the good work.'

'I try.' He smiled and waited, knowing what was coming.

'It is a pity my forebears were not so clever,' Max

said. 'Particularly my father. He allowed himself to be cheated.'

'Yes, you have told me this before.' He did not like to be reminded of how he came to marry Rosamund. It was something of which he was ashamed, but Chalmers seemed to have no shame. 'How can I help you? I assume that is the reason for your visit.'

'I am being dunned all round. A couple of thousand should see me clear. Let you have it back when I can.'

Harry got up and went to his desk, where he wrote out an order on his bank for two thousand guineas, which he handed over without a word. It was worth it to try to atone for the wrong he was convinced he had done Rosamund.

'Thank you,' Max said, folding it and tucking it into the pocket of his waistcoat.

They had so little in common the conversation dwindled to a halt. Max stood up and yawned. 'If you will excuse me, my lord, I am for bed. I should like to make an early start in the morning, if that is convenient to you.'

'Oh, quite convenient,' Harry said, hiding a smile. The man had got what he wanted and could not get away fast enough. He wondered how often he would be asked to prop up his debts. For Rosamund's sake, he would do it.

Alone again, he poured himself more cognac and sprawled on the sofa with his feet up on its arm, and allowed himself to meditate. Apart from the months immediately after Beth's death, he had always enjoyed his life. He loved his home and looking after his estate; talking to his tenants and the men who toiled in the fields and their wives, who worked just as hard as their menfolk. He was especially jovial towards the children and made sure that none on his estate was in want of a good meal and a stout pair of boots.

On the other side of his life was his work for the Piccadilly Gentlemen, which was varied, demanding and often dangerous. It added a spice to his existence and he revelled in it. His busy life had, until he met Rosamund, stopped him from brooding about the past, a past he could not change, however hard he tried. But now there was a third dimension: his wife and daughter. And that was where his unease lay. He wanted to make her his wife in more than name, but the old fear kept returning. He imagined her suffering as Beth had suffered, heard her cries and saw the blood and his desire abated and left him dissatisfied and restless. The only cure was action.

* * *

Rosamund came down for breakfast as she usually did. It was often the only time she and Harry could talk; he was always going off somewhere. He looked up from his plate of ham and eggs when she came in. 'Good morning, my dear,' he said, rising to greet her and see her to her chair while noting the pink crepe dress with its cross-over bodice, which emphasised the fullness of her breasts and narrow waist. 'It is another warm day. I think the harvest might be early this year.'

'Yes, I noticed the corn was ripening. A good harvest will be a boon to the farmers after so many years of poor yields.' She paused. 'Is Max still abed?'

'No,' he said, resuming his seat. 'I am told he left very early. Pressing business to attend to, I believe.'

'Paying his debts with your money, I do not doubt,' she said, looking sideways at him as she helped herself to bread and butter and some of Cook's damson preserve. His expression was unfathomable.

'Now what makes you think that?'

'I know my brother. Besides, he as good as admitted it to me. You do not have to indulge him, you know. I should not hold it against you.'

'No, but I should not like to see him in a debtors' prison, if I could prevent it with a small donation. He is my brother-in-law, after all. Families should look after each other.'

'I sometimes wonder if his need of money was not the reason he was so anxious I should marry you.'

'And were you also influenced by that when you agreed?'

She looked startled. 'Do you believe that?'

'Perhaps not, but I sometimes ask myself what your reasons really were.'

She managed a laugh. 'It was the alternatives I found unacceptable, my lord: to live with Max and his unruly children or be a puppy dog to Lady Bonhaven. Besides, I had hoped to find the men who cheated my father, something I would never have been given time for had I chosen either course. I thought the prospect of being the mother of your children would compensate for—'

'Compensate for what?' he prompted. They had both abandoned their breakfasts.

'Compensate for a lack of...' She could not say it, could not tell him the word she was searching for was love. He would laugh at her. It was not, had never been, a part of their bargain.

'You think I have wronged you.' It was a statement, not a question.

'No, I did not say that. You most certainly have not wronged me. Why, you have been kind and generous to a fault.'

'But is kindness enough?' he asked softly.

'I think it must be.'

It was an enigmatic reply that did not address the question. 'You said you hoped to find the men who cheated your father,' he said, changing the subject abruptly. 'How did they cheat him exactly?'

'They sold him worthless shares in a company I feel sure does not exist. I cannot think why he was so gullible. He lost everything.'

Her version tallied with her brother's, so he was inclined to believe it was true. 'What was the name of this company? I might be able to track it down for you.'

'The Barnstaple Mining Company.'

'I have never heard of it. Do you know anything else about it?'

'According to the family lawyer, who says he advised my father against investing, its headquarters was the Nag's Head, Covent Garden, and the man who sold him the shares was a Mr Michael O'Keefe.'

Harry managed to turn his exclamation of shock

into a grunt. He took a gulp of coffee to gather his wits. 'Rosamund, the Nag's Head is a low tavern, hardly the place from which to run a legitimate business.'

'I realised that as soon as I saw it.'

'You went there?' She continually astonished him. 'When was this?'

'The week after Papa died. I hoped to meet Mr O'Keefe and persuade him to buy back the shares. I was angry. I am still angry when I think about it. The man should not be allowed to profit by his crime.'

The conversation was becoming unreal and he had to be careful what he said. If she had met, or even been seen by, O'Keefe, they could all be in trouble. 'The Nag's Head is a dreadful place, a den of thieves,' he said. 'It is a wonder you were not set upon and robbed.'

'Do you know it?' she asked. It was hardly the sort of place someone in his position would fre- quent. There was so much she still had to learn about him.

'Only by reputation,' he said guardedly. 'Did you see this Mr O'Keefe?'

'No, the landlord denied all knowledge of him.'

He breathed a sigh of relief and put out his hand to cover hers and it had the same effect his touch always had; her heart began to race and she felt the warmth flooding her face. 'Rosamund, my dear,' he said, apparently unaware of the tumult he caused in her breast, both by his touch and his endearment. That neither meant anything to him she was well aware. 'You must never go there again. You are married to me now and you do not need anything from that man and his Barnstaple Mining Company. He would not give it to you anyway. He would undoubtedly say your father invested of his own free will. You have no legal redress at all.'

'Max says neither the man nor the company exists. The names were invented to fool my father.'

'In that I am inclined to agree with your brother,' he said, patting her hand and pouring more coffee. It had gone cold and he rang for a servant to bring more. 'Now, what are you planning to do today?'

As far as he was concerned the subject was closed and she knew better than to persist. 'Mr Travers has found a quiet little pony for Annabelle,' she told him. 'I was planning to teach her to ride, with his help. And I thought we might go for a walk later. Would you like to join us?'

He hesitated. The more he was in her company, the more he realised he was becoming enmeshed in a life he had never intended. Him, playing the family man! It was laughable. And yet he did not laugh. Instead he said, 'Why not? Travers has his work to do. I can teach the child to ride.'

They spent the morning teaching Annabelle to ride the little grey pony. She was an apt pupil and they were soon laughing at her enjoyment. In the afternoon they took a picnic with them on their walk. They found a quiet spot under a tree which hung over a stream and spread the cloth and unpacked the basket while Annabelle discarded shoes and stockings and paddled in the shallows, bunching her skirt up in her hands.

'She has made great strides, thanks to you,' Harry told Rosamund as they sat side by side on the ground beneath a tree, both fondly watching her.

'She is her father's daughter. Bright as a button. I only have to tell her something once and she has the measure of it. Have you noticed she is speaking so much better? There is hardly a trace left of the vulgar tongue she learned at the farm.'

'Yes, I had. Has she forgotten her life there?'

'Not entirely. Now and again she says something that makes me realise that her early upbringing is engrained deeply.'

'I am sure, with your help, she will soon put it behind her.'

'Thank you, my lord. Already I love her dearly.' She paused, took a deep breath and went on. 'But I think she misses the other children. To her they are her brothers and sisters.'

'Ridiculous! I am not having them at Bishop's Court if that is what you are thinking.'

She turned to him in shocked surprise. How could he be so obtuse? How much more of a hint did he need? 'No, my lord, I was not thinking of other people's children at all.'

'Good.' He called to Annabelle to come and sit down to eat and Rosamund realised she was getting nowhere at all. From being happy and relaxed, they became tense and distantly polite with each other and the walk home was a silent one and, on her part, miserable. She had done what she had warned herself against: she had fallen hopelessly in love with her husband.

Chapter Eight

Harry was nowhere near as obtuse as Rosamund thought he was. He could readily believe she wanted children of her own; he could see she was a born mother. After all, she had agreed to marry him to give him an heir. So why could he not oblige her? What had Ash said to him? *Women do have a choice, to marry or not to marry, and most, if you ask them, would certainly say they want to be married and to have children. It is their lot in life and they know it.*

Until today he had not thought Rosamund minded that he had done nothing to bring it about, might even have been relieved. But it seemed he had been wrong. His whole being was doing battle with itself. Duty fought compassion, desire fought fear, his newfound love for his daughter fought the image of a dead face. If only he could talk to Rosamund about it, tell her how Beth's dying curses haunted him, ask her if she knew what was involved; not just the sexual act, but the giving birth, the pain and the risk. But whenever he came close to it, he shied away. For a man who took risks as a matter of course, who could hold his own in a fight, both physical and verbal, who prided himself on his sang-froid, he was behaving like an untried boy.

He went back to town the next day. There was a meeting of the Piccadilly Gentlemen to attend and he wanted to go to the Nag's Head. If O'Keefe was there, he would try to persuade him to initiate him into the gang, not only to bring about the arrest of some of the most daring and blatant coiners, but to find out what he could about the Barnstaple Mining Company. Like Max, he did not think it existed, but O'Keefe had managed to convince Sir Joshua that it did. And Sir Joshua had conveniently died, leaving O'Keefe with his ill-gotten gains. If he did nothing else for Rosamund, he could try to obtain redress for her and prevent the man from gulling others in the same way. But nabbing the coiners had to come first.

The members of the Society for the Discovery and Apprehending of Criminals were all in attendance and the main item on the agenda was the security of George III, both at his wedding, now only a few days away and, more importantly, at the coronation, which would follow two weeks later. The wedding would be a private affair, but the coronation was for the populace who loved a grand pageant. London was crowded with sightseers coming to see the king and queen in their magnificent robes being conveyed to Westminster Abbey. Even those who had retired to their country estates for the summer were coming back. Entertainments were being arranged, balls, routs and fireworks, almost as if it were a second Season.

'And in any crowd there are bound to be pickpockets,' Jonathan added.

'And people passing counterfeit money,' Harry put in. 'The coiners haven't had such a golden opportunity for years, if you will forgive the pun.'

'I have spoken to Sir John Fielding,' James went on, smiling at Harry's little joke. 'He is recruiting more Bow Street Runners to mingle with the crowds. I have said we will all be available to give assistance. I hope I may have your co-operation.'

They murmured agreement.

'I have had an invitation to the coronation,' Jonathan said. 'Louise can think of nothing but what she will wear.'

'You are not the only one of us invited,' James said. 'I think we all are, in recognition of the work we do.' He gave them each an envelope inscribed with the royal coat of arms, though Sam Roker, not being a man of rank, was omitted. He took no offence, knowing he would feel like a fish out of water in that company.

'With all of us in attendance, who would dare raise his hand against the king and queen?' Harry said, with a laugh.

They went on to discuss the role each would play on the days leading up to the ceremony. When the meeting was concluded, Harry and Ash left together as was their wont. 'Have you heard any more of your coiners?' Ash asked.

'No, I have a feeling O'Keefe is avoiding me. I went to the Nag's Head earlier today, but I was told he had not been in the tavern for weeks. He knows I want to be admitted to the gang and he is reluctant to share the profits any further than his existing cohorts, but I shall persist. With the festivities drawing near, he might emerge on the streets. The opportunities for passing bad coins will be too tempting to ignore.' He could not say anything about the Barnstaple Mining Company without implicating Rosamund and that he would not do.

'Will you bring Lady Portman to London for the celebrations?'

'Naturally I will.'

Rosamund was not sure she wanted to go. It meant leaving Annabelle and as the child was settling into her new home and taking lessons with a governess, she felt it might put her back to be left.

'What about Annabelle?' she asked, when Harry showed her the elaborately decorated invitation that evening, having returned from town only an hour before.

'What about her? She will be perfectly happy with Miss Gunstock and Mrs Rivers. And we will only be gone three weeks.'

'But do you really need me?'

'Of course I need you. What would it look like among the *ton* if I turned up without my wife on such a formal occasion? The gabble grinders would have a field day.' It was said rather impatiently, but he was well aware that his need of her went much deeper than his reluctance to invite gossip. It was at the core of his being and nothing could shift it.

'Very well,' she agreed, admitting to herself that she would enjoy going to town as Lady Portman and taking her place in Westminster Abbey along-side her husband. 'When do we leave?'

'Tomorrow. Do you think you can be ready?'

'Yes, of course. I will give Janet her instructions when I go up.'

'Did you have a good day today?' he asked.

'Yes. Annabelle rode her pony round the yard. She is keen to ride out, but I told her it was too soon, she must become more proficient before she goes on the road, on account of other traffic. We walked into the village and took comforts to the sick and stopped to watch the harvesters. This afternoon we read a book together and Miss Gunstock gave her some arithmetic problems to do.'

'A busy day by the sound of it. You will perhaps be glad of a change of scenery.'

'But I love it here. The air is so clear and fresh, not like the dirt and fog of London. The villagers are so friendly. And I love being with Annabelle. You know, she called me Mama for the first time today.'

'And that pleased you, I do not doubt.'

'Oh, yes,' she said. There was only one thing that worried her about that. If she never had a child by him, never gave him the heir he wanted so badly, then he might send her away and annul the marriage and she would not see Annabelle again. Or him. But how did he expect her to fulfil her undertaking if he did nothing to bring it about? He had given no indication that he was repulsed by her; on the contrary, he was careful of her, frequently complimentary, and often took her hand or reached out to push a stray curl from her cheek. His touch always made her breath catch in her throat, as if it might be a prelude to something more intimate, but then that strange haunted look would come over his face and it was a minute or so before he had himself under control and was smiling again.

'Mrs Rivers has been singing your praises,' he said. 'And that is no mean achievement on your part. She is very particular.'

'Thank you, my lord.'

'Rosamund, I wish you would not address me so formally when we are alone. You know my name, pray use it.'

'Yes, my lord.' They both laughed aloud when she realised what she had said. 'Habits are hard to break, aren't they?' she added.

'Yes,' he said thoughtfully. 'And the longer you have had the habit, the harder it becomes.' He paused, wondering whether to go on and try to explain himself. 'I have perhaps become too used to my own ways to change easily. I fear I am poor company.' Which was not what he meant to say at all.

'You are not ill company, my...Harry, quite the contrary. When you are at home, you are always ready to accommodate me and fall in with whatever I am doing. I like having you at home.' Which was not what she meant to say either.

'Thank you, my dear. When you come to Portman House with me, we shall be more in each other's company. Besides the coronation, there will be any number of social occasions to which we shall be invited. We could perhaps hold our own entertainment. What do you think?'

'If you wish, but I have had no practice at being a society hostess, although when my mother was alive she entertained a great deal and I often helped her.'

'I am persuaded you will do splendidly. Shall we hold a Coronation Ball?'

A ball was rather grander than she had bargained for, but she wanted to please him. If she pleased him enough, he might remember why he had married her and make her truly his wife. 'That would be splendid.'

As always when Harry was at home, he spent some time in the library going over accounts and investments, some time with his steward and Travers, keeping up to date with events on the estate and discussing future plans, but more with Rosamund and Annabelle. The child had lost her fear of him and would chatter away about things she had seen and what she was learning, not only from her stepmama but from Miss Gunstock. The governess was the daughter of a baronet fallen on hard times, which was one of the reasons Rosamund had hired her; she was only too aware that she had only just escaped a similar fate herself. Miss Gunstock could not have been more inaptly named; she was thin and pale and softly spoken, but she was a good teacher and Annabelle had taken to her.

Rosamund saved telling the child she was going away until bedtime when she was tucked up with a favourite rag doll, waiting to hear the nightly story Rosamund always told her, often one invented especially for her. When it was finished, Rosamund tucked her up. 'Tomorrow, sweetheart, I am going to London with your papa and you must be a good girl while I am gone and do as Miss Gunstock bids you.'

'How long will you be gone?'

'Three weeks, I think.'

'Three weeks is for ever.'

'No, it is only twenty-one days. Miss Gunstock will help you to count them. I am going to King George's coronation, so I will have wonderful stories to tell you when I come back.'

'What's a coronation?'

Rosamund was in the middle of explaining this when Harry crept into the room and joined in. By the time they had finished Annabelle was reconciled to their absence and was drifting off to sleep. They crept from the room and returned downstairs.

'I have to do some paperwork,' he said, as they reached the library door. 'I doubt I shall finish before midnight so I will say goodnight now.' He took her shoulders in his hands, looked down into her upturned face as if studying her features, then bent and kissed her on the mouth. She felt herself responding to the pressure of his lips with delighted surprise. It was not a duty kiss of a man dismissing a wife for whom he had little affection; it was real and gently demanding and aroused them both to undeniable passion.

The sound of footsteps impinged on his ears before she heard them, and he pulled away from her with a wry smile. She felt so weak, she had trouble keeping upright and put a hand on the back of a chair that stood against the wall to steady herself. The night-duty footman emerged from the back regions of the house to take up his position at the door. He walked past them, looking straight ahead, trying to pretend he had not seen them. It broke the tension and they both laughed.

'Goodnight, my dear,' Harry said and disappeared into the library, shutting the door after him.

She wondered whether to follow, but decided against it. If she tried to push him too soon, she would defeat her own purpose. 'One step at a time,' she murmured to herself and made her way to the drawing room where she sat on a sofa and tried to read a book. She was still trembling, still in a cloud of pure euphoria and the words danced on the page. Giving up, she went up to her room where Janet was doing the last of the packing.

She could not believe she would need all those clothes for a three-week stay, but the maid insisted she did. 'You will need to buy more when you arrive, my lady,' she said, trying to fold a quilted petticoat into a small enough parcel to go into a trunk that was already overflowing. 'You must be a credit to his lordship when he takes you to all the grand occasions. Mr Sylvester says he always sends his lordship out in the pink and it is important to send out your mistress befitting her lord and if I need any advice to go to him.'

Rosamund laughed. 'I think Mr Sylvester has an exaggerated idea of his own importance, Janet. Lord Portman is perfectly able to make up his own mind what to wear.'

'So he may be, Miss Rosie, but I often wonder why he puts himself about as a coxcomb when he is nothing like that when he is at Bishop's Court.'

'Country wear is not the same as town wear, Janet.'

'That,' said Janet in triumph. 'is what I have been trying to tell you. You will need to go shopping.'

The packing finished, Janet helped Rosamund undress and then retired to her own room. Left alone, Rosamund lay in bed, wondering if Harry would come to her that night. But he did not. Still in a dreamlike state brought on by that kiss, she was disappointed, but not downhearted. Perhaps when they were in London…

Harry sat at his desk looking at the report he was compiling for the Piccadilly Gentlemen, but his mind was elsewhere. He had been foolish enough to kiss his wife! He felt again the pressure of her lips as she responded and he knew something he had not been sure of before: she wanted him as much as he wanted her. The knowledge did nothing to ease his torment; it exacerbated it. He could still feel his arousal and it was damned uncomfortable and needed relieving. He was tempted to go to her and take her to bed. He had every right to do so. It was his duty to do so. It was his desire to do so. Only his tormenting ghost prevented it.

If only Rosamund had been plain instead of lovely, foolish instead of intelligent, if only he had been able to keep her at arm's length and not come to enjoy her company so much, he could have been business-like about their bargain, like bedding a lightskirt, here today and forgotten tomorrow. Now it was impossible. She was his wife in every way except one. He groaned and went to the cupboard beside the fireplace and extracted a fat brown bottle and a large glass and proceeded to drink himself into oblivion.

They arrived at Portman House in Berkeley Square soon after noon the following day and almost immediately Harry went out again. 'Business, I am afraid,' he told Rosamund, handing her a pile of invitations. 'Go through these while I am gone and decide which you would like to attend. When I come back we will answer them together and talk about our own ball.'

There were so many invitations, routs, balls, picnics, concerts, all with a coronation theme, that Rosamund had no idea which they ought to attend. She knew hardly any of the senders, most of whom were aristocrats from the upper echelons of society and until her marriage would have been way above her touch. She decided to leave them until Harry came back and instead went to explore the house, which she had never been in before.

It was a solidly built house in the middle of a row on the western side of the Square, with a kitchen below ground level and steps up to the front door with a lamp above the middle and extinguishers for the linkmen's torches at shoulder height on each side. Inside on the ground floor there was an anteroom and two large drawing rooms, which could be opened up into one large room for entertaining. On the floor above was a dining room and a library and a small parlour and above these the bedrooms and dressing rooms. All the servants except Mrs Crossley, the cook-housekeeper, slept in the attics from where a separate staircase took them down to the kitchens. Mrs Crossley had her own room on the same floor as the kitchen, as did James, the butler.

It was all tastefully decorated and furnished in the French style, but it was perhaps too perfect and, unlike the comfortable untidiness of Bishop's Court, did not feel lived in, which told her Harry only used it as a place to sleep when he was in town.

Her tour finished, she went to talk to Mrs Crossley about holding a ball. The cook was enormously fat, due perhaps to too frequent sampling of the fruits of her labour. She wore a vast grey cotton gown and an even vaster apron. On her greying hair was a frilly white cap tied under her chin with a ribbon. She received the news that there was to be a ball with enthusiasm and was soon amusing Rosamund with tales of the entertainments Lord Portman's mother used to arrange.

'What about his lordship's first wife?' Rosamund asked, when at last the woman drew breath. 'Did she entertain?'

'No, my lady. They were no sooner married than she began increasing. Not that you would have known in the beginning. She was such a little slip of a thing, not yet seventeen when they married, and it did not show at first. She was so well, no one could have foretold the trouble she would have giving birth. That was terrible. Her screams filled the whole house. They lived here then, his lordship not having succeeded to Bishop's Court. She shrieked on and on for her mother and cursed her husband, yelling that God would punish him for what he had done to her. The handywoman and the doctor both tried to quieten her, but she was past listening to them.'

'How dreadful,' Rosamund murmured.

'I don't know how they got the infant out of her, but she was dead soon afterwards. His lordship was distraught. He would not look at the child, let alone touch her, and did not speak to anyone for days.' She paused. 'Mayhap I should not have told you.'

It was one more item to be added to those she had already learned about her complex and enigmatic husband and it explained a great deal. He had loved his first wife and she had died cursing him. There was a mountain to climb if she were going to help him overcome that. 'I am glad you did, Mrs Crossley,' she said. 'But I will not tell his lordship you told me.'

They were interrupted by a footman who came to tell Rosamund that Mrs Bullivant had called. Wondering how her aunt knew she was in town, she made herself put the cook's revelations to one side, gave orders for the tea tray to be prepared and hurried to the front drawing room, where the lady was busy inspecting the pictures and ornaments.

'Aunt Jessica, how are you?' She went forwards and kissed the old lady's rouged cheek. 'How did you know I was here?'

'Word gets about. Servants talk to each other, you know. Your cook told my cook and she told Miss Davies, who told me.' She stepped back to look her niece up and down. The petticoat she was wearing under her blue silk open gown was only lightly padded and her figure was as slim as ever. 'Not increasing, Rosamund?'

'Not yet.'

'What's the matter with you?'

'Nothing that I know of.'

'Well, it can't be his lordship.' She sat on the sofa, her wide skirts billowing round her. 'He already has a daughter.'

'There is time.' She remembered saying the same thing to Max and wondered how many other people would be blunt enough to ask.

'Have you met the child?' her aunt went on. 'I am told Portman will not have her to live with him. Is there something wrong with her?'

'There is nothing at all wrong with Annabelle,' she said firmly. 'She is living with us at Bishop's Court now. She is a delightful child and already I love her dearly.'

'Hmph,' the old lady said. 'Not the same as having your own, though is it?'

She was saved answering by the arrival of a maid with the tea things and a plate of cakes. Rosamund busied herself with these and there was silence between them for perhaps a minute, then her aunt took up the conversation again.

'Well, I am glad you have come to town. It is about time the *haut monde* saw you as Lady Portman.'

'Of course I am Lady Portman. Whatever do you mean?'

'Francis Portman has been putting it about that all is not well between you and his lordship. He says his lordship cannot stand the sight of you, which is why he is so often in town alone. According to Portman, he belongs to some drinking and gaming club called The Piccadilly Gentlemen. They are up to all manner of rigs, so I am told.'

Rosamund was shocked, but endeavoured to treat the gossip lightly. 'Oh, Aunt, I cannot believe that.'

'It is true. He told Maximilian and Maximilian told me.'

'Francis Portman is a troublemaker and Max is not much better,' she said firmly. 'They both sponge on Harry's generosity and then disparage him behind his back. I do not believe a word of it and I am surprised at you repeating it.'

'I am only telling you what is being said. You must get Portman to escort you out more. Oh, I know it is not often done for husbands and wives to live in each other's pockets, but if you want to survive as Portman's wife, you must assert yourself and bring him to heel.'

'Aunt, you need have no fears on that score and you will oblige me by informing anyone else who has nothing better to do than gossip that there is nothing amiss with our marriage.'

'Then why are you not increasing?'

'Give us time, Aunt. We are neither of us in the first bloom of youth.'

'I am only thinking of your good.'

'I know.' She put on a brave smile and handed her aunt a cup of tea. 'If it makes you feel better, I can tell you we are going to hold a coronation ball here at Portman House. That should silence the critics.'

'Oh, wonderful!' The old lady clapped her hands. 'Tell me all about it.'

It was at this point Harry returned. He bowed to Mrs Bullivant and asked her how she did, then turned to Rosamund. 'I see you have the tea tray there, my love. Shall I ring for another cup?'

'Please do. I was telling Aunt Jessica that we are planning a ball.'

He rang the bell and sat down opposite the two ladies. 'Yes, the house hasn't been used for entertaining for goodness knows how long and what better opportunity than the coronation?'

'When is the ball to be?' Jessica asked. 'There is the Royal wedding tomorrow and with the coronation only two weeks away, everyone's diaries are full.'

Harry looked at Rosamund, his eyebrow raised in a question. She nodded and he turned to the old lady. 'Then we will leave our entertainment until the 25th. That will give everyone three days to recover and be a fitting end to the celebrations.'

'Oh, yes,' the old lady agreed. 'And you must make it outshine them all, something to be remembered long afterwards. If you need any help...'

'I think we can manage,' Rosamund said. 'Mrs Crossley is very competent, But I thank you for the offer.'

There was a moment's silence while Jessica debated whether to insist on helping, but decided she could do without the bother. 'Have you met the bride, my lord?' she asked. 'I am told she is not at all comely and the King is not enamoured of her. Her nose and mouth are too wide and they do say her forebears came from Africa.'

'Gossip,' Harry said. 'I deplore gossip. The poor child is only seventeen and must be frightened almost to death, especially after that terrible crossing.' The future queen had been collected from Cuxhaven by a squadron of British yachts and warships, but the westerly gales had been so bad they had taken ten days to reach Harwich. 'I think we should all make her welcome.'

'Why, of course,' she said, backtracking quickly. 'I am sure everyone will come to love her.' Having absorbed the put-down, she rose to leave, bringing Harry to his feet. 'I must be going. I expect I shall see you out and about while you are in town.'

He executed an elaborate bow. 'Indeed, yes, Rosamund and I have every intention of making the most of our stay before we return to our daughter. We are engaged at Viscount Leinster's soirée tomorrow evening.'

'Then I shall see you there.' She turned and made her stately way to the door, where a footman waited to conduct her to her carriage.

As soon as she had gone, Harry turned back to Rosamund, grinning. 'That should give her something to think about.' And they both laughed, though Rosamund's was a trifle hollow.

They were so much in accord, so well matched, laughing at the same things, sharing the same tastes in almost everything, loving Annabelle, it was difficult to believe they were still not truly man and wife. Mrs Crossley's revelations went some way to explaining that, but it was difficult to believe a man like Harry Portman could not overcome his reluctance. His desire for her had been evident when he kissed her outside the library at Bishop's Court and, if the footman had not come along when he had, who knew if he might have succumbed? How soon would it be before another opportunity arrived? she wondered. And the awful thought came to her that if he did, he might regret it. There was more to the problem than the physical act of copulation.

Unaware of her tumbled musing, he was still smiling. 'Shall we go through those invitations while we have time?' he suggested.

The Royal wedding took place at the Chapel Royal in St James's Palace the following day. Few of the public witnessed it, but those privileged to do so said the twenty-three-year-old groom was tall and dignified and the seventeen-year-old bride was tiny beside him. The crowd who waited outside were disposed to wish them well. After all,

George, unlike his father and grandfather, had been born in England and English was his native tongue.

'I feel sorry for her,' Francis said, when he called at Portman House later that afternoon. 'She was far outdone by Lady Sarah Lennox, who looked magnificent; the old Earl of Westmoreland had to be restrained from mistakenly doing homage to her instead of the Queen.'

'I did not know you had been one of the congregation, Frank,' Harry said in his lazy drawl, knowing perfectly well the young man had not been invited, though to look at his clothes one might think he had. He was dressed in a full-skirted lilac coat faced with silver, white small clothes and stockings and a purple waistcoat covered in pink-and-green embroidery. His cravat was a huge lace bow, fastened with a diamond pin. His hat was a large tricorne, which would not have disgraced an admiral. Harry did not doubt he had been the one to pay for it and while the debts for which Francis had importuned him remained unpaid.

'No, I wasn't, but it's the latest *on dit*. I wonder Sarah Lennox had the face to go at all, let alone be a bridesmaid. 'Tis common knowledge she had set her heart on becoming George's queen.'

'Well, I hope the King and Queen will be happy together,' Rosamund said. 'And I am looking forward to the coronation.'

'You mean you have been invited?' Francis queried in disbelief. 'How did that come about? Harry ain't no more than a baron.'

'I must have done something right,' Harry said wryly.

'I can't think what it could be,' Francis went on. 'You don't do anything and you ain't sat in the Lords above twice this year.'

'Harry works very hard behind the scenes,' Rosamund said.

Harry looked sharply at her, wondering what she knew. He had never hinted at what he did when he was doing business in London and she could not have guessed, surely? Could anyone have told her? But the only people who could have said anything were the Piccadilly Gentlemen and he could not believe they would do so. She was simply being supportive. 'Thank you, my dear.'

'How cosy you are,' Francis said. 'Are we to expect a happy event shortly?'

'Mind your own business,' Harry snapped. 'Are you staying to dine? I must tell you we are going to Viscount Leinster's soirée this evening, so we dine very early.'

As an invitation, it was grudging and Francis knew it. 'No, thank you, coz, I am off to a cock fight at the Nag's Head, but if Lady Portman would like someone to escort her when you are busy with your *affairs*, I will gladly offer myself.'

Rosamund sensed the tension between the two men and decided to intervene. 'Thank you, Francis, I will bear that in mind.' She rose as she spoke. It was a gesture of dismissal and he bowed and took his leave.

'He is going to the Nag's Head,' she said to Harry when he had gone. 'Do you think he knows Mr O'Keefe?'

'I doubt it,' he said, though he was wondering the same thing himself. It was a little worrying. 'I doubt O'Keefe returned there after he had ruined Sir Joshua. He would not risk being traced and made to pay up, would he?'

'Have you made enquiries?'

'One or two, but so far I have learned nothing. I will keep trying.'

'Thank you,' she said. 'But please do not put yourself at risk over it. I would as lief forget the whole affair than have you hurt.'

'Why, my dear,' he said in delighted surprise. 'I do believe you care.'

'Of course I care. You are my husband and

Annabelle's papa. We would both be lost without you.'

'I am flattered, but if anything should happen to me...'

'Harry, you are frightening me. Do you expect something bad to happen to you?'

'No, no, I only meant if something *should* happen, I have made ample provision for you and the child—'

'Children,' she corrected him. 'Had you forgot our agreement?'

'No, how could I forget that? It is etched indelibly in my memory. But there is no hurry, is there? I want you to enjoy being my wife first.'

'That is kind of you, my lord—Harry—but I cannot help wondering if something is holding you back. Am I not what you expected and hoped for?'

'No, you are not,' he said, suddenly sounding angry. 'Nothing like.'

'You are being unfair,' she retorted, realising, with a sinking heart, that her words had not encouraged him to confide in her. 'I did nothing to deceive you. You knew exactly who I was and what I was.'

'Did I?' He looked at the woman he had married, longed to take her in his arms and tell her the truth, but a raucous voice, full of pain and yelling hatred at him, echoed in his brain. Would Rosamund be the same when giving birth? Would he kill her as he had killed Beth? He could not bear it if it happened again.

'If you have disappointed me it is only that you have turned out to be altogether more lovely, both in appearance and nature, than I deserve. There are things about me you do not know, would never understand…'

'You could try telling me.'

'One day perhaps I will.' He stood up and held out his hand to bring her to her feet. 'Go and change for dinner. We must not be late at Chaston Hall or Louise will ring a peal over us.' It was said light-heartedly, Lady Leinster was the most easy-going of hostesses, but Rosamund knew the question of having children was not to be broached again. His first wife was like a ghost hovering over them and she did not know how to banish her.

She found herself wondering about the gaming club her aunt had spoken of and what he had called the rigs they got up to. And something Francis had said echoed in her head and would not go away. He had offered to escort her when Harry was busy with his affairs. It had been said with heavy emphasis as if he were goading Harry about amorous

affairs in front of her. The little green god of jealousy fluttered in her stomach. If Harry had a mistress, and she supposed many men did and he was
no different, then he had no problem making love
to her.

In the two weeks between the Royal wedding
and the coronation, Harry and Rosamund were
rarely at home. If they were not attending entertainments, Harry was at the meetings of the Piccadilly
Gentlemen, more frequent now than they had been,
or Rosamund was shopping for gowns and fripper-
ies because to appear twice in the same gown was
not to be considered. And on the few occasions
when they were both at home, they were busy with
the arrangements for their own ball. Invitations,
food, music, flowers and costumes, all involved
endless discussion before decisions were made.
There was no time at all to continue their conversation about fulfilling the terms of their marriage
contract. Rosamund suspected it was deliberate on
Harry's part.

She had no intention of taking Francis up on his
offer, but he was frequently at the same occasions
they attended and he did his best to ingratiate himself with her, which puzzled her considering the
gossip he had been spreading about her and her

husband. Her nervousness of him was increased one evening at a concert given at Vauxhall Gardens in honour of the Royal couple. He minced up to them, hailing them and kissing Rosamund's hand, as if it were a foregone conclusion he would be invited to join them. 'You are in looks tonight, Cousin Rosamund,' he said. 'I felicitate you on that gown; blue is certainly your colour.'

She thanked him and he positioned himself between her and Harry as they promenaded, listening to the music. Harry, knowing how resentful his cousin was of his wife, wondered what he was up to.

'Do you know,' Francis murmured after a while, 'I was given a milled guinea at White's the other evening.'

Rosamund gave a stifled gasp, which Harry noted with puzzlement. 'Were you now?' he said nonchalantly. 'I believe there are a lot of them about.'

'Yes, but at a place like White's...'

'Do you know who passed it to you?'

'Oh, yes, it was Chalmers.'

Rosamund gasped and held her breath, something not lost on Harry, though he pretended not to notice. 'You mean Sir Maximilian?' he asked Francis.

'Yes. What other Chalmers is there? Of course I challenged him, but he said he had not noticed it was counterfeit and someone must have passed it to him.'

'That is more than possible,' Harry said evenly. 'I don't know why you had to bring the subject up.'

'Thought you might be interested.'

'Struth! Why should I be interested?' Harry asked, using the exaggerated drawl of the macaroni while dusting imaginary fluff from the deep cuffs of his coat sleeve.

'You are married to the fellow's sister.'

'What is that to the point?'

'Can't have the family name blackened, can we?'

'Take care, Frank,' Harry said, dropping the accent. 'You are as like to blacken it as Chalmers. And I beg to remind you Lady Portman is present.'

'I beg my lady's pardon,' Francis said, turning to her and executing a flourishing bow. 'But it don't look good, it don't look good at all.'

'I am sure my brother did not know it was a counterfeit coin,' Rosamund said, wondering if Harry had heard the gossip his cousin had been spreading about their marriage and whether it bothered him. 'I understand that it is easy to mistake the genuine from the counterfeit.'

The concert was then beginning and they strolled towards the orchestra and took their places, but Harry could not concentrate on the music. He found himself wondering how Rosamund knew so much about counterfeit coins, unless she knew Max was passing them and had seen and handled some of them. That would make her an accessory and put a whole new complexion on his dealings with the coiners and with his wife. He did not want to believe it, but Max Chalmers was present when he found the first coin at White's and there had been others since.

He was impatient to return home and study the lists Mr Mackreth had given him. And if it transpired that Max's name appeared on each list, what would he do? He had spent a year tracking down the coiners and one of the biggest operations was within his grasp. O'Keefe. Rosamund had mentioned the man's name. True, it was in a different context, but how much did she know?

It was on the way home in the darkness of the carriage, he introduced the subject. 'Rosamund, I have not made any headway in tracing the Barnstaple Mining Company. Are you sure there is nothing else you can tell me about it? Any little thing…'

'No, I have teased my brain over it, but that is all Mr Tetley was able to tell me.'

'Perhaps I should ask him,' he said to test her. If she had something to hide, she would not want him quizzing the lawyer.

'My lord…' she began.

'Harry,' he corrected her. She was definitely ill at ease; he could feel the tension in her body as she sat beside him and, dark as it was in the carriage, he felt, rather than saw, that she was twisting the cord of her reticule in her lap.

'Harry, I know I said I wanted that man O'Keefe brought to book, but on reflection, I can see that nothing can be gained by it and Mr Tetley's advice was sound. He said men like that are dangerous and I should leave well alone. I do not want you to be hurt. I would as lief forget the whole thing.'

'As you wish, my dear.' He put his hand over hers and felt her muscles slowly relax, which only served to confirm his suspicions. Could the business of the shares be connected with the counterfeit coins? The more he thought about it, the more convinced he was. And his wife, whom he had married in haste without affection and who had since become the pivot of his life, might be implicated. He prayed she was not. Never before had his duty been in conflict with his personal feelings and it was tying his gut into knots.

As soon as he arrived home, he said goodnight to Rosamund and shut himself in the library to study Mackreth's lists. Sure enough, Max Chalmers had been in the club on each occasion when fake coins had been passed. It was not proof, of course. There were others whose names appeared more than once on the list, but it was enough to set him thinking. Chalmers could have bought wine at the vintners where he had picked up the first one. He had certainly provided an ample quantity of drink at the wedding and the second guinea was found at the same wine merchants soon after that. The proprietor of Ranelagh Gardens had given one to the Excise the day after he had met Rosamund and her brother there. He fetched out all the coins he had collected and studied them carefully. Each one, including the one Francis had given him, had been clipped in exactly the same way, done by the same craftsman. It was beginning to look damning, damning enough for him to sit with his head in his hands and groan aloud.

Rosamund lay awake with tears trickling unheeded down her cheeks. Francis and Max between them had ruined any chance she might have of becoming closer to Harry. Why, oh, why did Max have to pass those coins instead of handing them over to the Excise men as he had been advised? Mr Tetley knew about them and he knew she knew. Why had she been so foolish as to tell Harry about Mr O'Keefe and the Barnstaple Mining Company? If he went to see Mr Tetley, the whole dreadful truth would come out and though she had always wanted to know what had happened in the days before her father died, now she wished with all her heart that it could be buried and forgotten. Once Harry found out about the counterfeit coins, she would be banished and the marriage annulled. He would not risk his good name being tarnished; that was what Francis had said and he had been right. Where could she go if that happened? How could she live without the man she loved? The future looked very bleak.

She fell asleep at last, but was suddenly awake again. There was someone outside her room. She waited a moment and then heard the sound again. Whoever it was had passed and was going downstairs. She left her bed and went to open the door a crack to peer out. A man was creeping down the stairs in the dark, his shoes in his hand. There was a lamp glowing in the hall as there always was and as he reached the bottom stair it revealed her husband in a brown stuff coat, thick breeches and a brown scratch wig. He tiptoed to the front door, slipped into his shoes and quietly let himself out. She went back to bed to lie awake, trying to make sense of what she had seen. He would hardly go to a mistress dressed like that. What could he be up to?

She had been sure it was Harry, but now doubts began to surface. Perhaps it had not been Harry, but an intruder. He had looked uncommonly like that highwayman who had held up Harry's carriage. Ought she to raise the alarm? It was too late now, he had gone. She left her bed, slipped into a dressing gown and went to Harry's room, smiling to herself as she did so. Was this the opportunity she had been waiting for? A frightened wife needing comfort? She knocked and entered. Harry was not there. He had not been to bed.

Chapter Nine

It was becoming more and more difficult to leave the house as Gus Housman and Harry was afraid he had missed O'Keefe at the Nag's Head. If only he knew where that farm was, he could set others to watch it. He had employed trustworthy men to follow O'Keefe from the tavern but the man seemed to have a sixth sense when anyone was on his tail and soon threw them off. For the first time since he had joined them, Harry was half-regretting his membership of the Piccadilly Gentlemen. He hated deceiving Rosamund, especially since that acquisitive cousin of his had hinted of affairs. It was not hard to see that he wanted to undermine their marriage. And why.

Late as it was, the Nag's Head was noisome and noisy, but for once O'Keefe was there. But so was Francis. He was in a crowd of drunken companions who evidently thought it great fun to visit taverns and mix with the low life. Harry hurried past him, his face averted, and slipped into a seat opposite O'Keefe with his back to the room. 'It's too crowded in here,' he complained. 'Can we go elsewhere?'

'They won't bother us,' O'Keefe said. 'Too drunk. And they are off to a dog fight soon. I need more genuine coins. What have you brought me?'

'Naught. I've a mind to see 'ow they're worked on. What say I bring 'em to your ken?'

'You ain't proved ye'self yet.'

'I reckon I 'ave.' Harry said, using the rough tones of the uneducated. 'Didn' I 'old up tha' there carriage and bring you a purse full of good yeller boys? Seems to me I'm takin' the risks and I ain't gettin' a fair return. Le' me in, a fair share same as the others.'

'Not my decision.'

'Then whose is it?'

'That would be tellin'. I'll give you a few milled megs to pass on. See how much you can get in real change. Meet me two days from now at noon. Bring me more genuine yeller boys and I'll see what I can do.' He put his hand in his pocket and produced a purse that jingled as he passed it across. 'There's ten 'ere, an' fer Gawd's sake don' confuse good with bad.'

'D'yer wan' to see what I've bought with 'em?'

'No. Just make sure what you buy don' cost much. The more change the better.'

Harry put the purse in his pocket and stood up. The noisy party, which included Francis, had left looking for new entertainment. Much relieved, he set off for home, musing as he went. He would hide the coins with the others in his safe and use his own money again for the change. His life was becoming very complicated, made more so by having Rosamund in town with him and having to escort her to functions. But he did not regret that. He enjoyed having her with him. But that was more than half the problem. He liked her and admired her and felt horribly guilty about the way he had persuaded her to marry him. He ought to set her free. And yet the thought of that depressed him more than he would ever have believed possible at the outset. She had become an important part of his life.

'O'Keefe wants more genuine coins, but I can hardly rob myself again,' Harry told Ash the next morning. They were sitting at the table in their usual meeting room at Trentham House, waiting for the rest of the Piccadilly Gentlemen to arrive, and Harry had been updating his friend on the progress he had made, though he had been careful not to mention Max. That was something he would have to sort out himself. 'And until I provide them, he is not inclined to take me to the farm.' He paused. 'Would you object if Gus Housman robbed you?'

Ash laughed. 'Not at all. But surely they trust you now and you can simply say you have done it without having to make a theatrical performance of it?'

'No, they are a cagey lot, and I need someone to witness it and describe the robber, which is why I wear that ridiculous spotted neckerchief.'

'You are laying yourself open to arrest, you know that, don't you? And then what would your wife say?' He regarded Harry with his head on one side. 'Or is that of no consequence?'

Harry looked sharply at him, wondering if his friend had guessed that his relationship with Rosamund had grown from where it had started to something deeper and far more important than simply getting her with child, but decided not to comment. 'I have to risk it, just once more. I am close to being admitted into the gang.'

'On your head be it,' Ash said. 'When and where do you propose to do the deed?'

'It will have to be done at night because I have

to creep out of the house without Rosamund seeing me.'

'Why don't you tell her what you are doing?'

'I cannot.'

'Why not? I am sure she can be trusted not to
blab about it. And she is no wilting violet, not
likely to swoon, is she?'

'No, she is not, but I have my reasons. Perhaps
one day…' His voice tailed off and he was silent
for a moment, then, suddenly pulling himself together, added, 'When will it be convenient for
you?'

Ash roared with laughter. 'I never yet heard of a
robber asking his victim when he would like to be
robbed.'

'Be serious, Ash.' But his own lips were twitch-
ing. 'Tomorrow is Coronation Day and I am going
to be at Lord Trentham's ball in the evening.'

Ash stopped laughing. 'Do it then. I am going
to a celebratory reception given by the Admiral I
served when I was at sea, at his house in Piccadilly.
It is just down the road from here. I will point it
out when we leave. When I arrive at precisely
nine o'clock, I shall leave my purse on the carriage seat, but remember it and go back for it five
minutes later. You will, by then, have taken it and

be making your escape and I will make a hue and cry over it.'

'Rosamund will be with me.'

'You do not need to be at her side all the time, do you? It ain't done to dance attendance on one's wife, you know.' He received no answer to this and went on. 'His lordship will arrange for you to have somewhere to change and you can slip out and be back before you are missed. It will give you an alibi if O'Keefe should be sharp enough to twig who Housman really is.'

'You may be right,' Harry admitted, delving into his pocket and withdrawing a purse, which clinked as he put it on the table in front of Ash. 'Take this. Don't want you losing your own money.'

'You should not have to lose yours either, my friend. How much has this quest cost you to date?'

'It is of no consequence. I can bear it and it will be worth it to see O'Keefe hang.'

Ash put the purse in his pocket just as James arrived, followed by the other members of the Gentleman's Club, including Lord Trentham, who said he was glad to escape from the turmoil the ball was causing in his household. They discussed the plan with him and then settled down to other business.

* * *

Rosamund was sitting opposite Mr Tetley again. She was relieved that Harry had not been to see him, but it left her wondering just what her husband was up to. She put that to one side as she explained why she had come. He was gravely courteous as he listened.

'But, my lady,' he said when she finished, 'I cannot refuse to tell Lord Portman what he wants to know, an' it is in my power.'

'But you said you did not know any more than you have already told me.'

'Nor do I, but if his lordship were to ask to see the documents relating to the shares, I cannot refuse him, can I? As your husband, he has a right.'

'I know, but if you were to destroy them…'

'My lady, why are you asking this? Have you discovered something about the Barnstaple Mining Company?'

'No, nothing.' She hesitated. 'It is just a feeling I have that whatever we discover will not be to my father's credit and I am afraid…'

'You are thinking of those counterfeit coins?'

How sharp he was, she thought. 'Yes,' she admitted. 'I cannot help but think the two things are connected.'

'But I understood Sir Maximilian had handed the coins to the Excise as I advised.'

She did not enlighten him. 'But that does not absolve my father, does it? I am convinced he was duped, but I doubt I would be believed.'

He looked at her with his head on one side and she felt as if he could see right through her and could sense she was not telling him everything. 'You do not wish me to continue my enquiries into Mr O'Keefe and the Barnstaple Mining Company?'

'Have you been making enquiries?' she asked in surprise. He had seemed reluctant to do so when she spoke to him previously.

'Yes, my lady. If the law has been broken...' He shrugged. 'One must do one's best to bring criminals to justice.'

She wished she had not come. Instead of ensuring Harry would learn nothing about that bag of coins, she had roused the lawyer's curiosity. She thanked him and left, wishing she could throttle that brother of hers.

She climbed into her coach, unaware that Harry and Ash were strolling down the road towards her and had seen her leave the lawyer's premises.

'I am going to leave you here,' Harry said. 'I have a call to make.'

* * *

Those privileged to be at the abbey to witness the coronation were required to be in their places hours before the ceremony began and Rosamund was woken at dawn by Janet with her chocolate drink and hot water for her to wash. Early as it was, the crowds were already gathering; she could hear them in the street, calling to each other and cheering the little road sweeper who came to clean the road of ordure.

'It'll be a good day for it,' Janet said, busying herself about the room, fetching out the clothes Rosamund was to wear.

Unable to break the habit of being frugal, even when Harry had told her to spend whatever she needed, she had bought a blue silk gown trimmed with satin bows and lace inserts. When she showed it to Harry, he had told her very forcefully it would not do. 'It is nothing but an ordinary everyday gown,' he had said. 'I see I shall have to come shopping with you.' And with that he had ordered out the carriage and taken her to one of the most expensive mantua makers in town, which had astonished the good lady, who had fallen over herself offering him a seat and bringing out bolts of silks, satins, brocades, gauze and lace in all the colours of the rainbow, striped, plain and flowered.

He had been at his most foppish as he fingered them all, talked knowledgeably about fashion and insisting on looking at patterns, commenting on each—this is not at all flattering, this will make you look too thin, this colour would not suit you, now this is better, but not rich enough—until Rosamund's head was spinning. She wanted very much to please him and be a credit to him and he did seem to know what would suit her, so she had fallen in with his choice. Now, as Janet helped her to dress, she knew she had been right to do so, though the dress and its accessories had cost a fortune. The brocade gown, embroidered in silk thread with long swirls of silver, pink, palest green and sky blue, was worn over a panniered satin petticoat. The stomacher was of pleated net over cream satin. She could hardly breathe when she was laced into it.

'Janet, for heaven's sake, loosen it or I shall swoon,' she said.

Janet, smiling to herself, let some of the silk cord out and then helped her into the bodice, which was of the same material as the skirt and had a square neckline that was rather more revealing than she was used to, but a handkerchief swathed round her shoulders and pinned into the top of the corsage with a diamond-and-amethyst brooch, a present from her husband, made her feel a little more comfortable about it. The sleeves were straight to the elbow and ended in net ruffles.

'Beautiful,' Janet breathed. 'Now for your hair.'

Rosamund suffered her maid to pull the front of her hair up over some wool stuffing to make buckle curls. The back was tied in a knot on top and the ends allowed to curl naturally over her ears. The whole creation was decorated with silk flowers and plumes. Looking in the mirror afterwards, Rosamund was confronted with a fashion plate that she was not sure she liked. At least it would allow her to look the part of Lord Portman's wife, even if she did not feel like it.

Slipping into her satin shoes and taking up her fan and reticule, she made her way in stately fashion to the drawing room where Harry waited for her.

He was in cream silk: plain breeches, tied at the knee with red ribbons, his coat and waistcoat embroidered in gold and silver. Unusually for him, he was wearing a white wig with three buckles at each side and the back confined in a large ribbon bow. He swept her an elaborate leg and then examined her through his quizzing glass. 'La, madam,' he said in his macaroni drawl, waving the glass in a circular movement around her. 'Stap me, if you won't outshine the whole company.'

In spite of her nervousness, she laughed. 'Harry, I wish you would not act the coxcomb. You are far too sensible and clever for that.'

'Ah, but this is the public me,' he said, mincing round her to inspect her from the back. 'And today we are to be in the public eye.'

'I prefer the private one.'

'Do you, my dear? I am gratified.' He was back facing her, the quizzing glass once more dangling from his neck. 'But we shall keep that to ourselves, shall we? What would the *ton* make of me if I suddenly changed my ways?'

'Would that matter? I had not thought you were one to mind what people thought of you.'

He was pensive for a moment. He could tell her the reason that he had started it was to disguise his hurt and guilt over Beth, but, as Rosamund had pointed out to him, habits were difficult to break. And since his involvement with the Piccadilly Gentlemen it was a good cover for what he was really doing; the fop could not be further from the dirty Gus Housman. He could have said all that and might have done, if he had not been plagued by his cousin's revelations about Chalmers and the clipped guinea and the little he had learned from

Mr Tetley, who had been decidedly cagey in answering his questions. He had to get to the bottom of that, which made his determination to inveigle his way into the counterfeiters' gang doubly important. He prayed she was innocent. If she were not… He could not bear to contemplate the consequences.

'They might think marriage had wrought the change,' he said, a half-smile playing about his lips because it had—a big change. 'And we cannot have that, can we?'

She did not answer, realising there were three Harry Portmans: the coxcomb who stood in front of her, the gentle, caring husband and father she knew at Bishop's Court and the scruffy individual who crept about at night and gave her nightmares. She pulled herself together and smiled. 'No, I can see it would be a dreadful blow to your pride.'

He did not answer. Instead he picked up her heavy velvet mantle and draped it about her shoulders before putting on his own, then offered her his arm. 'Come, my dear, our carriage is at the door.'

The crowds, spilling into the road and lining the route of the procession, cheered every carriage that passed, regardless of whether they knew its occupants. Rosamund, stiff with nerves, hardly noticed them.

Arriving at the Abbey, they were conducted to their places and prepared for a long wait. Many of those around them had brought packets of food and bottles of drink and the whole place hummed with conversation and gossip waiting for the arrival of the king and queen. Rosamund filled the time looking about her at the glittering array of churchmen and nobility and asking Harry to identify them. He had a tale to tell about each and kept her entertained until the cheering outside rose in volume and a few minutes later the Royal couple arrived.

They made their way through the nave to the coronation chairs and the service began. The Archbishop presented the sovereign to the people who responded with a cry of 'God Save the King!' Then the king took the oath. His crimson robes were removed, leaving him in a plain white tunic and he was seated in the coronation chair to be anointed while the choir sang the anthem. This done, the king was dressed in cloth of gold and invested with the regalia and crowned with St Edward's crown over the Cap of State. From there he moved to the throne and received the homage of the people, in strict order of hierarchy. Then the queen was crowned and silver coronation medals were thrown into the congregation. Harry, retrieving one, wondered how long it would be before these were counterfeited and being sold for genuine.

After Holy Communion, the newly crowned monarch and his queen went to St Edward's chapel where he put on a purple velvet robe and then proceeded in state to the west end of the Abbey, carrying the orb and sceptre. It was over and the congregation filed out behind them to celebrate in whatever manner they had arranged. Harry and Rosamund returned to Portman House to eat a quiet meal together, while outside the noise of singing and cheering and the explosions of fireworks filled the air. On the surface they appeared content with each other, but both were nursing secrets that made ordinary conversation difficult and they separated to go to their rooms and rest until it was time to go to Lord Trentham's ball.

Harry wanted to establish himself among the company so that he would not be missed when he later disappeared, and he had to make sure Rosamund did not come looking for him. Luckily most of the Piccadilly Gentlemen were there with their wives whom she had met on her wedding day, so she was soon in conversation with Louise and Amy. Amy rarely came to town, preferring to stay at their country home in Norfolk, but the coronation was a special occasion and so she and James were staying with Jonathan and Louise at Chaston Hall, a few miles out of town.

When the dancing began, they paired off; Rosamund was partnered by James and Amy by Jonathan. Harry swept Louise an extravagant leg and offered her his arm. They followed the others into the dance. Somehow he managed to make a wrong turn and drew everyone's attention to him as he endeavoured to get back into the set. 'My apologies, Lady Leinster,' he said loudly in the high voice of the fop. 'Don't know what I was thinking of.'

She smiled. 'Your lovely wife, I should imagine.'

'She is lovely, ain't she?' he murmured.

'Does she know?'

'That she is lovely? I doubt it. She is too modest.'

Louise laughed. 'No, I meant about the Piccadilly Gentlemen.'

'No. Too dangerous.'

'But I know and Amy knows,' she said.

'That's different.'

'Why?'

He paused, wondering how to answer her. 'Because of the way her father died,' he said with sudden inspiration. 'Very smoky, that.'

'Is that what you are investigating?'

'Among other things,' he answered enigmatically.

The dance ended. He bowed, she curtsied, then he took her back to Jonathan. He took a turn with Amy and then stood watching with tolerant amusement as Rosamund, smiling and relaxed, stood up with several youthful and not-so-youthful partners. He looked at his watch. It was time to go. 'There is someone I must see,' he said, to the company near him. 'Beg to be excused.' Flourishing a bow, he made his escape.

Looking about him to make sure he was not being watched, he dropped his lazy gait and hurried to the room Lord Trentham had set aside for him, which was at the rear of the house on the ground floor and close to an outside door. Jack Sylvester was waiting for him with his Gus Housman clothes.

The valet did not bother to hide his disgust; the garments were even filthier and smellier that they had been and his lordship would not allow him to clean them. 'Don't know why you want to go out in these things,' he said, trying to brush the coat down with his hand, as Harry threw off his white wig and began stripping off his finery.

'Reasons, Jack, reasons you do not need to question,' he said amiably, stepping out of his small clothes and into the disgusting fustian breeches. 'I hope you remembered the make-up, I am not keen to rub real dirt over my face.'

'Yes, my lord.'

Once the disguise was on, he dirtied his face and hands with make-up and put on the mouse-bitten brown wig. 'Will I do?' he asked, clapping a dirty black hat on top of it. 'Haven't forgotten anything, have I?'

'Your own mother would not know you, my lord.' It was said with a perfectly straight face. 'But I fancy red heels are a little out of place.'

'Good God!' Harry, who had absent-mindedly slipped his feet back into his shoes after putting on the breeches, kicked them off again and replaced them with the down-at-heel footwear of Gus Housman, then looked at his fob watch which lay with his quizzing glass, rings and other accessories on a table, ready for his return. 'I'm late. Don't stir from here until I come back, I shall need you.'

He left Jack muttering that he didn't know what the world was coming to, and peeped out to see there was no one about. The coast was clear and he was soon out and hurrying down a side road and out on to Piccadilly. He breathed a sigh of relief when he saw Ash's phaeton standing outside the Admiral's house and, unusually, no one in attendance. At once he went into character, sidling along, looking shifty. The street was still busy with pedestrians, a cab or two and a couple chairs being escorted by linkmen.

He had half his body in the carriage when Ash came out of the house to raise the hue and cry. He was too early or Harry was too late, but he could not retreat and there was nothing for it but for Ash to pretend outrage and grab the offender. 'You were late,' he muttered as they pretended to struggle. 'Now what am I supposed to do?'

'Let me get away and fall over your own feet coming after me.'

Ash obeyed, but others had seen the robbery and gave chase. This was not in Harry's plan, but there was nothing for it but to run for all he was worth. His closest pursuer dived for his legs and brought him down, making him hit his face on the cobbles. Desperation lent him strength and, after a brief but intense struggle, during which his neckerchief was torn from him, he squirmed away, scrambled to his feet and set off again. The man made a half-hearted attempt to follow, but gave up and went back to Ash, who had gathered the witnesses about him and was loudly lamenting the loss of his purse.

Harry could not go back to Lord Trentham's house until he was sure he was not being followed. He turned the corner into Tyburn Lane and risked a look behind him. There was no one on his tail. Another turn and then another and he was at the mews behind Trentham House. Making sure there was no one to see him, he slipped back into the house and rejoined Jack.

'My lord, what has happened to you?' the valet asked, shocked by the sight of him.

Harry was so breathless he had to sit down before he could answer. 'Nothing of any moment.'

'Nearly got caught, didn't you?' Jack said. 'I knew no good would come of it.'

'Come of what?' Harry demanded, stripping off the dirty coat and noticing there was blood on it. 'Where did that come from?'

'Your nose, my lord. You look as though you have been in a mill.' He sighed and wrung a cloth out in a bowl of water set ready to wash off the make-up and began dabbing at Harry's nose. 'It was a wager, I doubt not. I only hope it was worth it, though what Lady Portman will say when she sees you, I can but guess.'

'Ouch! That hurt.'

'I must clean the blood off, my lord, and get rid of this brown make-up, but you will have to use the lighter make-up to cover the bruise. I assume you mean to rejoin the company.'

'Of course I do.' He brushed the valet aside and stood up to look in the hand mirror, which he kept with his box of make-up. 'Good Lord, I did not know it was as bad as that.' He fingered the end of his nose tenderly. 'That comes from not looking where I was going and walking into doors.'

'You don't say,' Jack commented laconically, handing him a pot of make-up.

Harry could easily have admonished him for that but, busy smearing the paint over the bruise and blending it in, decided not to. Then he took off the rest of Housman's clothes and dressed again as the foppish Lord Portman, cramming his hair back under the white wig and sitting down again to put on his shoes. Restoring his fob and quizzing glass to his neck and the rings to his fingers, he left Jack to bundle up the other garments and return with them to Portman House.

'Where has Harry has got to?' Francis murmured, leading Rosamund down the line of dancers. 'Deserted you already, has he?'

'He is about somewhere. I saw him dancing not two minutes ago.' It had been considerably longer than two minutes, but she did not intend to let Francis know she had wondered the same thing herself. 'He might have gone to the card room.'

'Ah, yes,' he said, with an oily smile. 'Harry does so like a gamble.'

Why did everything the man said sound as if he meant something more than the words he was uttering? 'He is no different from most other men and I do not think he risks too much.'

'Oh, he risks a great deal,' Francis said enigmatically.

'I cannot think what.'

'No?' He stepped away from her and down the outside of the double line of dancers to find her again at its head. He bowed and took her hands to duck beneath the arch of outstretched arms. 'Marrying you was a risk and embroiling himself in your affairs an even greater one,' he murmured so only she could hear.

'Whatever do you mean?'

'I blame that play acting he was so keen on before he inherited. Thinks he's another David Garrick, I shouldn't wonder. It wouldn't be so bad if he confined his acting to the stage and didn't enjoy dressing up like a muckworm and consorting with the low life in the stews.'

'I am sure you are mistaken,' she said, as an image of Harry creeping from the house in that strange garb came to her. This was all to do with Papa and that mining company and Max and those coins, she was sure of it.

'I've seen him myself. Funny that, after your brother passed me a clipped guinea the other day.'

'That was an innocent mistake, you know that.' She tried to sound convincing but was not sure she had succeeded.

'Oh, undoubtedly it was a mistake,' he said airily. 'A big mistake.' He stopped suddenly because Harry was waiting for them at the end of the line.

'I will take over now,' he told Francis, holding out his hands to Rosamund. 'Do find something else to do.' Defeated, Francis left them.

'My lord,' she said, taking his hands and stepping to the side and then back again. 'That was discourteous of you.'

He matched her steps with his. 'I have no doubt he was filling your head with nonsense.'

'I took no note of what he was saying,' she said. 'Good.'

The dance ended, he gave her a flourishing bow and she curtsied. It was when he held out his hand to raise her and she looked up into his face, she noticed his nose was swollen and there was the beginning of a bruise on the end of it. 'Harry, what has happened?'

'Happened, my dear?' He was at his most infuriating as he tucked her hand beneath his arm and strolled to the side of the ballroom. 'Why, I have been dancing with you. I know it ain't done to dance with one's wife, but I don't care for that custom when the wife I have is making the whole population of London green with envy of me.'

'That is a foolish thing to say,' she said, unaccountably pleased with the compliment. 'I did not mean that.'

'Oh?' A dark eyebrow was raised towards her.

'You look as though you have been fighting.' It was said in a whisper.

'Fighting, my dear? Me?' He feigned astonishment. 'I am the world's worst coward. Besides, it would ruin my clothes.' These were as pristine as they had been when they arrived, but he ran the back of his hand down the lapel of his coat as if stroking it in affection.

'But your nose is swollen and I do believe I can see a bruise.'

'Oh, that,' he said nonchalantly. 'Silly me, I walked into a door. Not looking where I was going. A little foxed, perhaps.'

She did not believe him, but could hardly call him a liar; still, something had happened when he absented himself, she was sure of it. The company was too wrapped up in the dancing and their own conversations to notice when someone disappeared, which often happened at functions like this: a call of nature, a stroll in the garden, the lure of the card room, a little flirtation. But she had missed him. It had not worried her until Francis Portman started filling her ears with his innuendo and Harry had come back with a bloodied nose.

'Then perhaps we should take our leave and return home before other people notice it,' she said. 'I will put some salve on it. You cannot go about looking as though you had been in a prize fight and come off worse.'

'If I had been in a fight, I would not have come of worse,' he said, attempting humour. 'But, by all means, let us make our excuses and go home.'

Their carriage was sent for while they took their leave of their host and hostess. James and Jonathan, who knew about the supposed robbery, pretended to believe the story of the door and chaffed him unmercifully, so that he was glad to escape.

* * *

They were silent in the carriage going home. Rosamund was worried. If Harry had not returned with that bruise on his face so soon after Francis regaling her with his tales, she might not have been concerned. What had Francis meant by 'embroiling himself in your affairs'? She did not think for a moment that Harry would confide in his cousin about Mr O'Keefe. Or had Max been so foolish as to tell him the truth about those coins? And where had Harry got that bruise?

He would have gone straight to his room as soon as they entered the house if she had not taken his arm and propelled him towards her boudoir. Here she pushed him into a chair. 'Sit still while I find that salve. It is a recipe my mother used when my brother used to hurt himself as a boy and I always keep some by me.'

'There really is no need,' he said, watching her go to her dressing table and wring a cloth out in water, and then fetch out a pot of ointment. 'It's nothing. It will be gone by the morning.'

'It is already spreading,' she said, coming back to him and surveying him critically. 'It was only faint before, now it is a rainbow of colours. You must have run into that door full tilt.' She began dabbing at it with the cloth. It came away stained with make-up. 'Oh, Harry, do you have to wear this stuff, you really do not need to, you know. You have a very good complexion.'

'Too good,' he said, grinning. 'The fashion is to be pale.'

'I do not care for that fashion. You do not wear make-up at Bishop's Court.'

'That's different.'

'I like you best without it.'

'Do you, my dear?' he asked softly.

'Yes.' She was standing over him, carefully smearing the salve on his nose. As her hand came close to his lips, he caught her finger in his mouth. Startled, she pulled it away. 'Harry, I can't do this if you don't behave.'

'I am not sure I want to behave.' He put his arm about her waist and pulled her on to his knee. The pot went flying from her grasp. She heard it break, but could do nothing about it because he was kissing her. Her worries about Max and Frances and how he had come by that bruise flew from her head. He did want her, after all. Her heart began to thump in anticipation, but then he seemed to shudder, as if coming out of a deep sleep, and stood up, depositing her back on her feet. She stood and waited expectantly. Now, surely he would consummate their marriage?

Her hope dwindled to nothing as he murmured, 'Thank you for the salve, my dear. I shall be as good as new in the morning.' Then he dropped a kiss on her forehead and was gone, leaving her in tears to clear up the broken glass and ointment. They seemed as far apart as ever. But something had to be done, if she was not to lose the happiness the last few months had brought her.

Harry stumbled up to his room. He must have been more foxed that he realised. Good God, he had nearly succumbed to temptation. She had looked up at him, lovely eyes searching his face, her lips slightly parted as if in invitation. It was becoming unbearable, this longing to make love to his wife. Every time they were alone together, he felt himself spinning ever closer towards a whirlpool, which pulled him in and down. He must resist. Not only because of what had happened to Beth, but because of O'Keefe and the coiners.

It was not only his duty to the Piccadilly Gentlemen driving him, but the need to find out about Rosamund's involvement with O'Keefe, to discover if it was anything more than her father's foolishness. That was what Mr Tetley had assured him was the case. He would have been satisfied with that, if the lawyer had not also mentioned a bag of counterfeit guineas that had been found in the old man's room and which he believed had been handed over to the Excise. It had confirmed Harry in his belief that Max Chalmers had been passing them. He needed a clear head to bring that business to a conclusion and, more importantly now, keep her safe.

He slept fitfully and rose next morning, more determined than ever to try to distance himself from her. It was too early to go calling, so he took a gallop in the park and then, instead of going home, went on to Ashley's bachelor apartments in Lincoln's Inn Fields.

Ash, who was suffering from overindulgence at the Admiral's the night before, was wearing a quilted dressing gown and a wet cloth on his forehead. Having offered his early visitor a cup of coffee, they sat down to discuss the events of the night before. 'I made enough fuss to be sure word of it would be all round town,' Ash told him. 'According to the witnesses, I very nearly caught you in the act, but you are slippery as an eel and managed to escape, in spite of being pursued by half the population of London. It is strange how stories become more exaggerated with each telling.' He paused, surveying his friend's swollen nose with interest. The bruise had come out, red, yellow and purple, and he looked like a prize fighter. 'I didn't do that, did I?'

'No, it was that linkman who came after me. Put me down on the cobbles, curse him.'

'How did you explain it to your lovely wife?'

'I walked into a door when I was foxed.'

Ash laughed. 'You foxed! I never met a man who could hold his drink better. Did she believe you?'

'I am not sure. She pretended she did.'

'I sincerely hope that is the last time you set up a caper like that. You were as near as dammit caught. James would not have liked that. You know he is a stickler for keeping above the law and he would not be happy if he were forced to defend you by explaining that you were working for the Piccadilly Gentlemen. It would do the Society's reputation no good at all.'

'I know. I would not ask it of him. And it would not help to catch the coiners.'

'Now what?'

'Off to the Nag's Head and this time I think I will be taken to the farm.'

'Let me come with you.'

'No, I have to go alone, but you could follow and keep watch, in case anything goes wrong.' He paused. 'But keep well back and do not interfere unless I give you the signal.'

'You cannot arrest them all single-handed.'

'I am not going to try. Arresting people is the job of the Runners; besides, I do not want my disguise penetrated. It is too convenient and might be needed again. Once I have located the farm and told Sir John Fielding where it is, my work is done.' Then he could concentrate on his wife, he told himself. There were still problems to be overcome, not least the not-so-little matter of consummating the marriage. And then there was her brother and the clipped coins. Both seemed insurmountable.

'Speaking of disguise,' he said to Ash, 'I could not leave Portman House in broad daylight as Gus Housman, so I brought his clothes with me. I would deem it a favour if I could change here.'

Ash laughed. 'That would have caused some raised eyebrows. I'll send my valet out to collect my new waistcoat from the tailor and take you up to my dressing room.'

This was soon accomplished and Harry emerged in his usual disguise, though the spotted handkerchief was missing; it had done its work and was needed no more. He clamped his greasy black hat back on his head and rejoined Ash, who had dressed in his bedchamber and was wearing the dark blue coat of a naval officer.

'You look even more disgusting by the light of day,' Ash commented, wrinkling his nose.

'Good,' Harry said, filling his coat pockets with small coins from the bag he had brought with him. 'I had better be off.'

'Leave your horse in my mews,' Ash suggested. 'We must not make the mistake we made before and risk it being recognised.'

'Horse?' Harry laughed. 'Gus Housman could never afford a mount. He must walk, but it would help if you could have Hector on hand in case I need to make a swift getaway.'

O'Keefe was waiting for him in his usual place. He had a tankard of ale on the table in front of him and was in no hurry to leave until he had finished it and his cohorts had established that Housman had not been followed. Seeing Harry's face, he chuckled. 'Nearly had you, did they? Heard all about it. Serves you right for working alone.'

Harry fingered his nose as he slipped into the chair opposite the coiner. 'Tha's the way I like it.'

'So, what have you brought me?'

Harry emptied one of his pockets. There were half-guineas, shilling and sixpences, plus a few copper coins. O'Keefe picked them up and examined them one by one, biting into each with blackened teeth. 'Good,' he said, putting them in a leather pouch he wore about his waist. 'But I asked for yeller boys, too.'

Harry dipped into the other pocket and produced a bag, which he jingled enticingly. 'There's fifty 'ere, but it comes at a price.'

'I could tek it off yer.'

'Yer could,' Harry conceded thoughtfully. 'But you ain't goin' to, are yer? I know too much.' That was a risky ploy, he knew. They'd kill him as soon as not, but he didn't think they would attempt it in the Nag's Head in broad daylight. And he hoped Ash was not far away.

'Right.' O'Keefe drained his tankard and stood up. 'Let's be goin' then.'

Harry followed him out of the tavern down to the river, where the mudlarks paddled about in bare feet retrieving flotsam and jetsam, like coal and timber, to use or sell to make a few pennies to spend on food. The Thames was still the main artery of the capital and full of shipping of all kinds, sea-going sailing ships, small yachts, barges and hundreds of rowing boats, both privately owned and those for hire.

O'Keefe made his way down to the water's edge

where two men sat in a boat, resting on their oars. When they saw O'Keefe and Harry they picked up the oars and began pushing the boat off the mud with them. O'Keefe and Harry clambered in. No one spoke.

Going by water was something Harry had not considered and he wondered if they would go straight across, upstream or downstream; unless Ash was close by and could see them, he would not know which way they had gone. The two oarsmen pulled out into deeper water and turned upstream, sending the craft skimming along, helped by the incoming tide. Harry, pretending to be unconcerned, looked about him at the houses, shops and warehouses that lined the river, trying to catch a glimpse of Ash, but there was no sign of his friend. He had a feeling he was on his own.

'That gallowsgood has been at it again,' Janet said, as she helped Rosamund to dress.

Another day had dawned, a warm sunny day outside, but there seemed to be little warmth or sunshine in Rosamund's heart. Still worrying about her husband and her future, she answered unthinkingly. 'What gallowsgood?'

'Why, that highwayman that robbed his lordship on the heath. He's struck again, this time in

London. Last night it was, when the streets were crowded with revellers. He robbed Sir Ashley Saunders.'

'Who told you this?' Rosamund asked, suddenly alert.

'Mrs West, what comes in to do the laundry. She heard it from her son. He's a linkman and was walking alongside a chair in Piccadilly. He gave chase and brought the man down, but he managed to escape.'

Rosamund could not help thinking of Harry in those dreadful clothes, creeping out of the house at dead of night, although last night he had been at Trentham House with her, dressed extravagantly as the coxcomb everyone believed him to be. Except for the time he had been missing, she argued with herself, and he had certainly been hurt by someone or something. She stopped her ridiculous suspicions—why, in heaven's name, would one of the richest men in London want to rob anyone, let alone his friend?

'How do you know it was the same man?' she queried. 'It could have been anyone.'

'From his description,' the maid said. 'The clothes and his spotted neckerchief. They picked that up and handed it in to the Watch. Course the Watch are never there when they're wanted, but I reckon if the shagbag keeps on this way, he'll soon be caught. His lordship said he would be.'

'His lordship?' queried Rosamund. 'When did he speak to you about it?'

'He came to the kitchen to ask for an early breakfast and when Cook told him what we had been talking about, he said not to worry about it, but to be careful when we went abroad and not walk out alone.'

So Harry had risen early and gone out—did the man not need to sleep? 'Did his lordship say when he would be back?'

'No, my lady.'

'What was he wearing?'

'Why, a riding habit, my lady. He left on horse-back.'

She let her breath out. It was a stupid question to have asked. Her husband would never have gone out in daylight dressed like a vagrant. But where had he gone? Why all the secrecy? The last person she expected to answer that question was Francis Portman.

The young man arrived just as she was trying to make up her mind whether to call on Lady Trentham, which was the polite thing to do after enjoying her hospitality, or to wait until Harry came back and they could do it together. Francis was unctuously polite, but she could see as soon as he entered the small parlour where she sat that he was bursting to tell her something. She was not sure she wanted to hear it.

'It is early for making calls,' she told him. 'And I am afraid his lordship is not at home.'

'I know that.' He could not disguise the satisfaction in his voice as he refused to take the chair she indicated and stood facing her. 'I reckon he's got himself into a hobble he won't easily get out of.'

'What do you mean?' She clenched her fists into the folds of her skirt to stop her alarm becoming obvious. 'What has happened?'

'I saw him, not more than half an hour go, with a shady character in the Nag's Head, handing over a pile of coins. They left together.'

'Coins?' This time she really was shaken. 'Do you mean guineas?'

'I wasn't near enough to see. Could have been. Unless you want to see your husband hanged for treason, you had better do something about it. After all, it's on your account he's in trouble.'

'My account?' she repeated, though she was afraid he was right.

'Yes. He was always susceptible to a damsel in distress. He sees himself as a knight errant, but I never dreamed he would go so far as to marry one of them. Of course, I could let him stew in his own mess. If he hangs, then I inherit, but I do have a proper regard for the good of the family. It wouldn't do.'

Her resolve not to react to his nastiness went by the board. 'Do you know where he went with the man?'

'Yes. I heard the fellow talking to his mates before Harry arrived. He said something about a boat to Chiswick.' He paused to watch the effect his words were having on Rosamund. She had gone ghostly white and her hands were shaking. He gave a satisfied smile. 'If we make haste and ride to Chiswick, we will get there before the boat, taking into account the bends in the river.'

She did not stop to ask him what they would do then. Or why he thought she could rescue her husband, but if Harry had got himself mixed up with criminals, then she would have to do something. Anything. She stood up. 'I will go and change. Go to the mews and ask to have my horse saddled, will you?'

'With pleasure.' He paused; she was already halfway to the door. 'Don't dress too grand, will you? You do not want to embarrass Harry, do you?'

Ten minutes later she was mounting up beside

him, dressed in one of her old gowns covered with an equally shabby cloak. She should have thrown them away when she married, but had not done so in case Harry decided to annul the marriage and send her away with nothing and she might need them. The thought of that weighed her down, but she pulled herself together and concentrated on riding as fast as was possible given the amount of traffic there was on the road. There were coaches, wagons, carts, hackney carriages and sedans, costers with their barrows, children bowing hoops, dogs running in and out and the occasional cow being driven to Green Park. She had to get to Chiswick before that boat, though what she would do when they got there, she had no idea. It all depended on Harry.

Chapter Ten

Once the rowing boat had passed under Westminster Bridge it left the crowded buildings behind and the houses became grander and more widely spaced with gardens coming down to the water's edge. Further on there were market gardens and fishermen's cottages, and the tide was no longer helping them. 'How far?' asked Harry, breaking the silence.

'Ask no questions and yer'll soon find out,' O'Keefe told him.

Harry lapsed into silence, wondering if they meant to kill him and take the bag of coins. They could throw his body in the river and it might not surface for days, even weeks, and then it would be one of hundreds of unidentified and unidentifiable corpses pulled from the mud of the Thames every day. No one would know what had happened to him and Rosamund would be relieved of the encumbrance of a husband who could not bring himself to make love to her. She would be a very rich widow. And a beautiful one. Every unmarried man in the kingdom would court her. And that idiot Frances would inherit the estate.

He shook himself. He was not dead yet and he did not intend to let it happen. He began to think of ways of protecting himself. He was still thinking of and discarding ideas when they rounded the great bend in the river and were approaching the village of Chiswick. They passed the osier beds where men and women were at work harvesting the reeds, than drew in at a landing stage on the north bank. O'Keefe and Harry disembarked and the boat pushed off again.

O'Keefe led the way up through the village to the high road, followed by a still silent Harry. Was the farm close at hand? Or was the whole trip a wild goose chase, meant to get him out of the way? He considered making a run for it; the road was busy with vehicles, one of which would surely stop and take him up, but that could be a dangerous thing for those who had helped him; having come so far, he would not abandon his quest now.

They went round to the back of the Packhorse Inn where an old-fashioned closed carriage stood in the yard ready harnessed to a couple of mismatched horses. As they approached it, Job Smithall and Thomas Quinn came out of the inn with tankards of ale in their hands. 'You've no time for that,' O'Keefe told them. 'Put them pots down and, Tom, you get up there.' He indicated the driver's seat of the carriage.

Quinn gulped down the last of the ale, set the tankard on the window sill and climbed on the box, leaving O'Keefe, Smithall and Harry to travel inside. Two minutes later they were on their way, moving in a westerly direction. It was a road Harry knew well, having travelled it any number of times going back and forth from Bishop's Court to London. He wished he could have let Ash know that was the direction they were to take, but O'Keefe was a cunning operator; he was making it as difficult as possible for them to be followed.

They had not been going very long when O'Keefe opened his money pouch and handed Smithall the change Harry was supposed to have got from passing the clipped guineas. 'Do y'think that's a fair return for our work?' he asked him.

Smithall counted it. Harry was ignoring them, looking out of the window, making a mental note of their route.

'Fair enough,' Smithall said, handing them back.

'Good. He's sitting on fifty yeller boys. He's goin' to give 'em to us when we arrive.'

'You lettin' 'im see where the work is done then? Ain't that a bit risky?'

'No, for he'll 'ave no idea where he is.' He put his head out of the door and called up to the man on the box, 'Draw up before we get to the crossroads.'

They stopped in the entrance to a farm yard and O'Keefe jumped down and indicated Harry should get out. Harry stood on the road beside O'Keefe and looked about him. He could hardly believe they were at the farm where the clipping was done; it was too close to the main road, which was always busy with traffic, a road he knew like the back of his hand. The crossroads just ahead of them was where the way divided to go to Hounslow on the one hand and Bishop's Court on the other. He was less than five miles from his home. Had they penetrated his disguise, after all? Were they taking him to Bishop's Court? They could cause havoc there by terrorising the servants and stealing whatever took their fancy, and would no doubt think it a great jest. And there was Annabelle with only Miss Gunstock and servants for protection. For the first time he began to feel a real *frisson* of fear.

'Job, fetch some good stout cord from the basket,' O'Keefe said.

Smithall rummaged in the basket at the back of the coach for a length of rope with which they proceeded to bind Harry's hands behind his back. With two of them holding him fast, his struggles were in vain. 'What you want to go an' do tha' for?' he demanded, aggrieved. 'I ain't about to cut and run.'

'No, but we don't want you seein' more'n you oughta, so we'll blindfold you an' we don' want you rippin' it off.' And with that, he took a black kerchief from around his neck and bound it over Harry's eyes. That done, he prodded him in the back. 'Get back in the coach.'

Harry did as he was told and they set off again. Unable to lean back with his hands tied behind him, he sat uncomfortably in the corner, straining his ears and every other sense to make out the direction they were going in. He would need to find it again if the Runners were to catch the gang red-handed.

The horses slowed to turn off the main road and he sensed that they had taken the Hounslow turn and were making for the Heath. After a while, the coach took another turn and then began to roll and bump over deep ruts. He could hear a ferocious dog barking and could smell farmyard smells. He thought he heard a child crying and a woman scolding, but they carried on past them and a minute later drew to a stop.

O'Keefe climbed out. 'Out you get,' he said, grabbing Harry by the arm.

'A'right,' he said, pulling away and getting down awkwardly by himself. 'Untie me, can't you? I can't see where I'm goin'.'

'Tha's the way it's meant to be,' O'Keefe said, leading him. 'Duck yer head, the door's a low one.' He pushed Harry's head down and he found himself in a building which was unbearably hot. His hands were untied and his blindfold removed. He was not surprised to find himself in a forge, but it was all he could do to hide his astonishment when he found himself face to face with Alfred Chappell. He was at Feltham Farm!

He realised they would not have brought him here if they had any idea who he really was. He needed all his acting ability now; not by a flicker of an eyelid must he be anything but the acquisitive and inquisitive Gus Housman. He looked about him with the open curiosity that Gus Housman would have shown. The building they were in had been a barn converted into a forge with a brick fireplace, in which a red hot fire glowed. On it a cauldron of shining liquid bubbled. There were several tables used for the separate processes: stamping, milling, polishing. Bert Ironside was setting out the moulds on the one closest to the fire to take the melted gold. Sitting at another table under the only window a man, whom Harry recognised as Alf Chappell's brother, Bob, was busy clipping coins, catching the clippings in a dish. He was being very meticulous, but looked up as Harry entered.

'Alf, Bob, this 'ere's Gus Housman what I told you about,' O'Keefe told them. 'He's prepared to get us yeller boys to work with if we cut him in.' He turned to Harry. 'Alf's the boss o' the outfit and Bob's his brother.'

''Ow do,' Harry said.

'Did anyone follow you?' Alf asked O'Keefe.

'Not a chance. I was watchin' out the whole way. And he's been blindfolded the last five miles.'

'You wanted to see the operation,' Alf Chappell said. 'It's not something we'd allow everyone, so are you satisfied?'

Harry gave a non-committal grunt as Thomas Quinn helped Ironside pour the liquid gold into the moulds. Beside them were the dies used to stamp the image on the coins. 'Where d'yer get them dies from?' he asked, moving forwards to examine one of them.

O'Keefe tapped his nose. 'Thomas, 'ere, were once employed at the Mint. They're the real thing.'

'Where's the yeller boys?' Bob got up from his seat and came over to face Harry. 'We could do with them, I've just about run out. How many have you got?'

'Fifty.'

'Let's be having them, then.' He held out his hand.

'I want in, first,' Harry said.

'For a paltry fifty guineas! You must be jesting.'

'Not just fifty guineas. I gave you more'n that when I held up Lord Portman's coach. There were near a hundred there and some small change. An' I c'n get more.'

'Lord Portman!' O'Keefe laughed. 'I nearly split me breeches when I saw that. Neat as you like, it was.'

'Wha's so special about Lord Portman?' Harry queried, genuinely mystified. 'He ain't no different from any other gentry. More of a coward than most, which is why I picked 'im.'

Bob Chappell joined in the laughter. 'His lordship has been supplying us with gold coins at the rate of five guineas a month for years. I reckon he'd wet hisself if he knew that.'

'How so?' Harry asked, though he fancied he knew the answer.

'To keep his brat. Fancy thinking it took five guineas to keep a scrawny little thing like her for a month!'

Alf Chappell grunted. 'Well, she's gone now, took away by his lordship's new wife.'

'Do he know what he's married, I wonder?' O'Keefe said, musing aloud. 'I reckon she'd pay good money for him not to know.'

'Know what?' Harry demanded, almost forgetting his role as Gus Housman, but quickly added in Gus Housman's vernacular, 'You got summat on 'er?'

'Never you mind.'

He did mind, of course, but had to pretend indifference. O'Keefe intended to blackmail Rosamund. He hoped sincerely that when that happened she would confide in him and not meekly pay up. Did that depend on how guilty she was? Guilty of what? Coining, along with her brother? He had no answer to that, but had to admit it was one of the reasons he had come on this escapade alone when he would have done better to involve the rest of the Piccadilly Gentlemen to bring the gang to justice. In doing so he had as good as incriminated himself.

He watched as O'Keefe emptied his pockets of the loose change he had given him and spoke to Alf. 'Here's the change from Gus's shopping trip. It's a fair return.'

'Give it to Tilly,' Alf told him.

'How many more you got in this gang?' Harry demanded. Tilly was a new name to him.

'Oh, Tilly ain't part of our gang,' O'Keefe said. 'But she's come in with us since her pa and ma and her old man got took two or three months back for the silver lay. Bordes and half-bordes she specialises in, though she ain't half as good as her old man was.'

Borde, Harry knew, was their slang for a shilling, but that was not what had grabbed his attention, it was the fact that her parents and husband had been sentenced to hang, a sentence which should have been carried out a month before but all hangings had been postponed on account of the royal wedding and the coronation. It was felt that those happy celebrations should not be marred by the public spectacle of a hanging. Or perhaps those arranging them thought the hanging might prove the better entertainment. Could Tilly be Matilda Watson?

She had sworn revenge on whoever had informed on them and that had been Harry in the guise of Gus Housman. He had never spoken to her, simply watched her and her husband doing business in the Nag's Head and followed them to their lodgings. The Bow Street Runners had done the rest. But she might remember seeing him sitting alone in the corner of the tavern and put two and two together. He must be doubly careful.

While he was musing on how to deal with the situation, they heard the dog set up a frenzied barking and something being knocked over and Mrs Chappell shouting. Alf went out to investigate, leaving the door open. Harry could see the path leading to the farmyard and the side of the farmhouse itself. Rosamund was standing in the yard, facing Mrs Chappell who held the dog by its rope, ready to let it go if Rosamund so much as blinked. It snarled and showed its teeth. Harry's heart jumped into his throat as he watched the scene. Why was his wife here? Did she know his secret? Had she followed him? But that was impossible; he had left her asleep in bed in Berkeley Square. Did that mean she was in league with the coiners and her arrival was purely coincidence? He dare not go to her.

Alf grabbed her arm and pulled her away from

the dog, giving the animal a vicious kick as he did so. It yelped and subsided. 'You should know better that try to pass that animal, my lady,' Alf said, still holding her arm. 'What are you doing here?'

Rosamund had caught a glimpse of Harry in the doorway of the barn, along with several others. If she had not seen him at home dressed in that filthy garb, she would not have known him for her husband. Now she did not know what to say to explain her presence.

She and Francis had ridden to Chiswick as fast as they could, though she had little hope of catching up with her husband. Francis had entertained her on the way with stories of Harry's exploits as a boy and his unnatural affinity with the lower orders. 'There was nothing he liked better than climbing trees with the village boys for chestnuts to roast on a camp fire and fishing for roach and eels in the river,' he told her. 'He would invite them on to the estate and they would swim naked in the lake.'

'Did you join them?'

'Me? I was still in leading strings. Saw them once when I was out with my nurse. She was disgusted and hurried me away.'

'No doubt they were only enjoying themselves.'

He had sniffed his contempt of that remark and

reined in because they had reached the crossroads at Chiswick. They had been about to turn down the lane that led to the river, when a coach rumbled out of the yard of the Packhorse and Francis had a glimpse of O'Keefe inside it. 'They they are!' he had cried in triumph, as the vehicle disappeared up the road. They had followed at a discreet distance. Rosamund had begun to wonder if Harry was taking his companions home to Bishop's Court when they turned off. Following as closely as they dared, they had watched the coach turn down the lane to Feltham Farm. She had been no less surprised than Harry had been.

It was at that point Francis refused to go any further with her. 'You go on,' he had said, turning his mount. 'I will wait for you at Bishop's Court.'

'What am I supposed to do?'

'That is up to you. I only undertook to bring you to him. If you are not back at Bishop's Court by five of the clock I shall inform the Hounslow constable that there is devilment afoot. That's two hours from now.' And with that he had left her.

Cursing him under her breath, she had tethered her horse at the top of the lane and come the rest of the way on foot. So intent on reaching Harry and warning him what his cousin was threatening to do, she had forgotten about the dog. And now, here she was in the painful grip of a vicious man who showed no sign of releasing her, and faced by half a dozen stony-faced men, her husband among them, who had spilled out of the barn.

'Release me at once,' she commanded. 'May a lady not pay a call without being manhandled?'

'Pay a call?' Alf laughed. 'Last time you paid a call you went off with his lordship's bratling and cut off my wife's little income.'

'Yes, I am sorry for that,' she said, thinking quickly. 'I did not realise how much you had come to depend on it. I came to offer you some compensation.'

Harry, listening to her, could not believe that was the truth, but the alternative was worrying. He decided it was time he intervened, but he had to keep calm and stay in character, difficult though it was. 'Did I 'ear you call the wench lady?' he asked Alf. 'She ain't no lady.'

'No, she ain't,' Alf agreed. 'But seein's she married Lord Portman we have to bow and scrape to 'er.'

'Married Lord Portman!' Harry exclaimed, affecting surprise and looking directly at Rosamund, trying to convey a warning in his eyes. 'So tha's what you bin up to, Rosie, me girl, is it? I wondered why I 'adn't seen you about. 'Ow did you manage to 'ook a lord?'

'You know the wench, Gus?' O'Keefe demanded, looking from one to the other.

'Oh, Rosie and me 'ave known each other for…' He paused and addressed Rosamund. ''Ow long is it now, me darlin'?'

Rosamund swallowed hard. She had never aspired to be an actress, but she had to act now. Her life depended on it. 'That is a time I would as lief forget,' she said haughtily.

'Pity,' Harry said. ''Twere good while it lasted.'

'I reckon that fancy 'usband o' yours might give a lot for us to keep your past from coming to light, don't you think?' O'Keefe put in.

Harry could not help chuckling, but no one paid him any heed. O'Keefe turned to the other men. 'Her pa, for all his fancy ways, was one of us, until he lost his stomach for it and tried to double-cross us.'

Rosamund gasped, genuinely distressed. 'I don't believe you.'

'Don' matter what you believe, but d'you think your 'usband might believe it?'

She looked at Harry appealingly, but he would not meet her eyes. 'Of course he would not,' she said. 'My father was a gentleman.'

O'Keefe laughed and the others grinned and Harry had perforce to follow suit, though he was desperately wondering how to get them both safely away. 'Some o' the best rogues I know have been so-called gen'lemen,' he said.

'I came here in good faith,' she protested, pretending outrage. 'And all I have met with is ridicule and manhandling.' She tugged at her arm still in Alf Chappell's painful grip. 'Let me go.'

'I don't know if we can.' This from Bob. 'You know too much.'

'I don't know anything,' she cried, guessing these were the men who had given her father the counterfeit guineas. And Harry appeared to be one of them! Had he known about Papa all along? 'And I do not want to know.'

'There's my girl,' Harry put in. 'Shut yer eyes and pretend yer never was 'ere. Then your 'usband don' need to know about your pa, do 'e?

'What if she squeals?' Ironside said.

'She won't do that,' Harry said quickly. 'She's too much to lose.'

'Course, if we was to let you go, we'd need a little demonstration of good faith,' Alf Chappell said ruminatively. 'What say you restore my wife's five yeller boys each month? Genuine ones, naturally.'

She hesitated, wondering whether to tell them to do their worst, but before she could say so, Harry intervened again. 'You'd best agree, Rosie, m'dear,' he said. 'Your ol' man don' keep you on short commons, do 'e?'

'No, he's very generous,' she said.

'Glad to 'ear it,' Harry said and turned to Alf. 'I could act as go-between. Rosie pays me an' I bring it to you, alonga anythin' else I've got for you.' He laughed lewdly. 'I wouldn' mind remakin' the lady's acquaintance. We 'ad some good times t'gether.'

Alf seemed to take a long time considering this and Harry knew they were still not sure of him, but the man had released Rosamund's arm. She stood there, rubbing it. 'What makes you think I am desirous of renewing my acquaintanceship with you?' she demanded angrily of Harry.

'Oh, I think I can change your mind,' he said and before she could protest he had pulled her into his arms and was kissing her soundly. She struggled, but he held her firmly, his mouth on hers, his hands straying to her back; she could feel them spread over her buttocks, pressing her into him. In spite of her annoyance, she felt herself responding, felt her taut muscles relaxing and her mouth softening, but the raucous laughing of the other men brought her back to her predica-ment. She pulled her mouth away from his, freed her arms and beat at his chest with her clenched fists.

He laughed and stood back to look at her. 'Tha's my girl! I always did like a woman with a bit o' spirit.' But his eyes were telling a different story and she was thoroughly confused.

She wiped her hand over her swollen mouth and glared at him. 'You are a filthy beast. I hate you!'

'Oh, now tha's a pity,' he said, apparently uncon-cerned by her venom. ''Cos I reckon we could deal well together, if'n that 'usband o' yours could be got outa the way.'

'He's ten times the man you are!' She was not sure if she was acting or not. The words and the emphasis seemed to have a touch of reality about them. It was almost as if he were two separate men.

Harry's guffaw at that was Gus's, then realis-ing that the longer the exchange went on, the more they would risk giving themselves away, said, 'Never mind 'im. 'Ow did you get 'ere?'

'I rode,' she said. 'From Bishop's Court.' She looked hard at him as she spoke, but did not know if he understood.

'Oh, take the wench away,' Alf said, losing

patience. 'I've got other things to do than listen to you two bandying words. Take the first payment to the Nag's Head the day arter termorrer. If you don't...' He left the sentence hanging in the air.

'My pleasure.' Harry stepped forwards and grabbed Rosamund by the elbow. 'Come on, me lovely. You've no business 'ere.'

She allowed him to lead her away, at first in leisurely fashion, but once away from the farm-yard he quickened their pace, almost dragging her along. 'What were you thinking of, coming here?' he demanded angrily. 'You could have got us both killed.'

'I could ask you the same thing,' she snapped back. That the men had not known Harry's true identity was plain, but who did they think he really was? A criminal like themselves obviously. 'Your cousin was right...'

'My cousin?'

'Mr Portman...'

'What about him?'

'He said if we were not back at Bishop's Court in two hours, he was going to inform the Hounslow constable.'

'Inform him of what?'

'That you were up to no good. He said the men you were consorting with were criminals and you could hang…' She paused to get her breath. 'Do we have to walk so fast?'

'Yes. The sooner we get away from here the better.' His expression was grim. So Francis had recognised him at the Nag's Head, after all. He cursed himself for his carelessness. 'Where did you leave your horse?'

'At the head of the lane.'

They found the animal contentedly cropping the grass. Harry untethered it and hoisted Rosamund into the saddle, then he got up behind her, put his arms about her and picked up the reins.

Grasping the saddle in front of her, she could feel the warmth of his breath on the back of her neck as he held her close against his chest, but it was not a loving embrace. He was stiff with anger. And so was she. He had put himself and his whole household at risk, and for what? A cheap thrill, a rig, to use his cousin's words, for he certainly did not need the money, counterfeit or genuine. Was Francis right and it was done on her behalf? But how could that be? He had not known about Max and the clipped guineas the first time she had seen him dressed as vagrant. She did not doubt Francis would carry out his threat; the man could not wait to discredit his cousin and become the owner of Bishop's Court by default. She wished they could hurry, but with two on her back the mare could not go any faster.

As they neared Bishop's Court, he turned off and entered the grounds by a back lane. 'Where are you taking me?' she asked, screwing her head round to speak to him. 'We have to go home, before Mr Portman carries out his threat.'

'I can't ride up to the house like this,' he said, close to her ear, his breath making her shiver. He could still make her want him, in spite of what had happened. He reined in and slid off the horse's back. 'You go on. Placate my cousin. I shall join you as soon as I have changed.'

'Where are you going?'

'To the boathouse. I have some spare clothes there.'

She rode on, rehearsing what she was going to say to Francis. Angry as she was with Harry, she did not want him arrested. She wanted him to explain himself and make her believe in him. But it did not seem possible.

She rode round to the stable block, dismounted and made for the side door. Before she reached it, Annabelle tumbled out and threw herself into her arms. 'Mama, you're back!' Rosamund found herself hugging the child to her while the tears rained down her face.

* * *

Harry made his way to the boathouse to find Ash waiting for him. Two horses were cropping the grass nearby. 'Thank God!' Ash said. 'When I saw her ladyship and Portman going down that lane, I feared the worst.'

'It was touch and go,' Harry said, grabbing a bundle from a locker against the wall and pulling out a pair of white kid breeches. 'How did you manage to track me?'

'I saw you leave the Nag's Head and then Portman came out, grinning from ear to ear. He followed you and I followed him. When you got into that boat, your cousin turned away. I couldn't follow you by water so I decided to keep my eye on him, guessing he might know where they were taking you. He went to Portman House and soon after that he left with your wife. Where is she, by the way?'

'I sent her home.' He was busy changing his clothes as he spoke. The breeches were followed by a white shirt and a pink waistcoat. 'It appears Portman is waiting to inform the Watch of my lawlessness. I have to put a stop to that.'

Ash watched him doing up buttons. 'Did you find the coiners' workshop?'

'Yes. My dear wife was nearly my undoing, though.'

'What happened?'

Busy adjusting his fresh clothes and shrugging himself into a burgundy riding coat, Harry told him, mimicking the conversation, making Ash laugh. 'You may think it was funny,' he said. 'I didn't. I thought we would both be done away with. Luckily Rosamund kept a cool head.'

'Not one to panic, is she?'

'No.'

'So she knows what you have been doing?'

'No. She thinks I am one of the coiners and I discovered her father was in league with them and was probably killed because he lost his appetite for it. And there's her brother, almost certainly passing counterfeit money. How can I tell her that I am sworn to track them down? She will think I set out to trap them through her, especially as she mentioned O'Keefe's name to me.'

'She knows him?' Ash asked in surprise.

'I don't think she has ever met him, she showed no sign of recognition when he spoke to her. Unless, of course, she is a better actress than I thought.'

'Well, you should know.'

'That is the trouble, I don't.'

'You cannot let that gang get away with their crimes. James would never condone it.'

'Of course not, but how do I protect my wife?'

'Do you believe she is innocent?'

'Either that or she is the world's best actress. She was visibly shocked when O'Keefe said her father was one of the gang.' He was once again dressed as Lord Portman. He pulled his fingers through his hair, tied it back with its ribbon and crammed a bicorn hat on top. He bundled up Gus Housman's clothes and put them in the locker. 'I must go. Are you coming back to the house with me?'

'No, I thank you.' Ash chuckled suddenly. 'I am expected at a certain little lady's house in Leicester Square tonight. If I set off now, I should be in time.'

'I hope to be back myself tomorrow, but I have a private matter to sort out before then,' Harry told him. 'You would be doing me a favour if you could alert the rest of the Gentlemen and the Runners where they can lay their hands on that gang. The sooner the better. I am supposed to be taking more coins to the Nag's Head the day after tomorrow and I would as lief not be obliged to do it.'

'My pleasure.' Ash mounted up. 'I'll see you back in town.' He left at a canter.

Harry jumped into his own saddle and rode to Bishop's Court. He was not looking forward to a confrontation with Rosamund.

As soon as they were indoors, Annabelle had begun firing questions at Rosamund. 'Why are you back early? Miss Gunstock said you would not be back for another two days. I have been keeping a journal and crossing off the days in it. Where is Papa? Did you see the king and queen crowned?'

'Yes, I did.' Although her mind was on Francis Portman, wondering where he was and if he had already gone to carry out his threat, Rosamund did her best to satisfy the child, explaining that she had missed her so much that when she went riding, she had simply turned her horse in the direction of Bishop's Court without thinking.

The child had been delighted by that and did not question it.

When Rosamund said the same thing to Mrs Rivers a little later, the housekeeper was not so easily taken in. 'But, my lady,' she said, 'won't his lordship be worried about you?' If she wondered why her mistress should go riding in London in a gown that had seen better days and her hair all over the place, she did not mention it. Nor that

London to Bishop's Court was a long ride for a lady to undertake alone.

Rosamund gave a light laugh. 'Oh, he caught me up before I had gone very far and came with me. He stopped on the way to speak to the smithy. I think his horse needed a new shoe.' She paused. 'Have you seen Mr Portman? I believe his lordship was expecting him.'

'I think he is in the library, my lady. He arrived some time ago and has been prowling about the place ever since. Doesn't seem able to sit still.'

Rosamund sent Annabelle back to Miss Gunstock and went in search of Francis. He had taken several books from the shelves and had them spread out on the table. She noticed that they were all about Bishop's Court, its history and the men who had owned it. He looked up as she entered and scrambled to his feet. 'Where is he?' he demanded without the preamble of a greeting.

She made herself smile. 'How do you do, Cousin Francis? I hope the servants have been looking after you properly.'

'Yes, oh, yes,' he said vaguely. 'I thank you. Did you find Harry?'

'Yes, indeed. He was visiting the Chappells. If you recall, they looked after Annabelle for years. He wanted to ask them something about her health when she was with them. He will be here directly. He stopped to speak to the smithy.'

'Going calling dressed as a muckworm? I find that hard to believe.'

'He was not dressed as a muckworm, Francis,' she lied coolly. 'I fear your own exquisite taste in clothes has blinded you to what others are wearing. He is dressed in his usual attire.' She hoped fervently he would not ask her to describe what Harry was wearing. In order to prevent it, she picked up one of the books he had been looking at and rattled on. 'I see you have been amusing yourself with the history of Bishop's Court. It is fascinating, don't you think? The original Mr Bishop was a character to be reckoned with…'

She was greatly relieved when Harry put in an appearance. 'You here, Frank?' he said, as if surprised to see him. 'I shall soon begin to ask myself why I have suddenly become so popular. You used not to visit so often before I married my lady. Perhaps it is she who is the attraction.'

'No, no, course it ain't,' Francis blustered. 'Oh, I don't mean her ladyship ain't attractive. Very comely she is, but…'

Harry laughed. 'I understand, Frank, you do not need to empty the butter boat.'

Rosamund was becoming thoroughly embarrassed. 'I have been telling Cousin Francis that you stopped at Feltham Farm to ask Mrs Chappell about Annabelle's health while she was staying with them,' she told Harry. 'Did she satisfy your questions?'

'Partly,' he told her, without betraying by so much as a flicker of an eyelid that this was the first he had heard of it. 'I may have to pursue the matter further.'

'If you will excuse me,' she said, anxious to escape, 'I will go and change my gown. Mr Portman, will you be staying tonight?'

He bowed. 'If I may.'

Rosamund left them, thankful that she had not taken her entire wardrobe to London with her and wishing she had Janet with her, not only to help her change, but as an ally. She was feeling dreadfully lonely. And there was worse to come.

Harry refrained from saying anything but polite nothings to her during supper when Francis was present, but the atmosphere between them was icy. If Francis noticed it, he did not say anything, but kept up the conversation almost as a monologue. Rosamund said 'Yes' and 'No' in appropriate places and smiled a lot, though she ate nothing. Harry was unnaturally jovial, agreeing or disagreeing with his cousin in the politest way. On the surface it was a pleasant evening, though beneath the sociability the undercurrents were pulling each one of them in different directions. Rosamund was relieved when the meal ended and she was able to leave them to their cognac. 'I am very tired after my long ride,' she said. 'I think I will retire. Goodnight, Cousin Francis.'

She escaped to her room, but she did not undress. She sat on a chair by the window and looked out on the courtyard and beyond that to the park where a herd of deer roamed. Night was falling and the trees in the distance were black shadows, though the church spire stood out in silhouette against the night sky. No sound broke the silence except an owl hooting in a nearby barn and a dog barking somewhere in the distance. It was peaceful and she had come to love it, not because of the value of the land which must have been enormous, nor because she was the wife of the lord of the manor and must be addressed as 'my lady', but because it had felt like home from the first day she arrived and because she loved its owner. It did not matter what he had done, she could not help but love him.

She turned as the door opened and Harry came into the room.

'Now, madam,' he said, before she could protest at the intrusion, 'we will have that little talk, if you please.' He pulled up a chair and sat beside her at the window. Even by moonlight she could see he had pulled off his cravat and his eyes were dark-rimmed from fatigue. 'And do not say you are tired. I know you are. And so am I, but I do not intend that you should sleep on it.'

'I do not want to sleep on it. Nor could I. And do not look so fierce at me, I am not afraid of you and I have done nothing wrong.' She paused and went on to the attack. 'But you are...' She floundered under his steady gaze.

'Me?' He pretended surprise, watching her face, knowing that if she tried to dissemble he would see it in her eyes. Her eyes would always give her away.

She recovered her composure with an effort. 'Yes, you. You have joined a band of no-good outlaws and provided them with coins to mutilate. I cannot for the life of me understand why you did that or why you let your daughter stay in that den of iniquity. Is that how you got in with them, through Annabelle?'

'No. And leave Annabelle out of it.'

'How can we? Your behaviour is bound to affect her.'

'She need never know anything of it.'

'She will if you hang for it.'

He laughed harshly. 'I promise you, I shall not hang for it.'

'Francis thinks you will. Did you manage to convince him not to go to the Watch?'

'He has nothing to tell them. He listens at doors—' He stood up suddenly and went to the door, opened it and peered up and down the corridor, then he shut it and returned to his seat. 'He hears half a story and invents the rest...'

'Is that so? I think he must have heard more than half to know that you were going to Chiswick by boat. I caught you red-handed, Harry.'

'And I caught you. Why did *you* go to Feltham Farm? After more clipped guineas to take to your brother, were you?' He did not know why he was being so belligerent, but he had to get at the truth and if it meant turning the tables against her, then he must do it. How could he protect her if he did not know the whole story?

She was shocked to realise he knew about Max passing those coins. 'No, of course not,' she retorted, doing her best to retain her anger and sense of injustice. 'I knew nothing about what was going on there. We followed you there from Chiswick.'

'Francis denies taking you there; he said he rode

with you because you had no escort, but it was your idea to turn off at the farm and he did not want to become involved, so he rode on here.'

'I am sorry to say it, but your cousin is a liar and you do not have to look far to find out why. If he can ruin our marriage, he will.'

He had to concede that and smiled ruefully. 'Then why did you go there? And do not say it was to compensate Mrs Chappell for taking Annabelle away, for I will not believe that.'

'Of course that was not true, but I had to say something, didn't I? I was shocked when I realised where you were going and even then I did not know it had anything to do with forging counterfeit coins. That was what they were doing, was it not?'

'You know it was. Oh, you were clever enough not to recognise O'Keefe when you saw him—'

'O'Keefe?' she queried. 'Was he there?'

Was she really surprised or was she still acting a part? He could believe Sophie Charron, the real actress, could do it, but could the woman who sat facing him? His voice softened. 'You did not know?'

'I never met him. Which one was he?'

'He was the one who tried to blackmail you with

telling your husband of your association with Gus Housman.'

She managed a smile. 'Is that the name you go by? You know, I am beginning to think of you as two men, two very different men. The trouble is I am married to both of you.'

'And have no particular liking for either of us.'

'I did not say that,' she protested. 'I certainly have no liking for Mr Housman and I wish he could disappear before he finds his head in a noose.'

'Perhaps he will,' he said softly. 'When his work is done.'

'Work for that dreadful gang!' she retorted, too incensed to notice the change in his tone. 'Pulling the economy down with your illegal activities, making money from others' misery. I am sure they were responsible for my father's death…'

'But is that not why you married me, Rosamund?' he asked levelly. 'To root out Sir Joshua's tormentors?'

'No, it was not and I certainly did not ask you to join them.'

'But that was the way I chose to do it.'

'For me?' She gasped in surprise. Francis had been right, after all. He had assumed his disguise to help her and she had been angry and ungrateful. Oh, how she wished she had never mentioned Mr

O'Keefe to him! It had been the biggest mistake of her life.

'Partly. Partly to bring a rogue to justice.' It was only half a lie and justified under the circumstances.

'But I changed my mind.'

'Yes. That was when I began to have doubts about you. And they seemed to be confirmed when I discovered your brother was passing clipped coins. Now where did he get them from, I wonder?'

'I don't know.'

'A gentleman would never call a lady a liar,' he said evenly. 'Particularly if that lady happened to be his wife, but I do not know what else to call you.'

Rosamund remained silent, realising it was too late to retrieve the situation without betraying Max and much as she disapproved of what he had done, he was still her brother. And if he was arrested, she would soon follow, because she had known about the coins. Guilty by default. She sat looking at her hands folded in her lap and would not meet his gaze.

'I think,' he said quietly and reasonably, 'that we have reached the end of the road, my dear. I will make arrangements to have this marriage of ours annulled…'

She looked up then, her eyes betraying her dismay. 'So that you may have me arrested and give evidence against me?'

'Do you know,' he said slowly, 'I never thought of that. I assumed you were telling me the truth when you said you knew nothing of what was going on.'

'I was telling the truth.'

'Then there is nothing more to be said. I will not cast you out without a shilling. You shall have your own house and money enough to support you in comfort. And in the fullness of time, you will find a new husband. One you feel able to trust.'

'I am sorry I accused you,' she said dully, unable to take in what he was proposing, even though she had been half-expecting it. 'I did not know… And I am sorry about Max. I can quite see that you would not wish to associate with a family like ours.'

'You misunderstand me.'

'Yes, I suppose I do,' she said wearily. 'I do not understand anything about you.' She stood up. 'I think I should like to go to bed.'

'Very well.' He rose too and they stood facing each other, a chasm between them neither seemed able to bridge and yet they had only to reach out and they would be in each other's arms. But neither seemed able to take that small step. He picked up her hand, put it to his lips. 'Goodnight, my dear.'

Then he was gone and she flung herself on her bed in a paroxysm of tears.

Chapter Eleven

Harry went to his own room and sank wearily on to the bed, his hands dangling between his knees. His interview with Rosamund had not gone the way he had planned it. Their exchange had become more bitter and accusatory than even he had believed possible. How had it happened? Was his association with the Piccadilly Gentlemen and the criminal fraternity making him hard and cynical? Did he really believe she was hand in glove with the very coiners he had spent months hunting down? Of course he did not. Nor was her brother. That foolish man had simply taken advantage of a situation not of his making. Why had he not told her he understood that? Why had he pretended to be angry with her?

Oh, he had been furious at first, because she could have given the game away to Chappell and his gang and only his quick thinking and her swift reading of his mind had saved the day. But riding across the Heath with his arms about her, his nostrils full of the sweet scent of her hair, he had soon calmed down. If it had not been for the need to change his clothes and placate his cousin, he would have talked it over sensibly with her straight away, established her innocence and his reasons for doing what he did in an atmosphere of goodwill. He would have offered her the annulment for her sake, not his. Instead, his anger with Frank had taken him from that odious man to her room in the frame of mind for a confrontation. And what a confrontation! He groaned and put his head in his hands. There seemed no way back.

Rosamund rose bleary-eyed next morning, dressed in the shabby gown she had worn the day before and went down to breakfast to face a stony-faced Harry. He was eating toasted bread and boiled eggs, but rose as she entered the room. She bade him good morning and began helping herself from the dishes on the table.

He sat down again. 'Rosamund,' he said, 'you are still my wife. There is no need to dress like a servant. I wish you would wear something more befitting the lady of the house.'

'It is good enough for pottering about Bishop's

Court while I await my fate.' She spoke flatly, drained of all emotion.

'Your fate?'

'Yes. Am I not to be disgraced? Held up to ridicule? Banished?'

'Good God, no!' He reached out and put his hand over hers. 'I am sorry for the way I behaved last night. It was cruel and unfair. I should have explained myself better. You were never meant to see me as Gus Housman.'

'I am aware of that.' Oh, how difficult it was to pretend to be calm, when the very pressure of his warm hand over hers was making her heart beat wildly in her chest.

'Hear me out, please.' He paused, but when she did not reply, he went on. 'Have you ever heard of the Piccadilly Gentlemen?'

'Yes, according to your cousin, they are a drinking and gambling club who take on impossible wagers. I suppose pretending to be Gus Housman was one of those.'

He could have said yes, it was, but having made a start on his confession, he meant to finish it. 'No. And the Piccadilly Gentlemen are not like that at all. Their real name is The Society for the Discovery and Apprehension of Criminals. I am one of them and Gus Housman is the guise I wear when tracking down law-breakers.'

'You are a thieftaker!' she exclaimed. Of all the possibilities she had considered, being a thieftaker had not been not one of them.

'You could so describe me, but the Piccadilly Gentlemen are no ordinary thieftakers. We are all gentlemen, we do not do it for money, but to make the country a safer place for its honest citizens. I had no idea about Sir Joshua and O'Keefe until you told me the story. It shocked me because I had been tracking O'Keefe for some time.'

'Why did you not tell me?'

'It was safer for you not to know.'

'Did you know the forge was at Feltham Farm?'

'Not until yesterday. And when you turned up as well, I was so taken aback, all I could think of was to get us both out safely. And then O'Keefe said Sir Joshua was one of them...'

'He wasn't. I swear he wasn't.'

'But he did have false coins and your brother did pass them.'

'Yes,' she admitted. 'Max found them in Papa's study. He said Papa had been cheated and they should have been genuine and he did not see why we should be the losers over it.'

'He gave you some of them?'

'No, I never had any of them, nor the proceeds from them either.' She gave a mirthless laugh. 'Unless you count the wine at our wedding…'

He chuckled. It was the first sign of good humour he had shown for two days if you did not count the false bonhomie of dinner the night before. 'I drank some of that too, you know.'

'Then we are both guilty.'

'I think we can discount that.'

'I can see your predicament,' she said slowly. 'You cannot have your wife and her brother arrested; it would be uncomfortable for you, so you decided to rid yourself of the wife.'

'Oh, Rosamund, my dear, do you think so little of me that you can think I would stoop to that? I suggested an annulment because I thought that was what you wanted, that you might be glad to be free of a man who could not fulfil the role of husband.'

'Could we not talk about that?'

He opened his mouth to speak, but whatever he had been going to say remained unsaid, because Francis bowled into the room, a smile on his face. 'Good morning, my lady. Good morning, Harry.' He did not wait for them to answer, but went to the sideboard and examined the breakfast dishes.

'Ham and chops and hot oatcakes. I envy you your cook, Coz.'

'You are up betimes,' Harry said, assuming cheerfulness. 'Does that mean you are thinking of making an early start back to town?'

Rosamund wondered if her husband was glad of the interruption. It saved him having to explain himself and she was still left with that annulment hanging over her. She sat silently watching, trying not to let her tears betray her, as Francis sat down with his loaded plate.

'Are you coming?' Francis asked.

'Later. I have one or two things to see to before I can leave. But do not let me delay you.' He stood up, gave Rosamund a brief smile, which she could not interpret, and strode from the room.

Francis shrugged. 'I am afraid I am in bad odour with my cousin,' he said, tackling his breakfast with gusto. 'You were not meant to find out about his dark secret, but all I wished to do was warn you. I hope I have not caused a quarrel…'

Rosamund knew that was exactly what he had hoped. She smiled sweetly. 'No, Cousin Francis, you have not caused a quarrel, however much you might have hoped for it. Please excuse me.' And with that she hurried from the room in search of Harry. She was not going to let him off that easily.

She found him in the stables with Annabelle, having his horse and the child's pony saddled. 'We are going for a ride,' Annabelle said excitedly. 'Are you coming with us?'

'If you will have me.'

'Oh, we will, won't we, Papa?' she appealed to her father.

'Of course.'

While Honey was being saddled, Rosamund went to change into a habit and soon rejoined them. They rode out across the park.

'How did Hector come to be here?' Rosamund asked Harry, as they followed slowly behind Annabelle. 'You did not ride him out of London.'

He smiled. 'You and Francis were not the only ones to follow me. Sir Ashley was hard on your heels with my mount.'

'Is he one of the Piccadilly Gentlemen too?'

'Yes, and a staunch friend. He rode back to town last night to alert the Bow Street Runners to raid that farm. If the coiners are not all already behind bars, they will be before the day is out.'

'Do you think they will try to incriminate you?'

'La, what for?' he said lightly. 'I am nothing but

a foolish macaroni whom they made look even more foolish.'

'I meant your alter ego, Gus Housman. They will guess who informed on them and if any managed to escape arrest, they will be out for revenge.'

'I am afraid Gus will have to meet his end,' he said ruefully, remembering Matilda Watson and her threat. She was probably still at large, but there was no need to worry Rosamund about her. He chuckled. ''Tis a pity, he came in very useful. But there are other guises; he is not the only character in my repertoire.'

It was typical of him to make light of it, but she would not be easy in her mind until every last one of the gang had paid for his crime at the end of a rope.

'What will happen to Mrs Chappell and all those children? I could not like her, but the poor woman should not have to suffer for the sins of her husband.'

'I will take care of her.' He laughed suddenly. 'You are supposed to be paying her five guineas a month, to keep your sordid secret. We will not give her guineas but smaller coins, enough to bring up her children. Guineas are too much of a temptation.'

'I agree with you on that.' She paused and then

went on, 'I wish I knew how my father came to have those coins. I do not believe he was one of that wicked gang.'

'I am sure you are right,' he said lightly.

'Will O'Keefe name him, do you think?'

'What reason can he have for doing so?' He smiled reassuringly. 'It will not help to get him off. Put it from your mind.'

'Papa, Mama, watch me,' Annabelle cried, making her pony jump a narrow ditch.

'Bravo!' Harry called, as Annabelle, triumphant, reined in to wait for them.

'Harry,' Rosamund said, gathering her courage, 'I have come to love your little daughter as my own. It will break my heart to part from her.'

He turned to look at her. Her eyes were softly appealing, her lips slightly parted. A wisp of hair blew across her face and she pushed it away with an impatient gesture. How could he let her go? She had become part of his life, the person he returned to at the end of the day, the one with whom he most wanted to share his thoughts, his hopes, his plans. She had brought light and life back to Bishop's Court and given him back his daughter. Could she also banish his demons—given time?

'I had no idea you were planning to leave,' he said.

'I'm not, but I thought you...' She stumbled over her words. 'You seem to have forgotten our bargain.'

'I *have* forgotten it,' he said, making her heart falter. 'It was a foolish idea and one I have regretted making from the bottom of my heart.'

'Oh, then I must go.'

'Is that your wish?'

'Oh, no, you know it is not. I have been happy here.'

'Even though I have been less than a husband to you?' He spoke softly, reaching across and covering her hand with his own.

'Yes, because I believe there is a very good reason for it. And you are going to explain it to me, aren't you?' If she did not take the lead, he never would get round to it.

'Yes.' He retrieved his hand. 'Shall we turn back?'

Francis had left while they had been riding. They ate nuncheon with Annabelle and afterwards the child was sent back to Miss Gunstock, leaving them alone, sitting side by side on a sofa in the small parlour. The time for explanations had come.

'I hardly know where to begin.' he said.

She smiled. 'The beginning might be a good idea.'

'When I met your brother and he told me about you—'

'No, before that, long before that,' she said quietly. However much it hurt, she was determined to make him open his heart to her. Even if he could not love her as she loved him, she wanted to understand what made him the man he was. 'Back to when you were young, back to Beth.'

He sighed. 'I loved her, you know. When we married I was twenty-four and she was sixteen. I had known her all her life. Both sets of parents approved the match, both wanted grandchildren. In retrospect I do not think either of us was ready for that. Beth was tiny, almost like a doll, her body not yet fully formed. When she became pregnant everyone rejoiced—' He stopped, his voice faded and his eyes clouded as if he were far away from her. She put her hand over his and squeezed it gently to encourage him.

'All went well, until the birth.' He shuddered at the memory. 'It was her seventeenth birthday. We had been laughing together and saying what a grand birthday present a baby would be. Neither of us foresaw how difficult it would be. Beth had always been cosseted, she was not used to pain and the doctors had no patience with her; I could hear them scolding her. They sent me away. I paced the garden, but I could hear her, even there. She cursed me, Rosamund. With her dying breath, she cursed me. She said God would punish me for what I had done to her.'

'She was distraught, Harry. I am sure she did not mean it.'

'But I have been punished. Her ghost haunts me. I cannot bring myself to love again. Dare not, for how can I put someone for whom I have tender feelings through that torture?'

'It is not torture to someone who longs for a child, Harry,' she said, her heart lifting with joy that he seemed to be admitting tender feelings for her. 'What is a little pain compared to the joy of holding your own child in your arms? If Beth had lived, I am sure she would have said the same thing. If she had recovered and held Annabelle in her arms and felt her at the breast, she would have regretted those unkind words and begged your pardon.'

'Bless you, my dear. But I was wrong to make that bargain with you. And I cannot forgive myself for it. It was your brother telling me about your predicament after your father died that put the idea in my head. If I could marry a stranger, someone

I did not know, could coldly make her with child and beget me an heir, then I might lay the ghost to rest. But then I found I could not do it.' He paused, waiting for her to castigate him for it, but she said nothing and he went on. 'I came to know you, to appreciate your qualities and all my reasoning went out of the door. For that I beg your pardon and in return I offer you your freedom.'

'Supposing I do not want my freedom?'

He turned to look at her to find her smiling at him. 'But I might never…'

'I am prepared to risk that.'

He took both her hands in his and looked earnestly into her face, studying every contour, the expressive eyes which told him of her sincerity, the slightly parted lips, the high colour in her cheeks. He leaned forwards and put a gentle kiss upon her forehead. 'Oh, my dear, I do not deserve you,' he said. 'But if you will have patience…'

She would have all the patience in the world, she promised herself.

They returned to London the following morning to find Mrs Crossley flying hither and thither, trying to organise their ball and wondering if it should go ahead if the host and hostess failed to turn up for it. Janet was quite sure her mistress had met a dreadful end at the hands of robbers on the road somewhere and was in tears. Harry calmed Mrs Crossley and Rosamund assured Janet she was whole and hearty. When they had refreshed themselves and changed their clothes, husband and wife sat down to a meal together before Harry left to make his report to the Piccadilly Gentlemen.

He was more content than he had been since Beth's death. That his wife knew and understood how he felt was a great weight off his mind, though it had taken more courage than a little to admit he could not do what came naturally to every man and made him less than a man because of it. They would be companions, sharing their good days and their bad days, without secrets. He was glad he had told her about the Piccadilly Gentlemen.

Rosamund settled down in the small salon with a book, but it soon dropped into her lap while she sat musing. She and Harry had come to an understanding but that was all it was: an understanding. He had blessed her and said he did not deserve her, but he had not mentioned love, neither of them had, though her heart ached with it. He had loved Beth, still did, she supposed, which was why the memory of her death still haunted him.

She remembered when he had first suggested

marriage he had said, 'I am not disposed to fall in love again.' She had accepted that, but she had not, at the time, known the real man beneath the fop, had not expected to find herself falling in love with a gentle, caring, charismatic and courageous man. He made her heart beat faster when he gave her one of his enigmatic smiles. He made her legs weak and her whole body tremble when he touched her. What would it be like to have him desire her, really make love to her, to be told he loved her?

Sighing, she picked up her book again, but had hardly begun to read when a footman came to tell her that Travers had arrived and wished to speak to his lordship.

'Travers?' she queried. 'Is something wrong at Bishop's Court?'

'I do not know, my lady. I told him his lordship was out. He was somewhat agitated and asked to speak to you.'

'Then send him in at once.'

A moment later Travers rushed into the room, pulled up short in order to bow perfunctorily. 'My lady, Miss Annabelle has disappeared. We have searched everywhere for her, all over the house, in every nook and cranny of the grounds—there is not a sign of her. Her pony has gone too.'

'Oh, no!' Rosamund sprang to her feet in alarm.

The child was as fearless as her papa and would have thought it a great adventure to ride out alone. But she had undoubtedly taken a tumble and could be lying injured in a ditch. Or worse. It did not bear thinking about. 'How did you get here?'

'I brought the carriage, my lady. I thought you would have need of it.'

'I will come back with you.' She gave orders for someone to fetch Harry from Lord Trentham's. How long would he take to arrive? Should she wait for him or go on ahead? Supposing he was not at Lord Trentham's, but had gone on somewhere else, perhaps in one of his disguises? It might take hours to track him down. There was no time to waste. She scribbled a note for him and with Janet in attendance, set off to cover the same ground she had covered only that morning.

The journey, though only a matter of an hour and a half, seemed interminable and night fell before they arrived. Rosamund scrambled from the carriage before the coachman or a footman could let down the step and rushed into the house. Mrs Rivers and Miss Gunstock were in the hall, along with half-a-dozen outdoor servants, obviously in a huddle trying to decide what to do.

'Have you found her?' Rosamund demanded, looking at their anxious faces.

'No, my lady,' Miss Gunstock answered her. 'But her pony has come back alone—'

'She must have had a fall,' Rosamund said, deciding now was not the time to berate the governess for neglecting her duty or the grooms for saddling her mount and letting her go. 'She cannot have gone far. We must continue the search. If she is hurt and alone…'

'There is more, my lady.' This from one of the grooms. 'The pony had this attached to its saddle.' He held out a scrap of paper.

Rosamund took it and scanned it swiftly. 'Lord Portman, your daughter is safe for now. Bring one thousand guineas to Feltham Farm and she will be returned to you unharmed. Come alone.'

What she had dreaded had come to pass; not all the coiners had been arrested and whoever was left was determined on revenge. They had seen through Harry's disguise and were using Annabelle to wreak vengeance. She handed Travers the note. 'Don't unharness the horses. I need the carriage. His lordship can follow when he arrives.'

'My lady, I am not sure I should obey you,' the groom protested, after reading the note. 'His lordship would not like you putting yourself at risk. It is dark and that road is dangerous and you do not know what lies in wait for you.'

'Annabelle needs me now, not some time in the future.' She left the house with everyone behind her. 'I want three men in the coach with me and someone up beside you.'

He sighed and gave instructions to the biggest and strongest of the men to arm themselves and everyone piled in the coach and they set off towards Hounslow Heath at a swift canter.

The meeting of the Piccadilly Gentlemen had finished early and Harry had gone from there by chair to Newgate prison and requested to speak to Michael O'Keefe. The whole gang had been arrested at Feltham Farm, caught red-handed doctoring the coins Harry had given them. They were due for an early trial and a one-way trip to Tyburn before the month was up. It gave the Gentlemen, and Harry in particular, a great sense of achievement, but there was still one mystery that had not been solved and for Rosamund's sake, he would try and solve it.

Rather than conduct the exquisitely dressed fop through the filthy, noisome prison to the cells, O'Keefe was brought to him in the governor's office. The coiner stood facing Harry defiantly. 'What do you want with me?' the man demanded. 'Want to satisfy your curiosity, do you, and have a bit of fun at a poor prisoner's expense? Want me to sing for my supper, do you?'

'Yes,' Harry said. 'That is exactly what I had in mind. Sing me the tale of Sir Joshua Chalmers.'

'Sir Joshua Chalmers. Never heard of 'im. Who's 'e?'

'He was my wife's father.'

'Oh, now I place you. You're Lord Portman, him that got robbed on Hounslow Heath a month or so back. Did they ever catch the rascal, my lord?' And he grinned widely.

'No, I fear not. Do you know him?'

O'Keefe shrugged. 'D'you think I would tell you if I did?'

'It matters not. I am more interested in Sir Joshua.'

'What makes you think I know anythin' about 'im?'

'The Barnstaple Mining Company. You are listed as its proprietor. What did you mine? Gold, was it?'

O'Keefe laughed. 'You could say that.'

'What happened?' When O'Keefe stood stubbornly before him and refused to answer, he went on. 'You have nothing to lose by telling me; there is enough evidence to hang you already and it would be better to clear your conscience before you meet your Maker, don't you think? On the other hand, should you be obdurate, I am not particular as to the condition in which I send you back to the cells.'

O'Keefe laughed his contempt. 'You! A puff of wind would blow you over.'

Harry stepped forwards, grabbed the man's arm and twisted it behind him, pulling it up between his shoulder blades until he cried out in pain. 'This puff of wind is a tornado, O'Keefe.' He gave him another sharp tug.

'Leave off, can't you. I'll speak.' Harry relaxed his hold and the man stood rubbing his arm and shoulder. 'But it's atween you an' me,' he said. 'If you try bringin' it up in court, I'll deny it.'

'I won't do that. I simply want to set my wife's mind at rest.'

O'Keefe looked at him and decided it would be best to comply. 'I met Sir Joshua at the Cocoa Tree. There's a lot of business goes on there…'

'I know. Go on.'

'He was bemoaning his investments were not doing well, so I told him about the mining company. He bought into it…'

'With gold coins, I assume.'

'Yes. I don't know 'ow, but 'e smelled a rat and asked that lawyer fellow of 'is to look into the company and he found it only existed on paper. Sir Joshua asked for his money back.'

'And you would not agree to that, would you?'

'Course not. But he threatened to go to the law, so we offered half what we paid...'

'In clipped coins,' Harry interjected.

'Yes, you don' think we was stupid enough to give him real coins, do you? We needed them.'

'Did he realise they were clipped?'

'Oh, I told 'im, offered 'im a deal, passing the coins. He'd ha' made a good passer, bein's he mixed in high society where guineas don't raise eyebrows, but he refused and said he was goin' to take 'em to the law. Couldn't let that happen, could we? 'E had a little accident on the way 'ome. Trouble was we didn't know where he'd put the money. Had to lie low 'til we were sure the law weren't arter us and then we meant to search 'is 'ouse. But the lady moved out and took the coins with 'er.'

Harry did not correct him. He picked up his gloves and hat and went to the door.

'You goin' to put a good word in for me with the judge, your lordship?' O'Keefe called after him.

Harry turned. 'The only good word for you, Mr O'Keefe, is dead.' He nodded to the turnkey who had been waiting outside and strode away, out into the night, back to Portman House, back to Rosamund. He was smiling and humming a little tune as he went. He would tell Rosamund what he had learned, that her father had been innocent, but he did not think it was necessary to tell her that he had been murdered. It would only distress her.

He had begun to think she was right when she said Beth had cursed him *in extremis* and would have retracted had she lived. Did women really welcome the pain of childbirth? Was it a little like going into battle? You knew you might be wounded but you did it anyway for the reward of victory. If he thought of it like that, perhaps…

He left his horse in the mews, so absorbed in happy contemplation, he did not notice the carriage had gone. He even forgot to mince like the coxcomb he was supposed to be as he hurried into the house. His wife was not at home, the whole household was awake and buzzing and it was a minute or two before he could make out what had happened. And then he had Hector saddled again and galloped off in the direction of the Kensington Road, ignoring the shouts of chairmen, linkmen and pedestrians who had to dodge out of his way.

Rosamund's little force of men left the coach a little way short of the farm and scattered on foot, leaving only the driver to take the carriage right up to the house. The dog barked just as furiously as before and Mrs Chappell came to the door and stood watching as Rosamund stepped down and edged round it. 'Madam, I would be obliged if you would call that dog to heel,' she called out. 'I cannot speak to you above the noise of its barking.'

Mrs Chappell came out and smacked the dog on the nose and it slunk away as far as the chain would let it and sank down. 'What are you doin' 'ere?' she demanded. 'Send you in 'is place, did 'e? Too frightened to come 'isself?'

'Not at all.' Whatever happened she must remain calm, Rosamund told herself, at least until the men were in place. 'His lordship is not at home. I promised you compensation for the loss of your income and that you shall have, but only if you return Annabelle to me unharmed.' She looked up at the house. Apart from the light spilling from the open door, there were no lights to be seen. 'Where is she?'

Mrs Chappell shrugged. 'Le's see the colour of yer money first.'

'No. I want to see Annabelle.'

The woman jerked her head towards the barn where the gang had worked on the coins. Rosamund wondered how many of them had evaded arrest and were there waiting for her. But the thought of Annabelle and how frightened she must be drove her on. She walked purposefully towards the door. It opened and a woman stood silhouetted against the light behind her. There was no sign of the Chappell men or any of the others. 'So we have the lady of the house, do we?' The woman gave Rosamund a mock curtsy. 'Lady Portman, pleased to make your acquaintance. Or should I say Mrs Gus Housman.'

Rosamund stifled the gasp that came to her throat. 'I do not know what you are talking about,' she said. 'I came in good faith to recompense Mrs Chappell and take my stepdaughter home.'

'Can't let you do that,' the woman said, moving forwards and seizing Rosamund by the arm. 'It's 'is lordship we want and until 'e comes, you and the girl are stayin' right 'ere.' She dragged Rosamund into the barn and bolted the door.

Rosamund looked about her. A lamp on a table illuminated the small area around it, but the corners of the building were in darkness. Rosamund had no idea how many men lurked in the shadows. There was no fire, no liquid gold, no evidence that the coiners had ever been there. But the room was peopled with children, some big strong youths, some ten or eleven, some only toddlers, all dirty and ragged. They surrounded her in silence. 'Annabelle!' she called. 'Annabelle!'

A muffled sound came from a corner. The child was lying trussed up on a heap of sacks. Rosamund pushed her way past the children and ran to her. She pulled the gag from her mouth and began untying her bonds. 'It's all right, sweetheart,' she said, pulling the child into her arms. 'Mama's here.'

'And Mama stays here until we have what we want,' the woman said, watching them. 'If Portman thinks he can get away with sending my ol' feller to the nubbing cheat, 'e's about to learn different. Now I ha' got two hostages instead o' one.'

'Lord Portman is in London,' Rosamund said. 'He won't come tonight, you may be sure.'

'I can wait. I've already spent three months trackin' the muckgrubber down, another few hours is neither 'ere nor there.'

'His lordship has not been hiding,' Rosamund said. The longer she could keep the woman talking the better. 'It surely did not take three months to find him.'

'Not 'im. Gus Housman. I learned 'is name from the keeper of the Nag's Head. But 'e disappeared. I didn't know Micky O'Keefe knew 'im.'

'What has that to do with Lord Portman?'

'Ah, that I did not know until two days ago. I was

comin' 'ere when I saw you leave with Housman. It was the first time I'd seen 'im since my folks were took, so I followed. You went on to the big 'ouse, but the man went to the boathouse by the lake and changed his clothes. La! There was his lordship, as fine a gentleman as you please.'

'What do you want of him?' Rosamund asked while she rocked the weeping Annabelle in her arms and listened for any sound from outside. She did not want the men to start shooting; they might hit the children, though how she could warn them without also alerting the woman, she had no idea.

'For sending me whole family to Tyburn? What do you think? I want them pardoned.'

'You are mistaken if you think my husband has the power to overturn the judge's sentence.'

They heard the dog set up a frenzied barking. Immediately the woman arranged the children around Rosamund and Annabelle, ordering them not to move.

'Using children is a coward's way,' Rosamund said.

'Hold yer tongue! I gotta listen.' She went and put her ear to the door.

'Tilly! Tilly!' It was the voice of Mrs Chappell. 'He's come and he's alone. Let the children out, for Gawd's sake. They ain't done you no 'arm.'

Tilly slowly unbolted the door and opened it a crack in order to see what was going on in the yard. Immediately it was pushed violently open, knocking her back against the wall, and Harry strode into the room. 'Go to your mother,' he ordered the children. They scampered away, glad to be free and the doorway was filled with the men Rosamund had brought with her. They burst in, just as Tilly recovered from the impact and rushed at Harry. He turned swiftly and grabbed both her arms. 'Tie her up, Travers,' he said quietly. 'She can join her husband and parents.' Then he turned his attention to Rosamund and Annabelle, fell on his knees and put his arms round both of them and kissed first one and then the other.

'Are you hurt?' he asked, looking from one to the other.

'No,' Rosamund assured him. 'Annabelle was frightened...'

'But I am fine now you have come, Papa,' the child said. 'And Mama was so brave.'

'I know she is,' he said, smiling at Rosamund. 'The bravest woman I know.' He stood up. 'Shall we go home?'

Later, after Annabelle had been put to bed, Harry and Rosamund went downstairs to the small parlour where they sat side by side to talk over the day's events. The pros and cons, the sequence of events were soon dealt with and they fell silent for a moment. It was a pause full of expectancy, a kind of waiting, charged with emotion, fighting to find expression.

'I never expected to be back here again so soon,' she said at last.

'Nor I.' He took one of her hands in both of his and held it close to his chest. 'You have no idea what a shock it was to learn you had come racing back here to search for Annabelle. I ran poor Hector into the ground, unable to think of anything except that I had to find you. I had a presentiment that it was more than a small child lost. Your life and hers were in danger because of what I did. It was all very well to risk my own, but to risk yours…' He was almost too choked to go on, so he lifted her hand to kiss it. 'I could not imagine my life without you in it. It would be empty, meaningless. I love you, Rosamund Portman. I love you with every sinew of my being. It was the most fortunate day of my life when I married you and I wish I had never mentioned an annulment.'

'I thought we had dismissed that idea,' she murmured.

'So we have and if you are sure, it will never

be mentioned by me again. It is the last thing I want.'

'I am glad,' she said slowly, smiling at him through tears of happiness. 'We could put it out of the question...'

He looked into her eyes; it was easy to read the message in them. He stood up and drew her slowly to her feet. 'Upstairs?'

She nodded. It was going to be all right. She would make it all right. And it was. The ghost had fled.

They returned to London next day for their Coronation Ball, which turned out to be the most lavish of the season. It was also the jolliest, for the host and hostess were so evidently pleased with each other. Harry had been instrumental in ridding the country of two gangs of coiners, had helped the coronation pass off with only minor hitches that were not important, but most of all he had the love of the loveliest, the wisest and the bravest woman he had ever met. She was also an exemplary mother for Annabelle, who adored her. As he did. More he could not ask.

'Lucky fellow,' Ash said, coming to stand beside him as he watched Rosamund smiling and talking to their guests, being the perfect hostess. 'It is obvious you have overcome your scruples.'

'Your turn next.'

'Not on your life!'

'You will change your mind when you meet the right woman, I will put money on it.'

'Done!'

The two men shook hands.

Epilogue

Nine months later, Harry found himself pacing up and down the corridor outside Rosamund's room. She had woken him at dawn to tell him quietly, 'I think the baby is coming, Harry.'

He had sprung out of bed, trying not to panic, but failing miserably as he roused Janet and Mrs Rivers and sent one of the grooms on Hector to fetch the doctor and another with the gig to bring the nurses. Everything that could be done to ease his wife's suffering he was determined should be done. But then he was left with nothing to do but wait. He had been shut out of the room, as he had been once before, but instead of going downstairs or out into the garden, he had chosen to pace the corridor. He had told the doctor in no uncertain terms that if it came down to a choice of saving the child or his wife, they were not to hesitate: Lady Portman must come first.

They had been at it for hours and all he could hear was a low murmur of voices. It puzzled him. Why was she not crying out, why were the doctor and nurses not urging her to make an effort? Surely she was not already dead? If he had killed her as he had killed Beth, he could not live with himself. But Dr Marshall would have come out and told him if that were the case.

He was close to the door when he heard one muffled cry and that was enough. He burst into the room and then stopped in amazement. The baby had been born and had been wrapped in a cloth and handed to Rosamund. She was smiling and gazing down at their son and looking incredibly beautiful and contented. Harry fell on his knees beside them and gazed in wonder, speechless with happiness.

'I thought…I thought… You didn't make a sound.'

'No,' she said, determined to forget how hard it had been to stifle her inclination to cry out. She had known he was just outside and how anxious he was. 'I told you it was easy, didn't I?'

'Henry James Ashley,' he said solemnly, then laughed and kissed her, as Annabelle rushed into the room and pushed her way up between them. 'Let me see my little brother.'

Rosamund moved the swaddling clothes to reveal a very pink face, rosebud lips and the bluest of blue eyes, which seemed to be looking straight at his sister. 'He's pretty,' she said.

'I hope, young lady, you do not say that to his face when he is old enough to understand,' her father said with mock severity. 'He will not thank you for so effeminate an adjective. He is going to be a big strong man. A handsome man.'

'Like his father,' Rosamund added, picking up Harry's hand and cupping it about her face. 'I love you, Harry Portman.'

'And I adore you, Lady Portman.' At last he could let go the last of the past; it would not trouble him again. The future was what mattered. He took her hand and kissed the inside of the wrist. 'I have a family, a proper loving family. Was ever a man so blessed?'

Annabelle giggled.

* * * * *

HISTORICAL

Large Print

LORD PORTMAN'S TROUBLESOME WIFE
Mary Nichols

Forced to marry Harry, Lord Portman, Rosamund must produce an heir in return for a comfortable life! But self-controlled Harry is unsettled by his attraction to Rosamund, his convenient wife, and keeps her at arm's length. But Rosamund falls into danger and he has to find the courage to let go of the past and fight for the woman he loves…

THE DUKE'S GOVERNESS BRIDE
Miranda Jarrett

Dreading the end of her Grand Tour, former governess Jane Wood awaits the arrival of her employer, Richard Farren, Duke of Aston, with trepidation… Richard finds mousy Miss Wood unrecognisable as the passionate, carefree Jane. Will Richard overcome the shadowy demons of his past…and convince Jane to be his wife?

CONQUERED AND SEDUCED
Lyn Randal

Two years ago former gladiatrix Severina had no choice but to flee from Livius Lucan. Their fiery relationship threatened his safety – a risk she couldn't take. But now she needs his help. In his turn, Lucan is determined to conquer this runaway woman – and claim the wedding night he never had!

MILLS & BOON

HISTORICAL

Large Print
REAWAKENING MISS CALVERLEY
Sylvia Andrew

Lord Aldhurst rescues a cold, dazed lady one stormy
night – and now the nameless beauty is residing in his
home! Horrified at her growing feelings for her handsome
protector, she flees to London, where she regains her
status as the *ton*'s most sought-after debutante. Until
she sees James's shocked and stormy face
across a ballroom…

THE UNMASKING OF A LADY
Emily May

While she dances prettily by day, the *ton* doesn't know
that by night Lady Arabella Knightley helps the poor –
stealing jewels from those who court her for her money.
Upon discovering it's Arabella, Adam St Just should be
appalled. Instead, captivated by her beauty, he proposes
to unbutton Lady Arabella…or unmask her!

CAPTURED BY THE WARRIOR
Meriel Fuller

With the country on the brink of anarchy, Bastien de la
Roche will do what it takes to restore calm. So when he
captures the spirited Alice Matravers, a servant to the royal
court, he charms her into gaining an audience with the
King. Could Alice's courage and kindness begin
to mend Bastien's shattered heart…?

HISTORICAL

Large Print

INNOCENT COURTESAN TO ADVENTURER'S BRIDE
Louise Allen

Wrongly accused of theft, innocent Celina Shelley is cast out of the brothel she calls home and flees to Quinn Ashley, Lord Dreycott. Lina dresses like a nun, looks like an angel, but flirts like a professional – the last thing Quinn expects is to discover she's a virgin! With this revelation, will he wed her before he beds her?

DISGRACE AND DESIRE
Sarah Mallory

With all of London falling at her feet, wagers abound over who will capture the flirtatious Lady Eloise and her fortune. Dashing Major Jack Clifton has vowed to watch over his late comrade's wife, but her beauty and behaviour intrigue him. The lady is not what she seems, and Jack must discover her secret if he is to protect her…

THE VIKING'S CAPTIVE PRINCESS
Michelle Styles

Dangerous warrior Ivar Gunnarson is a man of deeds, not words. With little time for the ideals of love, Ivar seizes what he wants – and Princess Thyre is no exception! But to become king of Thyre's heart, mysterious and enchanting as she is, will entail a battle Ivar has never engaged in before…

 MILLS & BOON